D0556947

"If you're new to Shearin's work, and you enjoy fantasy interspersed with an enticing romance, a little bit of humor, and a whole lot of grade-A action, this is the series for you."

—*Lurv a la Mode*

THE TROUBLE WITH DEMONS

"The book reads more like an urban fantasy with pirates and sharp wit and humor. I found the mix quite refreshing. Lisa Shearin's fun, action- packed writing style gives this world life and vibrancy."

—*Fresh Fiction*

"Lisa Shearin represents that much needed voice in fantasy that combines practiced craft and a wicked sense of humor."

—*Bitten by Books*

"The brisk pace and increasingly complex character development propel the story on a rollercoaster ride through demons, goblins, elves, and mages while maintaining a satisfying level of romantic attention…that will leave readers chomping at the bit for more."

—*Monsters and Critics*

"This book has the action starting as soon as you start the story and it keeps going right to the end…All of the characters are interesting, from the naked demon queen to the Guardians guarding Raine. All have a purpose and it comes across with clarity and detail."

—*Night Owl Reviews*

ARMED & MAGICAL

"Fresh, original, and fall- out-of- your-chair funny, Lisa Shearin's *Armed & Magical* combines deft characterization, snarky dialogue, and nonstop action—plus a yummy hint of romance—to create one of the best reads of the year. This book is a bona fide winner, the series a keeper, and Shearin a definite star on the rise."

—*Linnea Sinclair, RITA Award-winning author of* Rebels and Lovers

"An exciting, catch-me-if-you-can, lightning-fast-paced tale of magic and evil filled with goblins, elves, mages, and a hint of love interest that will leave fantasy readers anxiously awaiting Raine's next adventure."

—*Monsters and Critics*

"The kind of book you hope to find when you go to the bookstore. It takes you away to a world of danger, magic, and adventure, and it does so with dazzling wit and clever humor. It's gritty, funny, and sexy—a wonderful addition to the urban fantasy genre. I absolutely loved it. From now on Lisa Shearin is on my auto-buy list!"

—*Ilona Andrews, #1* New York Times *bestselling author of* Magic Shifts

"*Armed & Magical*, like its predecessor, is an enchanting read from the very first page. I absolutely loved it. Shearin weaves a web of magic with a dash of romance that thoroughly snares the reader. She's definitely an author to watch!"

—*Anya Bast,* New York Times *bestselling author of* Embrace of the Damned

Magic Lost, Trouble Found

"Take a witty, kick-ass heroine and put her in a vividly realized fantasy world where the stakes are high, and you've got a fun, page-turning read in Magic Lost, Trouble Found. I can't wait to read more of Raine Benares's adventures."

—*Shanna Swendson, author of* Don't Hex with Texas

"A wonderful fantasy tale full of different races and myths and legends [that] are drawn so perfectly readers will believe they actually exist. Raine is a strong female, a leader who wants to do the right thing even when she isn't sure what that is...Lisa Shearin has the magic touch."

—*Midwest Book Review*

"Shearin serves up an imaginative fantasy...The strong, well-executed story line and characters, along with a nice twist to the 'object of unspeakable power' theme, make for an enjoyable, fast-paced read."

—*Monsters and Critics*

WEDDING BELLS, MAGIC SPELLS

Also by Lisa Shearin

The Raine Benares Series

The SPI Files Series

WEDDING BELLS, MAGIC SPELLS

A Raine Benares Novel

Lisa Shearin

Production Manager: Lori Bennett
Cover Designer: Aleta Rafton
Book Designer: Angie Hodapp

ISBN 978-1-62051-212-8

For all of my fans who never stopped asking me,
"What happens next?!"

ACKNOWLEDGMENTS

For my family—especially my husband, Derek—for all of their love, support, and understanding of an author's crazy schedule (and a crazy author).

For Kristin Nelson, or as I think of her, my Guardian Agent. A guardian angel protects and defends their charge from error and danger. Kristin does all that and more, only without the wings. There is, quite simply, no one better. Thank you for making my journey into indie publishing so easy. All I have to do is write the books. You and your awesome team (Lori Bennett and Angie Hodapp) do all the heavy lifting. Words cannot express my gratitude. You ladies rock!

To Betsy Mitchell, my beyond amazing editor. I've seen the words "legendary" and "superstar" used in industry publications next to your name. They both fit. I was beyond thrilled (squeeing, actually) when Kristin suggested you to edit my indie books. You have truly been a partner in each and every project with your uncanny sense of what is needed to make a book the best that it can be. You've helped me out of many a dark plot hole, and I'm honored to call you my editor.

To Martha Trachtenberg, my incredible copy editor. Just when I thought every typo, grammar goof, or inconsistency had been caught, you were there to prove me wrong. Your sharp eyes and attention to detail are truly awe-inspiring. (If there's a mistake in this book, it's totally my fault.)

To Aleta Rafton, my astounding cover artist. It's been so much fun to work with you to find the perfect look for each cover. Thank you for bringing Raine Benares to vibrant life. Our next project together will be the most fun yet—Tamnais Nathrach.

1

I'd spent entirely too much time in front of mirrors lately. For most people, that would simply mean they were vain. For a magic user like me, it meant you might have a death wish.

Mirrors let normal people admire how good they look, or how bad the morning after a night out.

The mirrors I had no desire to be standing in front of didn't exist for vanity. This room was a place of starting points and destinations, a way of traveling from one location to another, whether that distance was separated by a few miles or a few thousand. Most of the mirrors were large enough for at least one person to step through. Those were held upright by floor-mounted metal or wood frames, some ornately etched or carved, some just plain and practical. All of them were maintained and operated by Guardian mirror mages—magic users who were beyond skilled at opening, navigating, and closing the ways from one place to another, ways that were critical to the Guardians and the Conclave of Sorcerers that they protected. One such mage was currently preparing one of the larger mirrors for use.

All mirrors did for me was to give me a raging case of the creeps.

My name is Raine Benares. I'm an elf and I was a seeker. Well, technically I still am a seeker, only now I'm much more than a magical finder of people lost and things missing. The "much more" part wasn't my idea or choice. Three months ago, a soul-sucking stone of cataclysmic power called the Saghred attached itself to me like a psychic leech and gave me magical abilities I didn't want and that no sane person needed to have. Since destroying the stone, I didn't know if I still had those abilities, or if they'd been a package deal with the Saghred. In ancient times, armies that carried the Saghred before them were indestructible. That quality supposedly applied to the rock as well.

To destroy the Saghred had involved going through a mirror here to one hundreds of miles away in the goblin capital of Regor.

I'd been part of a strike team tasked with getting to Regor, hunting down, and destroying the Saghred. Our trip hadn't exactly been leisurely. We'd been under attack. The only escape route had been through that mirror. What was to have been an orderly, one-person-at-a-time scenario had degenerated into a dive-for-your-life trip.

If we had failed to stop the sadistic goblin dark mage controlling the stone, my soul would have been slurped up for an eternity of torment along with hundreds of thousands of others who'd been sacrificed to the Saghred over the ages. Destroying the stone first meant releasing all of the souls held captive inside. We'd done that, then I had smashed the rock into crystalline dust. The fact that I was standing here alive was proof that anything could be destroyed if someone was motivated enough.

I was someone and I had been seriously motivated.

The team had survived, the Saghred had been shattered, and the evil dark mage carried off by a nine-foot-tall bull demon into the Lower Hells.

I'd thought that meant mission accomplished.

Unfortunately, it was only the beginning.

With the destruction of the Saghred and a new, non-psychotic king on the goblin throne, an elf/goblin/human peace treaty was being negotiated on the neutral ground of the Isle of Mid. For as long as history has been written down, elves have hated goblins and goblins have despised elves, with humans just trying not to get caught in the middle of seemingly one war after another. That was the way it was, is, and how everyone thought it always would be.

We were going to do everything we could to change that.

Leading the charge would be the Conclave Guardians. The Guardians were mages and warriors whose primary job was the defense of the Conclave of Sorcerers, the governing body of all magic users in the Seven Kingdoms. The Conclave was based on the Isle of Mid, giving the Guardians the dubious honor of being peacekeepers on an island packed with mage bureaucrats, mage professors, and teenage mages in training at the Conclave's college—a volatile combination any way you looked at it.

The Guardians were also the most elite magical fighting force in the Seven Kingdoms, and as the Guardians' paladin and commander, Mychael Eiliesor was the top lawman on Mid. If it happened on this island, it was his business. He was an elf, a master spellsinger, healer, and warrior lethally skilled in battlefield magic.

He was also my fiancé.

Since the formation of the Seven Kingdoms, not only had the Isle of Mid been neutral, so had the Guardians. The Conclave? Not so much. It depended on who you were dealing with, which way the wind was blowing, and what was in it for them. But within the walls of the Guardians' citadel, they made the rules and enforced the law, so the peace talks would take place here. That was the one thing all of the delegates had agreed on. Now that the Saghred had been destroyed, no one kingdom had a military or magical advantage over the other. The chances to reach a peace agreement would never be better than they were right now.

It would be the Guardians' job to ensure that the delegates played nice and stayed safe.

It sounded simple enough, but I didn't kid myself that more than a thousand years of hate and distrust was going to evaporate overnight just because some diplomats got together and signed a piece of paper. Ink scratched on paper wasn't a guarantee of anything, not even good penmanship.

Trust was the biggest issue.

Neither trusted the other not to slaughter them while they slept.

Elves were awake during the day and slept at night.

Goblins were nocturnal.

And they differed from other races in more ways than one. Their skin was a pearlescent gray varying in shades from light to dark. But the big distinction—and what had kept elves reaching for their weapons for the past millennia—were the fangs.

Goblins had fangs and they weren't for decorative use only. Like elves, goblins were tall and lean and, also like elves, much stronger than they looked. While most elf children were still playing with toys, goblin kids were given blades and taught how to use them. Running with knives was encouraged, and intrigue was a way of life. Toss *fangs* and *nocturnal* into the mix, and trust was a hard thing to come by.

Since both races had pointed ears and a preponderance of magically gifted individuals, it was said that elves and goblins had a common ancestor. I didn't know if it was true or not, though it sounded logical enough to me. But it was an opinion best kept to one's self. There was no quicker way to be challenged to a duel with an old-blood noble of either race, whether mage or mundane, than to open that topic for debate.

However, not all elves and goblins wanted to use each other for target practice.

I was here in the mirror room to welcome a friend coming in from the elven capital of Silvanlar. Duke Markus Sevelien was coming for my and Mychael's wedding. He was also the director of elven intelligence and part of the elven delegation for the peace talks.

I'd done seeker contract work for Markus over the years, finding missing elven diplomats, agents, and assorted nobles who'd gotten involved in something over their highborn heads. It was gratifying work, and I'd been good at it. I considered him a friend, a good one.

And in about another hour the goblin delegation would arrive, and I was sure Markus would stay to welcome Tamnais Nathrach and Imala Kalis. The new goblin ambassador to Mid, Dakarai Enric, was already in residence at the goblin embassy here. Tam was the chief mage and chancellor for the goblin king Chigaru Mal'Salin, and Imala was the director of the goblin secret service.

I would be welcoming both of them with hugs. Markus would greet Tam with a warm handshake, but the last time he'd seen Imala, they'd done that double-cheek-kissing thing. That alone should communicate enough peace for anyone. Unfortunately, Markus and I were the elven exception and so were our goblin friends.

I trusted Tam, Imala, and Markus with my life. Who I'd never met, and had no reason to trust, were the people the other delegates would be taking the signed treaty home to. Those were the individuals in their respective governments with the power to enforce what would be decided here—or pick and choose what they liked and what suited their political agendas.

There was never a convenient time for the top lawman in the Seven Kingdoms to get married. We'd already had to put off the wedding twice for one thing or another. We'd picked a date during the peace talks for one reason only—our friends. Tam and Imala were on the goblin delegation, and Markus was on the elven. Mychael's younger sister was on the elven ambassador's staff. It was the only time we'd be able to get them all in one place at one time.

The world was watching us. It was the Guardians' job to keep the delegates safe, and ensure that the treaty was drafted and signed.

Screwing up any of the above wasn't an option.

Like I said before, my last name is Benares. My relatives make up the most notorious criminal family in the Seven Kingdoms. The Benares family is good at being bad, and proud of it. I was a member of the family, but not in the family business.

Yeah, I know. No one else believes me, either.

Archmagus Justinius Valerian is the most powerful mage in the Seven Kingdoms and has complete authority over the Isle of Mid and everyone on it. The Guardians take their marching orders from him. I wasn't technically a Guardian, but Justinius wanted me to be the first female in the order. I hadn't given him my final decision yet—though I'd already made it. During the past few weeks, I'd had time to think of something other than a way to survive the next few minutes. After everything that'd happened over the past months, I'd clearly seen a need, and I wanted to meet it.

I wanted to establish a program that would locate, protect, and educate magically powerful, at-risk children.

Right now, neither the Conclave nor the Guardians had anything in place to keep magical prodigies from being exploited by the Taltek Balmorlans of the world. He had used his position as an inquisitor in elven intelligence to front a black market kidnapping ring.

Yes, the Guardians had enough on their plate, but the people they protected—the Conclave and the Seat of Twelve—could take care of themselves, and if they couldn't, it was high time they learned. The Conclave governed the magic users of the Seven Kingdoms and was quick to prosecute if they broke any of the laws. I'd found that out firsthand. But as far as I'd seen, they didn't do a thing to protect the average magic user. And what about the children, the young ones, the ones who would never make it to the Conclave's college because their parents couldn't afford it? At worst, these kids were left to their own devices. Sometimes their parents (if they had any) hired tutors, who very often did more harm than good with a highly gifted child. There were mages, like my godfather Garadin Wyne, Piaras's grandmother Tarsilia Rivalin, and Tam's first teacher Kesyn Badru, who were amazing teachers of precocious prodigies. There had to be others out there just like them.

I'd already talked to Mychael about it. He thought it was a great idea and a program that was long overdue. After the peace talks, I'd sit down with Justinius and tell him that I would be a Guardian, but in my own way. Also, until I knew what level of magic I had, the less I slung spells around, the better—and possibly safer—for everyone.

The Saghred had taken all of my magic just before we went to Regor. After I'd destroyed the rock, my magic had begun coming back. Some of it was mine; some was what the Saghred had given me. So basically, I had no clue how much—or how little—I was packing. Justinius strongly suggested that for my own safety that I should keep that information to myself, as there were still plenty of people around who might want to take me on, or take me out—and I didn't mean for a night on the town.

I usually wore leathers—doublet, trousers, and matching boots. However, I was about to marry the paladin of the Conclave Guardians, and I was still considered to be one of the most powerful magic users in the Seven Kingdoms. Like I said, I didn't know if that was true anymore or not, and I hadn't had the time and privacy to experiment. So to reinforce my perceived badass image, Mychael and Justinius had strongly suggested that I upgrade my wardrobe as befitting my station and reputation. I was now wearing entirely too expensive, custom-made leathers of gray and midnight blue. Gowns had been out of the question. If I needed to run—either to chase someone or escape from something—I didn't want a bunch of extraneous brocade in my way. Neither one had objected. They picked their battles with me and had deemed this one not worth the fight.

While I'd been linked to the Saghred, I'd been the target of pretty much every power-grubbing megalomaniac in the Seven Kingdoms and most of the demons living in the realms under them. That I was still alive with my soul and sanity intact was the result of ten kinds of miracle, every form of luck, several world-class cons, and the magical skills and bravery of some of the best friends a girl could have.

I smiled. A big, goofy, love-besotted grin. In four days, I would be marrying one of them.

That earned me a confused look from my bodyguard, a blond Guardian by the name of Vegard Rolfgar.

"You've decided you like this room?" he asked.

"Are you kidding? Just thinking happy thoughts to keep my mind off what could pounce, slither, or run at us through any one of those mirrors."

Vegard smiled. "That's why they're arranged how they are, ma'am. I wouldn't be standing here without a sword in my hand if they weren't. The door's on one wall, the mirrors on the other. That way you don't have one of those things at your back unless you want to."

"Anyone who would want to is nuts," I muttered, so the mages wouldn't hear me.

Don't get me wrong, I was glad there were people who

were good at turning mirrors into doorways to essentially anywhere, and I wouldn't want to insult anyone's livelihood, but I'd seen someone cut in half while coming through a suddenly deactivated mirror. Sights like that stayed with you. And a couple of weeks ago, monsters had ripped their way out of the big mirror to our left—a mirror that was now an empty frame, thanks to timely shattering on our part. Also traumatic. And also not forgetting it anytime soon.

When I'd come to Mid for help getting rid of the Saghred's bond to me, Vegard had been assigned as my bodyguard. Even though the rock was gone, Vegard's assignment had stayed the same. I was glad. I'd gotten used to the big guy, and now going anywhere without Vegard would be like walking on a sunny day without my shadow. He was big, blond, bearded, and human—classic Myloran sea-raider stock.

Our backs were to the door, so I didn't see Mychael come into the mirror room.

I sensed him.

It sounded simple, but it wasn't.

Mychael and I had a connection, a bond that went far beyond that of two people who shared a bed and the fun that went with it. I'd only met him three months ago, but I knew him down to his soul and beyond.

The Saghred had wanted souls, and the more powerful the magic that went along with them the tastier. Part of our connection had been forged by the Saghred. The rest had been my magic reacting and melding with Mychael's magic, and the Saghred hadn't had a thing to do with it. Our magics had coiled and twisted, weaving us together, and I had been keenly aware of his every heartbeat, every muscle, the surging of blood through his veins. In that instant we had seen each other as we truly were, souls laid bare.

I smiled. The man had seen my soul buck naked and still wanted to marry me.

Mychael could move like a cat, but he wasn't doing that

now. He'd learned the hard way that if he wanted to put his arms around me from behind, he needed to make a lot of noise before doing it. To say I hadn't reacted well on his first attempt was an understatement. In my defense, I'd had too many people try to kill or kidnap me since the Saghred had invaded my life not to be left with residual jitters.

"You almost didn't make it in time," I said without turning.

He came up behind me, wrapped his arms around my waist, pulled me back into him, and brushed the top of my head with his lips. I felt his smile. "Is he here yet?"

"No."

"Then I'm not late."

I turned in his arms. Yes, Mychael was the Guardians' paladin and commander, but he didn't let that stop him from public displays of affection, and I loved him even more for it. I felt another goofy, besotted grin coming on.

My fiancé was wearing his steel-gray formal uniform. Under that uniform was a leanly muscled body that I'd gotten up close and very personal with this morning. His features were strong and classic, and his eyes were that mix of blue and green found only in warm, tropical seas. He wore his auburn hair short, but long enough to get my fingers into. I was feeling several urges along those lines right now and, like Mychael, didn't care who was watching.

"You sure you're okay being in here?" he asked quietly.

"Until you came in, my back was to the wall and I was mere steps from the closest door."

"And now, I'm in your way."

"Yes, you are."

"Want me to leave?"

I smiled. "Never."

"We just received the signal," the Guardian mirror mage said. "They're ready to come through."

"Whenever you're ready," Mychael told him.

The mage stood before a sturdy metal-framed mirror at

least seven feet tall and three feet wide, arms extended, palms out, fingers spread wide, eyes focused and unblinking. This mirror was linked to a similar one in the basement of the elven intelligence building in Silvanlar. The surface of the mirror began to ripple as it was activated on the other side. When the ripple turned to a swirl, my stomach tried to do the same thing, and I looked away. Buckets were discreetly kept in the mirror room for a reason. I knew what came next without having to see it. The rotation would quicken until the mirror's entire surface pulsed. At that point, our first visitor would arrive.

I looked back to the mirror as an armed elf stepped through.

No one went for their weapons. We had been told to expect a bodyguard to come through before Markus. It was about time he'd gotten himself one.

A woman. Average height, dark hair, brown eyes. Sharp eyes that darted aggressively around the room, taking in everything and missing nothing. Beautiful, yet belligerent.

If Markus thought she was up to handling the trouble he attracted on a daily basis, she must be hell on wheels. I didn't sense any magic coming from her. Considering the sources of the trouble Markus often found himself in, that said a lot about this woman's capabilities.

The elf wore sleek leathers and was armed with knives strapped to her arms, legs, chest, and the small of her back— all within easy reach. I wore my blades the same way.

The elf nodded in Mychael's direction. "Paladin Eiliesor."

She didn't look directly at me, though she'd seen me well enough, along with every other armed individual in the room—seen them, assessed them, and determined them to be of no danger to her boss.

"I'm Brina Daesage, chief of Director Sevelien's security team."

That was a new one. "Markus has an entire security team?" I asked.

The elf woman flashed a good-natured grin. "He does now."

"About time."

"Raine Benares, I presume?"

"Presumption correct. Is Markus coming next?"

"He is." She turned to the mage operating the mirror and indicated the signal pad. "May I?"

The Guardian glanced at Mychael, who gave a single nod of approval.

Brina Daesage stepped over to the pad, which consisted of a single flat crystal set into the mirror's frame. She tapped out a coded message to the mirror mage back in Silvanlar that the destination was secure and Markus could come through. After a few moments, the mirror pulsed once and then a pattern appeared on the surface, flickering and rolling in silver waves.

My stomach tried to roll right along with it, and once again, I looked away.

The Guardian mirror mage took a few steps back, arms down, but hands still extended, palms out toward the mirror. Once he'd opened the mirror here, his job was essentially done. The elf mage in Silvanlar was running the show now; our man was merely keeping the mirror stable on this end.

I was watching our mage, not the mirror, but I didn't need to see the mirror to know there was a problem. The Guardian suddenly started taking deep breaths and hissing them out through clenched teeth as if he was lifting way out of his weight class.

I looked at the mirror.

What had been silver waves had turned to corpse gray, ripening into poison green.

I was no mirror mage, but I knew something was wrong.

Deadly wrong.

Just because getting from one place to another through magically linked mirrors was like stepping through a doorway didn't mean things couldn't go wrong. I'd seen one malfunction and heard of others—all had been fatal to the person caught in between.

Mychael had already stepped around me, as had Brina. Her job was to protect Markus from assassins, but unless she was a mirror mage, there wasn't anything she could do to stop whatever was happening.

Mychael put a calming hand on his Guardian's shoulder. Normally, touching a practitioner in the middle of working powerful magic had bad consequences for the toucher, touchee, and possibly anyone within splattering distance.

Mychael Eiliesor wasn't normal; he was a healer, of mind and body. He was giving his Guardian added strength and calm to do what needed to be done. The man's breathing slowed, but it didn't change the fact that he appeared to be fighting a losing battle.

"Steady," Mychael told him, his spellsinger voice helping the man to do just that.

"Sir, I've lost—"

"No, you haven't. Hold on to what you've got."

"Something…inside." His hands, palms out toward the mirror, were slowly flexing forward, toward the sickly green swirl, as if what was inside was dragging him forward and into his own mirror. Then his booted feet began sliding on the stone floor.

Mychael held on and Vegard ran to help.

For an instant, I saw Markus.

On the other side of the mirror.

Trapped.

His eyes were open and vacant, his skin was blue, and something like black rope was wrapped around his chest.

Mychael saw and swore. "Vegard, hold him."

He released the mage, and in the next moment before any of us could stop him, his arms blazed with a protection spell, he grabbed the mirror's frame in his right hand and plunged his left into the mirror up to his shoulder. His eyes squeezed shut with effort.

If the mirror shattered, Mychael's arm would be severed. That didn't stop him.

And it didn't stop another black, rope-like thing from lashing out from inside the mirror and wrapping around Mychael's throat. I instantly had my sharpest dagger in my hands, slashing at where the rope and mirror met. It didn't even scratch it.

Mychael jerked, the side of his face flush against the mirror, the rope pulling him inside.

My vision narrowed until all I saw was that thing wrapped around the throat of the man I loved, the man who had put himself in danger again and again, risking his life and soul to save mine. Now some monster thought it was going drag him off to whatever was on the other side.

Oh. Hell. No.

I summoned my magic and grabbed the rope with my bare hand—a hand that was glowing dark red.

Red?

That was the only thought I managed to have before instinct and rage took over. I didn't care that I should be ten kinds of terrified at what the rest of the monster looked like. I didn't care what it would do to me. I forced every bit of strength, every shred of whatever magic I still possessed into my hand, constricting, crushing. Whatever the magic was, wherever it'd come from, it hurt what was strangling Mychael. It hurt it badly. I didn't know what I was doing, and I sure didn't know how, but I kept doing it until the rope dissolved in my hand, freeing Mychael.

The instant after Mychael pulled Markus out of the mirror, it shattered, covering us all in crystalline dust.

Markus's eyes were fixed and staring, he wasn't breathing.

I dropped to the floor beside his body.

Markus Sevelien was dead.

Mychael's hand held balled lightning. He pushed his spread fingers hard against the center of Markus's chest, and the elf's back arched with the charge.

Nothing.

Mychael sent another jolt into Markus's chest.

And another.

A tremor shook Markus's entire body, and he gasped. That gasp turned into a breath. Two breaths. Three. Markus was breathing on his own. It was ragged, but he was doing it.

Mychael sat back and blew out a breath of his own. "Welcome back, Markus."

To the Isle of Mid, or to life?

2

Under normal circumstances, an injured—or recently dead— intelligence director would be taken to his kingdom's embassy. But considering that Markus's own people had tried to kill him last month and that an elf mage had been in control of the mirror today, any elf was suspect, and the elves in the elven embassy were more suspect than most.

With the mirror on our end destroyed, the rest of Markus's security detail was stuck in Silvanlar at elven intelligence headquarters—supposedly the most secure building in the capital. The black-tentacled thing that had attacked Mychael and briefly killed Markus hadn't been an elf, but that didn't mean an elf hadn't set it loose.

I didn't know how something like that had happened, but I knew why.

Someone wanted Markus dead. Again.

Markus Sevelien had been presumed dead before.

It'd turned out to be a good thing then.

The house he'd been staying in here had been packed with explosives and set on fire, converting it instantly from a house to a crater. If Markus had been in there, he'd have been blown to bits. Mychael and I had gotten him out moments before everything had gone boom. Markus had worked behind the scenes to lure out some highly placed traitors both in elven intelligence and the elven embassy here. They'd been arrogant and had grown careless, and both had gotten them caught.

To keep whoever was behind killing Markus this time from getting a second chance, Mychael was entirely justified tossing protocol out the nearest window—or through what was left of the elves' sabotaged mirror.

As the head of a security detail that was now stuck in Silvanlar, Brina Daesage had agreed with his choice.

Archmagus Justinius Valerian's apartment in the west tower of the Guardians' citadel was as secure as a vault—although most vaults didn't have Guardian battle mages standing guard along both sides of the corridor leading to it, warriors who could kill you in various and sundry ways with a single spell. The old man had hosted security-compromised guests before, and not one of them had died while in his tower.

As long as he was here, Markus was safe.

I wasn't so sure about myself. Though the biggest danger to myself might be me.

Even when I'd been bonded to the Saghred, my magic had never manifested itself in dark red. Red and acid green were the colors of the darker magics. I'd seen a similar deep red radiance many times over the past few months.

In the glow of the Saghred.

The shade of red that I'd produced had been closer to the Saghred end of the spectrum.

I was feeling an overwhelming urge to scream and run.

While neither would accomplish anything, that didn't stop me from wanting to.

Everyone had seen what happened, and no one had said a word. Whatever had enabled me to do what I did had saved Mychael, who had saved Markus, so as scared as I'd been of what I'd done, my magic could have manifested in purple sparklies for all I cared.

Find who attacked Markus now, care about what had happened to me later.

Brina Daesage had just seen her security plans shattered as thoroughly as that mirror. She was expressing her displeasure in the only way she could at the moment, which was pacing the length of Justinius's bedchamber, scowling at not having anyone to punch or stab.

A woman after my own heart.

Markus was still unconscious. His heart was beating again mostly on its own and he was breathing, but he was far from stable.

Mychael and Dalis, the archmagus's personal healer, were working on him, and Brina and I were trying to stay out of the way. Vegard was across the room, waiting on our side of the closed bedroom door. If anyone tried to come in, they'd better belong here.

We had no idea why Markus had been attacked. And until we did, Mychael wasn't taking any chances. Most of the delegates had arrived yesterday and last night. Tam and Imala were due to arrive in another hour—by mirror. Mychael had ordered a message sent by telepath telling them to wait. It'd been successfully received in Regor. Santis Eldor, the elven ambassador, was on his way to Mid on a small agency ship that had set sail from Laerin two days ago. Mychael had ordered a message sent to the telepath aboard the ambassador's ship with news of what had happened—though that had just as much to do with being a protective big brother. I didn't blame him one bit. Isibel Eiliesor, Mychael's younger sister, was on the elven ambassador's staff and traveling with him—for the peace talks and our wedding.

Markus's color had improved just in the past few minutes. He may not have been completely out of the woods yet, but unless he took another long trip through a short mirror, his survival chances were looking really good. I recognized the spell Mychael was presently weaving. It would put Markus into a deep sleep to allow his body time to heal.

I took a breath and tried to relax my shoulders. "He'll make it," I said quietly. Brina Daesage glanced at me, expression unreadable. "You had doubts?"

I gave her a tired smile. "With any other healer, maybe. With Mychael, never. I've seen him do more in less time with worse injuries."

"Worse than death?"

"Try dead with a crossbow bolt through the heart."

Mychael had brought Tam back from the dead after I'd shot him through the heart with a crossbow. It was a long story, and nothing personal.

Brina grinned. "Chancellor Nathrach. I heard what happened."

I wearily rubbed the back of my neck. "It was a hell of a day."

"I imagine it was. You did what you had to do."

I nodded once. "I did it. I didn't like it, but I did it."

The apartment doors opened, and Brina and I both went for our blades.

Justinius Valerian.

I sheathed my blades. Brina hesitated, then did the same. She'd never met the old man, and if he hadn't been wearing his formal robes, she—or anyone else—wouldn't peg him as the most powerful mage in the Seven Kingdoms. He was lean to the point of appearing scrawny. What might have been a luxurious head of hair decades ago was now a fringe of white tufts on a liver-spotted head. Only a pair of gleaming blue eyes gave a clue to the power inside the man. Though at the moment, those eyes were as hard as agates. Yep, the old guy definitely wasn't happy.

It was his apartment, so I wasn't surprised to see him, but seeing the look on his face, I wouldn't exactly say I was glad. I'd seen the old man pissed before, but nothing like this. Even though I hadn't been the one to cause the figurative thundercloud over his head, I couldn't help experiencing an internal cringe with a side order of impending doom.

When I'd come to Mid, the first thing Justinius had done was a mind link to determine if—because of my link with the Saghred—I was too dangerous to live. He'd determined then that I wasn't. I wondered if he'd ever regretted that decision.

"You all right, girl?" he asked me.

"Physically, yes. Emotionally, I'm reserving judgment."

"There's a lot of that going around." He glanced at Markus in his guest bed and grunted in satisfaction. "Looks like he'll live."

"He will," Mychael said without turning or pausing in his work.

"I've got Cuinn Aviniel taking a look at that mirror," Justinius said. "Or what's left of it."

Since Carnades Silvanus's death, Cuinn Aviniel was now the best mirror mage on the island. Everyone had hated Carnades; no one felt the same about his replacement. Cuinn was a nice guy who actually liked sharing his knowledge of mirrors, unlike most mirror mages, who wanted to be the only ones who understood how and why linked mirrors behaved as they did. He was also a mirror-travel scholar. If anyone would know what had happened to Markus, it would be Cuinn.

Justinius held up an envelope. The seal was broken. "I've got news on the elven ambassador. A messenger was on his way from the communication room with this for you."

"It's been opened," I noted.

"By me."

"And you're entitled, sir."

"Yes, I am. And as winded as that squire was, I knew it was something I probably needed to read. Mychael?"

Mychael paused in his work and turned.

"It's something you need to read, son."

Oh no. Mychael's sister.

No one said a word as Mychael read the message. He then passed it to me and nodded to Brina. As Markus's security chief, she'd certainly need to know if anything had happened to the elven ambassador. She read over my shoulder.

"They couldn't make contact with the *Blue Rose*," I summarized. "Could the ambassador's ship merely be—"

"When you're dealing with our telepaths, no contact is the same as bad news." Mychael's expression was utterly blank. It was the face he wore when he'd been kicked in the chest with bad news, news so bad it had to be cast aside and dealt with later.

"I take it they're your best?" Brina asked the archmagus.

"They are. There was no distortion. The signal should have come in loud and clear."

If there'd been a signal to receive.

If there had been a ship still afloat to send a signal from.

I spoke into the tense silence. "Could a sky dragon patrol—"

"Already deployed," Justinius said.

"Thank you, sir," Mychael said.

"You're welcome. Occasionally I can pull my weight around here. If the ambassador's ship left Laerin two days ago, it would have been southwest of Mermeia by now. Those shipping lanes are heavily traveled. If that ship was attacked, it's likely there would have been witnesses."

"Witnessing is one thing," Brina said. "Few could or would have stepped in to stop it."

Not necessarily. I had a little spark of hope. "I know a captain in those waters right now who could and would have stepped in and ensured the attacker never did it again." I turned to Justinius. "Sir, I need one of your telepaths to reach out to the *Fortune*. Phaelan has a telepath on board."

Mychael glanced back at Markus, a muscle working in his jaw. "I can't leave him—even for Isibel."

I gripped the message in my hand. "I'll take care of it. Phaelan will find that ship."

If there was a ship left to find.

3

Brina Daesage stayed with Markus for obvious reasons.
Justinius and I went downstairs to the citadel's communication center. Vegard and the old man's four bodyguards followed, close enough for protection, far enough for privacy.

I took advantage of it, though I still kept my voice down. "How are you doing, sir?"

A perfectly normal question, usually the opening for polite small talk. Neither Justinius nor myself were known for our politeness. And most people who asked the question weren't interested in a response other than "fine." I knew the old man wasn't fine, and I wanted to help if I could, even if that help was just to lend a sympathetic ear.

Archmagus Justinius Valerian had his hands more than full. The old man had to be close to overwhelmed, though he'd never admit it.

The Conclave of Sorcerers had never been a squeaky-clean organization, but no one had ever attempted to clean house to the extent Justinius had in mind.

As archmagus, Justinius was the ultimate power and authority on this island and over the Conclave of Sorcerers, and he was using that authority to its limits and beyond. If anyone had a problem with him bending the law until it squealed to clean up the Conclave, they weren't speaking up. They probably fell into one of two camps: those who were cheering him on, and those who were plotting his death. Weeding out traitors was a lot like weeding a garden—unless you got the roots, those weeds were going to come right back.

"Good analogy, girl," Justinius said. "Though I was thinking more along the lines of bad apples."

I smiled a little. "I keep forgetting you can read minds."

"You're an easy read. Besides, you asked how I was doing, and you know what I'm trying to do. And you know better than anyone just how nasty the men and women on this island can get when there's power at stake."

"Power corrupts—to say the least," I muttered.

"And absolute power corrupts absolutely. Things had been bad for years; that was why I brought Mychael in as paladin. I knew it was too big a job to do by myself. The Saghred surfacing for the first time in centuries, and you being able to use the rock without going off the deep end…Well, it kicked the greed to new heights."

Mychael had brought the Saghred here to keep it safe. I'd come to Mid for help in ridding myself of the rock's bond to me. We'd set off the firestorm Justinius Valerian was trying to stomp out. If anyone could do it, he could, but that didn't make me feel any less guilty about striking the match.

I winced. "Sorry about that."

"It's not your fault that at least half of the mages here have the morals of a Nebian snake oil merchant. Besides, it lured the lot of them out in the open like the swarm of cockroaches they are. And since you've smashed the rock, now there's nothing left for them to get their power-grubbing hands on. I've started at the top and I'm working my way down. By eliminating the wealthy traitors first, though, we gave the little ones time to squirm their way back under the rocks they'd come out from under."

"So they got away."

Justinius waved a negligent hand. "Some. People like that won't risk anything—most of all their lives and livelihoods—if they won't be well paid for the trouble. I took away the people paying the bribes, and half the problems on this island vanished overnight. That leaves the other half of the problem—the mages with plenty of magical *and* political power. They're not rich; they're just dangerous. Some of them wisely turned in their resignations, so they can do their plotting in private. Others have been more reluctant to give up their lucrative positions."

I grinned. "I'll bet you ate their reluctance for breakfast and their excuses for lunch."

The old man snorted, a sort of laugh. "The smart ones were gone by dinner. That left the stupid and the stubborn. The stupid will take care of themselves, always have." Any sign of humor vanished. "That leaves the stubborn, the patient. They're biding their time and making alliances while they wait. And while they scurry around like rats behind a wall, I've got entirely too many vacant positions, important positions. As a result, I'm not exactly operating from a position of power here. Hell, only half the mages are left on the Seat of Twelve. It's more like the Park Bench of Six."

Damn. Six of the most powerful mages in the Seven Kingdoms had been corrupt, either living in a power broker's pocket or—like Carnades Silvanus—had minions of their own.

Justinius scowled. "With the bad guys down but definitely not out, and the good guys not all that plentiful, the winner's going to be whoever can get their feet underneath them first. I want mages who know what they stand for, and stand for it openly. I may not agree with a mage's politics and beliefs, but I respect their right to think that way. Say what you believe in and stick to it, don't skulk around in corners. Ass-kissers, bootlickers, and two-faced turncoats have no place in the government of this island or holding any power over the magic users in the Seven Kingdoms. I've started the ball rolling on making some appointees of my own."

"So…As to how you're doing, you're tired, but you know what your job is, and you're determined to dig in and do it."

"Damn right."

That job would be one of the most difficult I'd ever heard of, but it was the one he'd picked, and he was the best man for the job.

So was Mychael.

After what had happened in the mirror room this morning, I didn't know what I was best qualified for, but I suspected it wasn't anything I wanted to do.

I glanced down at my hands. Hands that had been glowing dark red only an hour ago. Red with unknown power.

Or worse, a power that I knew only too well.

I needed to find my father as soon as I could.

Eamaliel Anguis had been bonded to the Saghred for nearly nine hundred years. His life had been lengthened by contact with the stone. Maybe soul-sucking rocks got lonely, too, but I knew the real reason—the Saghred couldn't feed itself; it needed someone to sacrifice souls to it. My father hadn't fed it a thing, so the first chance it got, the Saghred had slurped him up and used its wiles to try and trick me into eternal servitude.

If anyone would know what magical remnants the stone could have left with me, he would.

I lowered my voice even further than it had been. "Sir, did you hear what happened in the mirror room with Markus?"

Justinius kept walking by my side in silence for at least a minute.

I swallowed with an audible gulp.

"Raine, whatever you've got going on in there, you saved two men today—Mychael and Markus Sevelien. Whoever almost killed Sevelien and latched on to Mychael didn't like whatever it was you did. In my opinion, that makes it good; I don't care what color your hands were."

"Thank you, sir."

"Don't thank me. I'm simply calling it like I see it."

If word got out, other people would be calling it something else—something evil.

"I don't give a damn what anyone else thinks," the old man said. "And neither should you. You possibly still being more powerful than anyone else is their problem, not yours."

I smiled a little. "Anything I can do to keep you from picking up my thoughts like dice on a table?"

"Nope. You don't play cards, do you?"

"I try to avoid it—for just that reason."

"Probably a good thing. For you, that is." He gave me an impish grin. "But if you ever feel the need to play a few hands, promise you'll let me know."

"I'll do that."

We walked in silence for the next few moments.

The attack on Markus might be enough to postpone the peace talks. If it turned out the elven ambassador was dead, they might be scuttled before they even got started. Not to mention, what Justinius was trying to accomplish by getting rid of the Conclave's corruption had never been attempted at this level.

"Sir, I don't mean to be the voice of gloom and doom—"

The old man snorted. "Since when?"

I pressed on. "Do you really think this stands a chance of working? Especially now with what happened to Markus, and whatever may have happened to Ambassador Eldor and his staff."

"This isn't just about the elves and goblins agreeing to

play nice and not enslave each other," Justinius said. "The elven queen Lisara Ambrosius has always had a level head on her shoulders, and now that Carnades and Taltek Balmorlan and their treason-plotting cronies have been exposed to the light of day, that little lady's taking a broom to her house, the same as I'm doing with mine. As to the goblins, I don't know their new king—"

"You're not missing out."

"I've heard he's about as easy to get along with as a boil on your backside."

"Let's just say that while he's finally started showing some redeeming qualities, he's not someone I'd choose to spend an evening drinking with."

"Trust?"

"Depends on what's in it for him." I paused thoughtfully. "And his. I think he really does care about his people."

"That's what Mychael told me."

"But I trust Tam and Imala and the people they're putting around Chigaru, so I think he'll turn out all right."

"For a Mal'Salin."

"That goes without saying."

"It's not the elves and goblins that concern me. They know what a thing like the Saghred can do, the level of destructive power. History says the Saghred fell from the sky. What are the chances of there being only one? Or what if there's something out there waiting to be found that's even worse?"

"I can't imagine what could—"

"Your papa led the team that got the Saghred away from Rudra Muralin. The damage was limited. A thousand years ago when he was the chief mage for the goblin king, there were fewer people around for him to sacrifice. There are a lot more now. Every kingdom has several centers of population; cities are larger and packed with people. Another lunatic backed by a government with a grudge against another, or a group of zealots with warped ideology—"

"Like the Khrynsani."

The Khrynsani were an ancient goblin secret society and military order, with even more outdated political ideas. The Khrynsani's credo was simple. Goblins were meant to rule, and if anyone disagreed, they weren't meant to live. Those who disagreed included every other race. Sarad Nukpana had been their leader. The night I'd smashed the Saghred and Nukpana had gotten himself carried off to Hell had essentially marked the end of the Khrynsani. I hoped.

The old man nodded. "If they get their hands on an object of power and the chance to use it…"

Justinius didn't finish. He didn't need to. I knew what could happen, what would happen when the next Rudra Muralin or Sarad Nukpana found a new magical toy and took it home with them. I also didn't need him to remind me just how close we'd come to Sarad Nukpana unleashing Armageddon—and using me to do it.

"The elves and goblins—at least those in charge now—know that such power should never be allowed to fall into anyone's hands," he continued. "The other kingdoms have only seen such power from afar. They've never been threatened with annihilation. They see power that has never been theirs, respect that has never been theirs. Some people think respect and fear mean the same thing. Are their leaders, and the powerful and influential who support them, content with what they have under their control? It's been my experience that mankind—and I use that to encompass all the races—is seldom satisfied with what they have. Most people's striving is harmless, beneficial even. But there are those who strive for subjugation, having control over others' lives, lives held in the palm of their hand."

"A treaty won't stop those people."

"No, but agreement now will get the kingdoms off their asses to stop them. If you don't help, you face consequences. Sanctions, embargoes."

"So, we won't like you or play with you anymore?"

The old man gave me a flat look.

I raised my hands defensively. "I'm simply playing devil's advocate here. The kind of people who would use something like the Saghred as a weapon to kill or conquer won't care about sanctions or embargoes."

"Which is why the treaty will give the Guardians the authority to go into any kingdom ànd do whatever they have to do to secure that weapon."

Silence.

"That could be nasty," I said.

"There's no 'could be' about it. And by signing a treaty, each kingdom promises to allow the Guardians free and complete access to their lands to secure that object. If they don't want a Guardian army inside their borders, fine. Get the thing and turn it over to us. I know what the delegates are going to say. They'll say that for the Guardians, and goblins, and possibly the elves, this 'treaty' is merely a means to secure all magical power for themselves and render the kingdoms unable to obtain their own object of power, like the Saghred, with which to protect themselves. They'll claim to want it as a deterrent. Then their neighbor across the border will get their hands on something even stronger." Justinius was silent for a moment. "Where that ends…It's not anyplace any of us want to be, or leave to our children and grandchildren to deal with. That's why I'm going to do whatever I have to do to ensure my Katie and your Piaras don't have to go through any of this ever again when we're gone and they're in charge. That is what we must accomplish."

There was no time like the present to tell the old man what I wanted to be when I grew up.

"Sir, speaking of the cadets and the talented children they were—and you wanting me to be a Guardian—I've got your answer and an idea."

Justinius stopped in the middle of the corridor. I did

likewise, and so did Vegard and the archmagus's guards. One wave from Justinius and they all backed out of hearing range and went to attention.

I hadn't meant to cause all that.

"Uh…First, I can't be a Guardian—at least not in the usual way."

Those intense blue eyes came to rest on me. Eyes that could make a battle-hardened Guardian stammer like a newbie cadet.

"I'm listening," he said.

"It doesn't have anything to do with being the first woman Guardian. I don't have a problem with that." I tilted my head down the hall toward the at-attention men. "Those men all went through years of hard work and training to get where they are. I can't just walk in and pick up a uniform. Plus, I'm about to marry their paladin and commander. I'll gladly fight beside them, but I can't wear a Guardian uniform without earning it. And don't say I have earned it. Getting a power infusion from a soul-sucking rock didn't earn me anything."

"So what do you want to do?"

I told him.

"There's the Conclave college, but there's nothing for younger children," I continued once I'd covered the basics. "*That's* when they need teaching and guidance—and protection. There needs to be a school for them. Here. I know the Conclave is shorthanded right now, but we would need mages who not only have experience raising and guiding young talents but who can go out into the kingdoms and recognize potential when they see it, and who know the signs that these children's gifts are being abused or are at risk for abuse. Too many of the rogue dark mages the Guardians end up hunting started out as kids with more talent than good sense and guidance. Then there are the kids whose parents were duped into apprenticing their child with a mage who was really a broker or a procurer for someone like Taltek

Balmorlan. Piaras was lucky. He has a supportive family who are talents themselves. He's in the minority. The kids who go to the Conclave's college have wealthy parents or families. Tam didn't know he had a son until Talon was a teenager. When his mom died, he spent his childhood on his own. And you know what that kid's packing and the trouble he can get into. And what about the poor kids? Or even the middle-class kids whose parents can't afford qualified tutors or don't even know how to find somebody who's qualified?"

I wasn't bothering to keep my voice down anymore. The Guardians could hear me. I didn't care. It was a good idea. A needed idea.

"And being a Benares, my family has connections to people who would know who the brokers are and where they operate. It'd help find the kids who would otherwise fall through the cracks—or into the wrong hands."

I stopped, mainly because I'd run out of air. I hadn't said everything I wanted to say yet, but I'd said enough to get an opinion.

"What do you think, sir?"

"I think it would fit right in with finding those power objects. The nastiest thing about the objects and those brokers is that they both have a reputation for wanting young magic users to latch on to. I guarantee you, if you find one, the other will be close by. The same people who want to get their greedy hands on the next Saghred will be looking for talent to use it for them, and they don't want someone like you—a grown woman who's not about to let anyone make her do anything she doesn't want to do. They want talent they can intimidate and manipulate."

"Children."

"The younger and more gifted, the better. It's happening in every last kingdom, and I have long wanted it stopped. As much as I would like to do it myself, I can't."

"You have enough asses to kick here."

"God's own truth." The old man grinned. "And I've known I would need someone I could trust and depend on to do it." He slapped me on the back. "You're in charge. Just let me know what you need."

4

Unlike the mirror room, nothing in here made me want to turn and run the other way. Anything that could come out of a crystal ball or scrying bowl would be small enough for me to stomp on.

I was thrilled that Justinius had not only approved my idea but put me in charge of it. I wanted to live long enough to get started.

The room had just enough light to keep the telepaths from bumping into each other. Each had a workstation consisting of a small desk next to a wide pedestal with a scrying bowl filled with water or a crystal ball mounted on top, depending on the practitioner's preference.

Justinius made a beeline straight for a stocky, dark-haired Guardian. He was in uniform, but it looked like he'd slept in it. He probably had. Mychael and the old man had been keeping the telepaths busy coordinating the delegates' arrivals—and gathering intelligence to use to ferret out any traitors with the mistaken impression that they'd escaped Justinius's personnel purge. The old man was relentless and ruthless. I, for one, was glad of it. It meant he was going to do it right the first time. Not that I had any doubt.

Every other man in the room snapped to attention as the archmagus swept through the double doors. The dark-haired Guardian/telepath merely looked up from his onyx scrying bowl, his expression as worn as his uniform.

"I expected the paladin, sir."

"Mychael's busy, so you got me."

The Guardian grinned crookedly. "Then I'll make do, sir."

"Still nothing?" Justinius asked.

"Not a word or image. I know the telepath on that ship. I've contacted him before, and I've spoken to him in person. I know how to reach him." The Guardian's face was somber. "He's not with us anymore, sir."

"Rest assured, Ben, whoever was responsible will be found and will pay."

The Guardian nodded. "Thank you, sir. He'd appreciate that."

A dangerous gleam lit the old man's eyes. "I will, too." He stepped aside for me. "Miss Benares here knows a ship that's in the area. They might have seen something."

"And if Phaelan saw it, he'd have acted on it—so if your friend was killed, he's already been avenged."

"The *Fortune*?" To Ben's credit, he didn't bat an eye at the thought of touching minds with the ship's telepath of the most notorious pirate vessel in the Seven Kingdoms.

"That's the ship," I said. "Can you reach her?"

The Guardian gave me a raised eyebrow and a look.

I returned the smile. "Of course you can." I glanced from the telepath to the archmagus and back again. "Do we need to step outside or something so you can work?"

Ben jerked his head at Justinius with a fond grin. "Ma'am, I've worked most of my time here with this one breathing down my neck. You standing right where you are won't bother me in the least."

With that, he laid his hands flat on the pedestal on either side of the scrying bowl, his eyes intent on the surface, and went absolutely still. There were conversations going on around us, and even though everyone kept their voices down, I knew I'd never have been able to do what Ben was doing, even with the Saghred's boost.

After about five minutes, he spoke without looking up. "I've got the *Fortune*'s telepath, ma'am. Captain Benares is there with him, and he wants proof that you're the one doing the asking."

"He would. Phaelan doesn't trust what he can't see, and magic is at the top of the list." I thought for a moment. "On Phaelan's sixteenth birthday, he invited a whole bordello's worth of ladies of the evening on board one of his dad's ships to help him celebrate." I gave an evil chuckle. "Ask him what his dad did when he found out."

Ben raised a bushy eyebrow. "Really?"

"And that wasn't even the first time Phaelan had done it. It was just the first time he got caught."

The Guardian looked back into the bowl. After about a moment, he grinned. "The captain believes you are who you say you are."

"Good, because I was about to really get personal. Ask him if he's seen the *Blue Rose*."

He silently asked, and we silently waited.

Ben raised his head from where it'd been bowed over the bowl, and squeezed his eyes shut for a few moments. I bet telepaths were constantly on the verge of a splitting headache.

"The captain said they captured a Caesolian schooner a little over an hour ago," Ben told us. "She'd been running under full sail away from a burning ship that'd been forced onto a shoal about ten miles northwest of Gruen. The captain says he knew she was a pirate and gave chase. They engaged her, crippled her, and boarded. They found and freed six prisoners."

"Was one of them…" I stopped and swore. "I don't even know what Mychael's sister looks like. Do you know?" I asked Justinius.

"Not a clue."

"Crap…uh, she's about seven years younger than Mychael, which would make her mid-twenties. Maybe auburn hair and blue-green eyes, though she might—"

"The captain says the paladin's sister is safe—though righteously pissed at the situation."

My shoulders sagged in relief.

"What about the elven ambassador, Santis Eldor?" Justinius asked.

I mentally kicked myself. Don't ask about the head of the elven delegation. Way to go, Raine.

Ben concentrated on the scrying bowl again. After less than a minute, he looked up at the two of us and grimly shook his head. "The captain says the *Blue Rose* wasn't chosen at random. She was targeted. When she was boarded, Ambassador Eldor was killed first, along with his two guards, the ship's telepath, and the crew. The ambassador's staff was taken captive."

Captives—or payment for the pirates from whoever had ordered the ambassador assassinated.

Either way…Thank you, Phaelan.

Ben lowered his voice. "And something the captain feels you should know now. The pirates had been paid in goblin gold, in bags still carrying the Mal'Salin royal seal."

The old man spat a word in a language I didn't recognize. If it wasn't a curse word, it should have been.

"I couldn't have said it better," I told him. "We do *not* need that. Goblin gold being paid to assassinate an elven ambassador before the peace talks even start. It wasn't Chigaru, sir. He's not my favorite person, but he wouldn't do this. He needs these talks to succeed. But plenty of nobles who lost everything when they allied themselves with Sarad Nukpana would love to see him fail. Bags of gold with the royal seal are too obvious. It's a setup. I'm sure of it."

Justinius gave a terse nod. "How about the ambassador's second in command?"

Ben looked confused. "The paladin's sister is fine."

"I said the ambassador's second..." The old man stopped, then whistled. "I didn't know that."

Neither did I.

And neither did Mychael.

Apparently neither did the assassins, or Isibel wouldn't have been left alive for Phaelan to rescue.

Isibel Eiliesor was the elven ambassador's second in command.

With Eldor's murder, *she* was the elven ambassador.

And if a killer didn't want the elven ambassador alive to participate in the peace talks, she was their next target.

5

The weight of the world dropped off of Mychael's shoulders when I told him that Isibel was safe.

I seriously considered letting her tell Mychael about her new title when Phaelan dropped anchor in Mid's harbor, but that'd be the cowardly way out. Mychael's job was ensuring the security of the ambassadors and the rest of the delegates. Isibel was now the elven ambassador. Since he'd be doing the overprotective brother thing anyway, at least now he could do it officially.

Besides, from what Mychael had told me about Isibel, I knew I was going to like her. And by taking the brunt of his initial reaction to her new job title, I'd earn serious sister-in-law points.

What shocked me was that this news was a surprise.

"You're the paladin of the Conclave Guardians and a virtual nexus of spy networks. How did Isibel hide being one step away from being elven ambassador?"

"Because she's not using her real name. At least she wasn't. She probably will now."

Well, that explained a lot.

"Let me guess. She wanted to get out from under big brother's shadow and do it herself."

Mychael's grunt told me I was right, and that as far as he was concerned Isibel had some explaining to do.

If Isibel Eiliesor had fought her way up through the elven foreign service to one step removed from an ambassadorship without using her family name and influence, she was one tough cookie, and I *really* wanted to be in the room when she and Mychael crossed verbal swords.

"Apparently she dropped the alias when Phaelan took her ship," I noted.

"I told her how close you were to certain members of your family," Mychael said. "I also told her that Phaelan and Mago are good men."

I chuckled. "I hope she didn't tell him that. As far as Phaelan is concerned, 'good' is a four-letter word. Mago would like it, though."

We were in Mychael's office in the citadel. Justinius had told Mychael to go get some rest. Markus was out of danger and Mychael had released him from the bespelled sleep. Markus was now sleeping on his own. Dalis would watch him and let us know when he woke up.

Mychael was slumped in his office chair. I stood, went around behind him, and began massaging his shoulders.

He groaned.

I smiled. A girl liked to have her work appreciated.

I didn't have the weight of the world on my shoulders, just my red-tinged magic corner of it. Mychael hadn't said anything yet. I had to. I needed to.

"Do you have any idea what happened with me this morning?"

He rolled his shoulders under my hands and laughed.

"That covers entirely too much ground. You'll have to be more specific."

"What I did in the mirror room."

Silence.

"The way I'm feeling right now, no answer is a bad answer."

"I don't know what happened, but I was grateful for it." He paused. "It's the red, isn't it?"

"Yes. My magic's never been red before. Quite frankly, it scares me."

"Red doesn't only mean dark magic. Kesyn Badru's magic manifests as red, and so does A'Zahra Nuru. They're not evil, far from it."

I winced and briefly squeezed my eyes shut. I had the mother of all headaches coming on. "I didn't mean to imply that goblin magic is evil. It's just that…"

"Others might."

"Others *will*. When I was bonded to the Saghred, my magic wasn't red, and now it is. I just want to understand why." I stopped massaging Mychael's shoulders, and came around in front of him. I needed to see his face, watch his eyes, for what I was about to say. "I want to understand who I am. I thought once the Saghred was destroyed I'd go back to being myself again, or at least someone I recognized. I don't know who or what I am anymore." I felt the sting of tears welling up in my eyes. "Or what I'll become."

Mychael pulled me down onto his lap, his arms gathering me against his chest.

My throat tightened in response. Oh great, I was going to cry. I sniffed loudly. "I don't want to cry."

"Then don't cry. You don't have a reason to."

I lifted my head and looked at him. The tears that had pooled in my eyes trickled down my face, but no fresh tears joined them.

Mychael smiled and gently wiped my tears aside with his thumb. "Not what you expected to hear, was it?"

"No, it's not. Though I think I like it. At this point I'll like anything that doesn't make me cry. I don't have time for that."

"We've had this talk before," he said. "You're not evil, you never were, and you never will be. And as I believe Tam has told you before, you don't even qualify for minions."

I laughed, though with the half sob that came with it, it sounded more like a hiccup. "I could have minions."

"No, you most definitely could not have minions." The humorous gleam left his eyes. "I've met evil face-to-face. You are *not* it."

"Thank you."

We sat there in silence, the tension slowly leaving me. Time to push it away and change the subject to something a little less terrifying. I eased myself out of his lap. "Any word on your parents?"

"Their ship was docked overnight in Mermeia. I've ordered two Guardian ships to escort them, but it will take some time for them to rendezvous. They won't arrive until late tomorrow."

"But at least you know they'll be safe." I bent and kissed the top of his head, wrapping my arms around his shoulders in a tight hug. "Think I could talk you into losing your uniform tunic? It's in my way. A real massage—or anything else that might occur to us—would make you feel a whole lot better."

Mychael groaned again, but this one wasn't happy. "You could talk me into anything, but we don't have time."

"We could make time."

"You have no idea how tempting that is."

I grinned. "Oh, yes, I do. It'd make me feel better, too."

"But we have to be at Sirens in two hours."

"Sirens?"

Sirens was the nightclub Tam owned here in Mid. The three times I'd been there I'd barely made it out alive, though to my knowledge none of his clientele had shared my experiences. If they had, Sirens wouldn't have been the most popular nightspot on the island.

"When I sent word to Tam and Imala telling them to delay their arrival," Mychael continued, "I said we were having technical difficulties."

I barked a laugh. "I don't believe that's what Markus would call it. So you think any telepathic communication could be intercepted?"

"I don't know what to think, but until we know what's happening, I'm being cautious. I included a coded message that hit the high points of what those technical difficulties were."

"So Tam knows?"

"He does."

"And we're going to Sirens because…?"

"Tam has a warded room in the basement that he's used as a workroom in the past."

"Does it have a mirror?"

Mychael sighed. "Not exactly."

Now it was my turn to be tense. "There's a lot of dislike in that 'not exactly.'"

"Before Tam returned to Regor, he told me the warding spell he was using so I could get into the room if I needed to."

"Why would you need to?"

"To unblock the Passage door inside the room."

My suddenly nerveless hands dropped from Mychael's shoulders. "A Passage door?"

He nodded once.

"I'd rather chance running through a mirror with a tentacle monster," I said.

"Me, too."

The director of elven intelligence had been mirrored to death and barely brought back to life. The ship carrying the elven ambassador had been attacked by assassins on the high seas, the ambassador had been killed, and the rest of his staff taken captive. Fortunately, they had been saved by pirates who, thankfully, were related to me. One of the staffers was now the ambassador, and she was related to my fiancé.

And it wasn't even lunchtime yet.

The Guardians were responsible for delegate security and safety during the peace talks. To say security and safety had gotten off to a bad start would be the ultimate understatement. Though technically, none of the above had happened on the Isle of Mid, so there was nothing we could have done to prevent it, that wasn't how a lot of the delegates would see it. As soon as word got around—and it would—the peace talks would be the talk of the Seven Kingdoms, and not in a good way.

Now, two of the most important people in the goblin delegation would be arriving via a Passage door.

There was bad—and there was worse.

The Passages were worse.

"Passages" was a misnomer. For those who weren't savvy about all things magical, the word "passage" simply meant a way to get from one place to another.

Problem wasn't with the Passages themselves; it was what could be in there with you.

The Passages were the areas between dimensions. Their boundaries flowed fog-like around our own reality. Where a Passage touched our world at one place could be just a short distance from where it touched our world in another, even though physically those points were far apart. From Mid to Regor via sky dragon was a three-day flight. Via a mirror, two steps. Via the Passages, about a mile.

A mile chock full of things waiting to kill and eat you every step of the way.

A Passage door was an opening between our world and the Passages. It could be naturally occurring, or it could have been torn by a mage. Dark mages practicing black magic were usually the only ones who would want to.

When it came to mirror magic, elves were the undisputed experts. The best mirror mages were elves, and it was through their research that mirrors had replaced the Passages as the preferred method to quickly get from one place to another.

There were things living in the Passages, and those things considered elves, goblins, and humans quite tasty.

And after what Mychael had told him, Tam and Imala had decided to take their chances with a run for their lives. I'd wondered why they hadn't taken a sky dragon, but Mychael said considering the circumstances of Markus's attack, Tam didn't believe we had three days of flight time to spare.

That made me feel all kinds of better.

I'd been living in Mermeia when Tam had come to town two years ago. He was a duke and a primaru, or mage of the royal blood. Primaru Tamnais Nathrach was the ex-chief mage of the soon-to-be-assassinated goblin queen and a grieving husband of a recently murdered noble wife. Rumor had it that Tam leaving the goblin court and his wife's murder were connected. Tam arrived in town as a goblin of wealth and influence. He purchased the palazzo of an old but impoverished Mermeian family and transformed it into Sirens—the most notorious nightclub and gambling parlor in the city. Before coming to Mermeia, Tam had already opened a Sirens location here on the Isle of Mid.

We'd met when a cash-strapped noble started working his way through his wife's jewelry to support his gambling habit. The wife hired me to find her grandmother's favorite ring. I tailed the ring—and her husband—right to Sirens' high-stakes card table. I'd heard that the owner of Sirens was a scoundrel and an opportunist, but he was also a savvy businessman. Working together—and after entirely too much risk to life and limb—we got the ring back and returned it to its rightful owner.

It looked good for him to return the lady's ring. Tam told me later he did it to impress me.

He needn't have bothered. Being a Benares, I'd always been attracted to rogues. Kind of like a moth to flame. Most times I had the good sense to steer clear, but with Tam, I'd come close to getting my wings singed more than once.

Tam had been Queen Glicara Mal'Salin's magical enforcer for five years. Chief mages for the House of Mal'Salin tended to have short lifespans. The lifespan-shortening was usually done by others who wanted to be chief mage. For Tam to have survived for that long at his queen's side meant that he'd left his conscience and any morals he possessed at the throne room door.

After his wife's murder, Tam left the court and sought out one of his early teachers, Primari A'Zahra Nuru. Like a drug, black magic was addictive—and it exacted a price you did not want to pay. With the help of A'Zahra Nuru and Mychael, Tam came back from magic's dark path. Even though he'd been through what was essentially black magic rehab, Tam was still a dark mage. When I'd been bonded to the Saghred, Tam had nearly fallen off the recovery wagon. Hard.

The Sirens nightclub in Mermeia was mainly a gambling parlor. The Sirens on the Isle of Mid offered spellsinging as the featured specialty. On the outside, Sirens looked more like an expensive manor house than a nightclub. The diamond-shaped, lead-paned windows belonged to the restaurant part of the establishment. We were in the interior theatre where the shows took place.

Small tables were scattered across the main floor of the theatre, each covered in a crisp white cloth and set with a single pale lightglobe in its center. There were either two or four chairs at each table, with enough room between each for servers to discreetly fill drink orders—and to give Sirens' guests privacy to enjoy the show. The second-floor dining suites were like private boxes in a fine theatre. Columns stretched from the floor to the high, vaulted ceiling, carved with mermaids and mermen—sirens that could sing men or women to their doom, or somewhere much more enjoyable.

The stage wasn't large; it didn't need to be. Sirens was about spellsingers and what they could do to an audience. Spellsingers didn't need space, just flawless acoustics, so that a whispered word sounded as though it was being whispered directly into a patron's ear even at the table farthest from the stage.

Shields at the base of the stage prevented spellsongs from having their full effect. They could be strengthened or lowered as needed. With spellsinging, the sex of the singer and the listener shouldn't matter. A truly gifted spellsinger could make you forget that you even had a sexual preference.

Entirely too much had happened here over the past three months—all of it bad. Justinius had nearly been assassinated with a spellsong, the queen of demons had sent her undead minions here to make me an offer that I could refuse and die, and I'd nearly been killed (twice) by a thousand-year-old goblin dark mage who'd basically been a reanimated corpse.

Good times.

At this time of day Sirens was closed, but Tam had told his manager that either Mychael or I were to be allowed in at any time.

Apparently Sirens' basement contained much more than stage equipment and old costumes. That was all I'd seen on my first and only trip down there.

The air smelled as if nothing had stirred it since then. After a misunderstanding of epic proportions with the city watch, Tam had run down here with me tossed over one shoulder like a sack of potatoes. Needless to say, what I'd seen had been limited to the floor and Tam's ass. And I'd been too pissed at Tam to notice anything else.

Mychael pushed aside a rack of costumes to reveal…a wall.

I'd been on Mid long enough to know that things you thought were common, weren't. There was no such thing as just a mirror, and walls very often concealed something else. Just because I couldn't feel magic coming from it didn't mean there wasn't any. Mychael confirmed it by placing his left palm flat against a particularly dusty section. There was no click of a hidden door unlocking. A door-sized opening simply appeared.

The room beyond was darker than dark.

I stayed right where I was.

I knew Tam, and Tam would never hurt me. I didn't have the same level of trust for Tam's stuff, especially stuff left in a secret room openable only by magic. He'd been a dark mage for most of his life.

Mychael glanced at his upraised palm and a lightglobe flared to life, awaiting instructions.

I looked past him into the room. Nope, that dark definitely wasn't natural. "Any chance of you being able to unblock that Passage door from here?"

"None."

"Any chance of you covering yourself in the best shields you've got?"

"That goes without saying."

"Good. Because that dark looks a little too dark."

"Tam did that on purpose. There's also a strong repelling spell woven in."

"It's working great. I'm repelled, repulsed even."

Mychael launched the lightglobe, freeing up both hands should spell or steel become necessary, and explored the room.

I followed his every move.

Thresholds were powerful. Spirits, evil or otherwise, couldn't cross a warded threshold unless invited by the mage who'd done the warding. The same applied to living magic users. If you crossed uninvited, your magic took a hit. Tam had known Mychael before he'd met me. Mychael had helped him to step away and stay away from black magic. I didn't know exactly what Mychael had done for Tam, and neither one of them had ever shared details.

Neither Mychael's lightglobe nor his shields had flickered when he crossed the threshold, meaning he had Tam's permission to be here. Tam had created whatever was in this room two years before he met me. Tam liked me now, but he didn't know me then. So when Mychael gestured me in, I hesitated.

"It's safe," he assured me. "It's not nice, but it's safe."

I started to step across.

Mychael held up his hand, stopping me.

I tensed. "What?"

"This was Tam's safe room and his escape route, if needed." He paused. "After creating it, he never came here again. The Tam who wove these wards then is not the Tam you know now."

Tamnais Nathrach, chief mage to the House of Mal'Salin, a dark mage practitioner of black magic, Queen Glicara Mal'Salin's right hand and magical enforcer.

I knew this, had been told this, but I'd never experienced it for myself.

Magic users could block entrance to a room with the same ward, and yet no two would be alike. Spells worked by a practitioner bore their imprint, their essence, a piece of who they were when a ward was created. Magic was a part of whoever was gifted with it. Part of the Tam of three years ago still existed in the wards he'd placed on this door.

"Mid was his first stop after leaving Regor," Mychael said. "A'Zahra Nuru was here."

A'Zahra Nuru was the mage Tam had approached when he realized he needed help.

Mychael had just warned me what I'd be stepping into, literally.

I swallowed nervously, took a deep breath, and crossed the threshold.

I winced as I crossed. There was a featherlike brush of Tam's magic against my shields, and I shivered. This was Tam, and yet not Tam. The wards on the door had been woven by a man who had just fled the goblin court. His wife had been murdered and he had been framed for the crime. Tam had been on the run from his enemies—those he'd known and those who still hid in the shadows awaiting their chance.

The magic that had gone into creating those wards belonged to a Tam I'd never known, but had been told about. Rage, fear, pain, soul-crushing grief. This Tam had already been plotting revenge even as he fled. Revenge that was breathtaking in its violence. Everything Tam had, was, and had planned and hoped to be had been torn from him when Calida Nathrach had been poisoned. The Nukpana and Ghalfari families had been responsible for it all. But the Tam who had created this hadn't restricted his anger only to them. Tamnais Nathrach wanted to lash out at anyone and everyone. All that magic from the dark depths of a well of power, aimed at all who dared to defy him, who were foolish enough to stand in his way. He would strike, swiftly and without mercy.

The same residue of unbridled violence permeated what appeared to be a simple wooden door on the other side of the room. The wood itself was old, ancient even. Runes had been branded into it; not with a branding iron, but with the finger of the practitioner who had traced them there, the very touch burning the runes into the door.

Tam's touch, superheated by black magic.

I recognized some of the runes, but not most. And judging from those I could read, I had no desire to have the rest translated for me.

They were runes of protection, runes to keep what waited on the other side where they belonged—as far away from the population of this world as possible.

"How is this thing safer than a mirror?" I asked.

"Because no one in their right mind would use one."

"And Tam and Imala are coming through that?" I'd instinctively lowered my voice to keep from being heard by the things on the other side. "When Tam comes through, what's to stop things from coming through with him?"

"Tam…and me."

An exhausted paladin and a danger-addicted goblin.

What could possibly go wrong?

Imala Kalis, director of the goblin secret service and protector of the goblin royal family, came through the Passage door first.

Considering that her feet weren't anywhere near the floor at the time, I didn't think her mode of entry was her idea.

She'd been thrown.

Mychael was there to catch, which was good because he was all that stood between Imala and a wall. Hitting that would've made her even less happy than she already was.

I got out of the way of who was coming next. The man who'd thrown her dove through the entry, hit the floor and rolled, kicking out with his booted feet to slam the door.

Something hit the door from the other side. Hard. With a shriek that threatened to make my ears bleed, the whatever hit the door again. Harder.

The goblin hadn't budged. Flat on his back, his long legs bent, bottom of his boots pushing with all he had to keep what was in there from joining us out here.

Goblins knew how to make an entrance—especially this goblin.

Tamnais Nathrach grinned up at us. To him, we were upside down. "Sorry I'm late."

Then he gave all his attention to the door. No works, no spells, no incantations, just intense staring and even more intense concentration. The runes blazed so brightly, I had to look away and squeeze my eyes shut. Too bad I hadn't done it fast enough to keep the runes' afterimages from glowing against my closed eyelids.

Black magic runes, there for the viewing for the next few hours whenever I closed my eyes.

Oh good.

The monstrous whatsit on the other side flung itself—or whatever it was throwing—against the door again. The sound wasn't nearly as loud, the door didn't budge, and the shriek that followed barely registered in my ears.

That apparently told Tam it was safe to take his feet off the door and put them on the floor where they belonged.

Tam and Imala were dressed almost identically in black from head to toe, including boots that came up to mid-thigh. Their armor was leather and both were wearing blades anywhere and everywhere they had the room. Both wore their hair pulled back in a long goblin battle braid.

I'd seen them wear this armor before; heck, I'd worn this armor before. It was functional and made a seriously fierce fashion statement.

Right now, that statement was less fashion and more ick.

What looked like blue dust had mixed with yellow slime, resulting in green foam that emitted a stench the likes of which I hadn't experienced since a pint-sized demon had crawled out of a latrine at city watch headquarters.

Like I said, ick.

Imala Kalis stood there, dripping, her glare saying loud and clear that all of it was Tam's fault.

I had absolutely no doubt that it was.

Tam stood and flicked his hand in distaste, sending a splat of foam against the nearest wall.

"Why don't we go upstairs, Imala and I will get cleaned up, and I'll tell you what you have in your mirror?"

6

The last time Mychael and I had been with Tam in his apartment over Sirens' stage, we'd been attacked by the undead minions of the Demon Queen.

I, for one, could do without a repeat.

Tam had insisted that the Passage door was securely closed and locked, but bad luck had been the only luck the three of us seemed to experience. If one of us hadn't done something to bring evil bad guys down on our collective heads, one of the other two could be counted on to pick up the slack.

It wasn't a matter of *if* but *when.*

I could do without a repeat of that, too.

None of us were holding our breath that Doom hadn't put us on his dance card and just hadn't told us yet.

The coded message Mychael had sent to Tam had given him the basics of what had happened to Markus. He'd just finished telling Tam and Imala the gruesome details while Tam fixed us all some much needed drinks.

The two goblins exchanged a glance when Mychael finished.

"And all this coincidentally happened less than two hours before Tam and I were due to arrive," Imala said, slouching down in her chair. "Wonderful. Just wonderful."

Tam took a fortifying swig of his drink. "What attacked Markus was a Rak'kari, a creature conjured from goblin elemental magic, like a Magh'Sceadu. But while Magh'Sceadu feed on magic and life essence, Rak'kari just kill. It's all they were made to do, and as you witnessed for yourself, they do it very well. Their webs are coated with a poison that can paralyze in seconds and even stop a heart. They have small mouths, which make it difficult to feed. So like some spiders, their bite injects venom into their victim that dissolves flesh and organs into a drinkable liquid."

I think my mouth was hanging open. "Doesn't goblin elemental magic make any fluffy creatures?"

Tam flashed a grin and took another sip of his drink. "It does, but you should see the teeth."

"I'd rather not."

I looked at Mychael. I didn't need Tam to tell me how close Mychael had come to sharing Markus's fate. The high collar on his tunic—and my hands glowing red with suspicious new magic—had been all that'd kept Mychael from certain death. Justinius was right; I didn't care what kind of magic had taken up residence inside of me. If it'd saved the life of the man I loved, it could stay. For now.

Mychael didn't tell Tam about his close call. I bit my tongue and followed his lead. It'd happened, it was over, and Mychael hadn't died. That was how Mychael's "man logic" saw it. As far as he was concerned he'd dodged that dagger and moved on. If I was going to be married to a man who ignored Death on a daily basis, I'd need to learn to do the same. I'd do it, but I wouldn't like it—or probably ever get used to it.

"I thought I knew about all goblin elementals," Mychael was saying.

"It's no surprise that you haven't heard of Rak'kari," Tam told him. "They're rarely conjured because they can't be controlled. They'll turn on and kill their creator as soon as they manifest unless they're immediately contained."

I was incredulous. "So the black 'rope' Markus was wrapped in was a *web*?"

Tam nodded.

"It was as thick as two of my fingers put together. How big is this thing? Or do we not want to know?"

"You probably don't want to know."

"Okay, I'm good with that." I raised my glass. "Here's hoping I'll never have to look one in its ugly face."

"Technically, it doesn't have a face."

"What part of I'm good with not knowing don't you understand?"

Imala sighed the sigh of the long-suffering. "Welcome to my world."

"And there's no recorded way to kill them." Tam continued. "They don't require air, they can live underwater, and their outer armor is indestructible."

I just sat there. "It's a spider monster with a *shell*?"

Tam nodded. "The entire body is armored."

"Of course, it is. Magh'Sceadu are Khrynsani. Whose bright idea was it to create Rak'kari?"

"Khrynsani."

"Please tell me you're kidding."

"I wish I could."

"Shit," I spat.

"We couldn't agree more," Imala said. "The night you destroyed the Saghred, we arrested as many Khrynsani as we could find, but just as many escaped. They have nothing to lose now and everything to gain."

"First being revenge on us," Tam noted.

"Whether they would have wanted to kill you and Imala as well would depend on their idea of revenge," Mychael noted. "Would they want you dead at their hands, or would they prefer to leave you to take the blame for their actions?"

"Yes," Imala replied.

"Pardon?"

"Yes, to both. They wouldn't see why they couldn't have both. Though they'd want blame to come first, death later, once they thought we'd suffered enough. When it comes to vengeance, we goblins prefer to drag it out as long as possible."

Yet another goblin quality that gave elves nightmares.

I looked from Tam to Imala to Mychael in disbelief. None of them appeared to be shocked that there were still Khrynsani running around among the living, and still organized enough to come after us. Come to think of it, I shouldn't be surprised. Roaches and Khrynsani, you couldn't get rid of either one of them.

"The Khrynsani have been active for over a thousand years," Tam told me. "They've always come back. They're like rats. Kill a few and the rest will either disappear down holes or vanish into the walls. Lying low for a few years—a century even—is well within their capabilities. They've done it before."

"I was thinking roaches."

"Just as hard to exterminate, but it doesn't mean we stop trying." Tam flashed a grin complete with fangs. "And occasionally you get lucky and get a few under your boot."

"Speaking of which, have your parents found Sandrina Ghalfari?" Mychael asked.

Sandrina Ghalfari was the mother of Sarad Nukpana, the late, not-lamented leader of the Khrynsani. The psychotic, rotten apple that had been Sarad hadn't fallen far from his mother's crazy tree. Sandrina had fatally poisoned Tam's wife and had come close to killing Tam's parents and his brother—

and me. For a few hours, Sarad Nukpana had been the goblin king, with Sandrina as the power—and evil—behind the throne. Tam's parents had led the goblin resistance. Tam's mom was a mortekal, which in Goblin meant "noble taker of life" or "righteous executioner." My translation was "badass assassin." Before we'd returned to Mid from Regor, Tam's folks said they'd be taking a second honeymoon/hunting trip, with Sandrina Ghalfari as the prey.

"They haven't found her," Tam was saying. "And yes, they're still looking. Mom doesn't give up, especially when it's personal. Sandrina Ghalfari is as personal as it gets."

Mychael raised his glass. "I wish them good hunting."

"Don't we all?" I muttered. "As to the rest of the Khrynsani crawling back out of their collective hole in the ground, isn't there anything—"

"To keep them from coming back?" Tam finished for me. "When they do try to come home, they'll find they don't have a home to come to. Those sea dragons gave us a good head start on demolishing their temple."

A family of sea dragons had been living in the caverns beneath the Khrynsani temple. Sarad Nukpana had summoned them up into the temple itself to kill and eat the goblin resistance fighters who were putting a crimp in what was to have been his night of triumph. The dragons had come up through the floors, and in their enthusiasm had brought down a big part of the ceiling.

"The stone used to build the temple is virtually indestructible," Tam continued, "but no one told that to the sea dragons. We have our best engineers and stone masons working on a way to dump every last brick into the caverns and tunnels below the temple, then build something useful where it used to be, something the people can enjoy."

Imala smiled, complete with dimple. "I'm in favor of a city park." Then the smile vanished. "Mychael, is there any theory on how the Rak'kari got inside that mirror? I thought that once two mirrors were linked, the way was sealed and nothing could get inside."

"It should be impossible, but obviously it isn't. We've got several of the kingdoms' top mirror researchers on the faculty here. Justinius has them working on it."

"If Khrynsani made it, couldn't they have put it in the mirror?" I asked.

Tam shook his head. "They prefer to travel by Gates."

Of course they did.

A Gate is a tear in the fabric of reality. It's not naturally occurring. Nothing about a Gate is natural—or legal or moral. Stepping through a Gate is like stepping through a doorway or a mirror. But unlike a doorway or mirror, it takes magic of the blackest kind to make one, magic fueled by terror, torture, despair, and death—the more the merrier.

"And with their preference for Gates, I've never heard of Khrynsani doing much, if anything, by way of mirror research," Tam continued. "That being said, I've been away from court for two years. Imala?"

The director of the goblin secret service shook her head. Imala made it her job to know everything about her enemies, and the Khrynsani were at the top of her list.

"If there was such a person, either Khrynsani or goblin mirror mage, we would have heard of them, or at least rumors of their existence and abilities. Elves, on the other hand, are known for expanding the boundaries of what is possible in mirror travel."

"The college's faculty expert's an elf," Mychael said.

Tam shifted uneasily in his chair. "Carnades wasn't the only mirror mage in his family. He wasn't even the best. The Silvanus family is known for producing highly gifted mirror mages. Legendary, even." He paused meaningfully. "A family full of expert mirror mages who blame us for Carnades's death."

"Sarad Nukpana killed Carnades," I said. "If Carnades hadn't kept trying to frame the three of us and have us executed, chances are we never would have had to go to Regor in the first place. But once we got there, he betrayed us, partnered with Nukpana, and then was stupid and suicidal enough to betray him. His death was his own fault."

"To his family, Carnades could do no wrong," Mychael said. "Everything he did was to reach his goal of 'purifying' the elven race. I know for a fact that they agreed with his views and supported any act he had to commit to achieve it."

"Just what the Seven Kingdoms needs, an entire family of bigoted, sadistic sickos."

"Don't forget powerful and influential—at least they were. It's not only Carnades's death they would want revenge for. It's the shame brought on the Silvanus name. Like most noble families, they take a great deal of pride in their honor, actual or perceived. The Silvanus family is ruined—financially, politically, and socially."

"And I was the one who dug up the dirt," I said. "I would do it again, I don't care who it would bring down on my head. Though if I hadn't kept trying to 'do the right thing' and save his hide every time someone or something tried to kill him, half our problems would've solved themselves." I thought for a moment. "Would a Silvanus be too proud to ally with the Khrynsani? Though Carnades wasn't too proud to buddy up to Sarad Nukpana."

"They wouldn't like it," Mychael said, "but they'd do it. Carnades came way too close to securing the ultimate power for himself, and by association, his family. Everything a Silvanus does is for the advancement of the family. You may have found the ledger that put the final nail in Carnades's coffin, but it was Markus who used it to bring him down."

"And I gave it to him."

"You did the right thing—the only thing. Exposing Carnades's treason was Markus's job, and I know for a fact that bringing down Carnades and his allies was the most enjoyable act of Markus's entire career."

"And it almost killed him."

"How much do we know about specific Silvanus family members?" Imala asked. "In terms of mirror talent."

"Carnades has a younger brother and an older sister," Mychael said. "He had a younger sister who died nearly twenty years ago—was killed, actually. Rumor has it the family did it themselves. An honor killing."

I blinked. "Honor?"

"She refused to marry the husband that had been chosen for her. She was in love with another."

"And they killed her?"

Mychael nodded once. "Carnades's older sister is said to be the best mirror mage in the family. However, they also believe in keeping their actual levels of talent secret, so their true powers are essentially unknown."

"So any of them could be capable of shoving a Rak'kari into a mirror."

"Now that we know it's possible, a Silvanus would be a viable suspect."

"We can safely assume that the Khrynsani were responsible for conjuring the Rak'kari," Imala told us. "I think it would be in our best interests to keep that information to ourselves. I could see the Khrynsani wanting to disrupt the peace talks, and killing Markus Sevelien and making it look like goblin work would be an effective first step. To many of the delegates, there's not any difference between a Khrynsani and the goblin government—they see them as one and the same. During his reign, Sathrik did all that he could to encourage that view. It intimidated his people, his enemies, and the other races. We want and need trust now, not intimidation and fear."

"Who is protecting Chigaru and Mirabai while the two of you are here?" Mychael asked.

"Kesyn Badru and my grandmother are with them," Imala

said. "And between me and Tam, we've provided enough qualified guards."

"They're as safe as they can be," Tam added. "Their food tasters have tasters."

"What about Talon?" I asked him.

"Safe with Kesyn, and considering what may be happening here, I want him to stay there."

"I take it that Markus will fully recover?" Imala asked.

Mychael nodded. "Once he wakes up, he could be back on his feet within three or four days. I'd prefer longer."

Imala's mouth curved in a bemused smile. "I imagine he'll let you know what he thinks about your bed rest prescription."

"I'm sure he will."

"If you hadn't been there…" She didn't finish. She didn't need to. We all knew that the peace talks would have suffered irreparable damage before they'd even started. Markus Sevelien was respected throughout the kingdoms as a man of integrity. But Imala had meant more than that. We all not only admired Markus, but considered him a close and good friend. Whoever was responsible for the attack was going to pay dearly.

"Have you taken any steps to suspend mirror travel to the island?" Imala continued.

"Only in the citadel," Mychael replied. "We haven't heard of any other incidences. Our expert is working on a way to safely test the mirror the two of you were going to use to see if it's infested."

"Infested is a good description," Tam said. "To produce a web of the thickness Raine described would make that Rak'kari, from the tip of a front leg to the tip of a back one… about as long as Raine is tall."

I shivered from head to toe and didn't even try to stop it. I knew what kind of nightmare I'd be having tonight. That is, if I managed to get to sleep.

Mychael didn't bat an eye. "All the more reason to keep

this quiet until we know whether there's a danger outside the citadel. I don't want to incite a panic, especially when there might not be grounds for it. There was only one attack. I have people listening for news of any other incidents. If there's another one, then I'll have to act, but the quieter we can keep this for now, the better."

"Then all of the delegates are here."

"All that made it here alive," I said. "Markus wasn't the only target. The ship carrying the elven ambassador and his staff were attacked by a Caesolian-registered ship last night. A pirate. The kind of vermin that gives my family a bad name. The ambassador, his two guards, the ship's telepath, and the crew were killed. His staff was taken captive. Phaelan happened to be in the area and rescued them."

"I take it the ambassador's second will be stepping in to fill the position."

"She will."

Imala smiled and arched a brow. "She? How delightful."

"Mychael's not thrilled."

Delighted turned to confused. "And why would that be?"

"The acting elven ambassador is my sister, Isibel."

"And you're having protective feelings." Imala didn't ask that as a question. Mychael's feelings—and the nature of those feelings—were obvious.

"I quite understand your concern," Imala continued, "but at the same time, you must be very proud that she has risen so high in the foreign service."

"I am, though the timing could have been better."

"In any government service, be it foreign or secret, good timing is a luxury we seldom receive."

"According to Phaelan," I said, "the pirates that attacked the ambassador's ship were paid in goblin gold in bags carrying the royal Mal'Salin seal."

Tam hissed a few choice words under his breath. In

Goblin. When any quality swearing needed to be done, Goblin was the way to go.

"Has there been a theft of an army outpost payroll or unauthorized transfer of funds from the royal treasury to a foreign bank?" Mychael asked him.

Tam leaned back in his chair, suddenly looking about ten years older. "Yes and yes. The transition from Sathrik's rule to Sarad's regency to Chigaru's reign has been far from smooth. Apparently Sathrik's royal treasurer kept himself in much better condition than he did the account books. There isn't any place royal treasury gold could be found that would surprise me. The elves have nothing to worry about from any goblin for at least the next ten years—with or without a treaty. Our courtiers and bureaucrats are going to be too busy trying to kill each other to even notice what's happening outside of Regor. We're doing everything we can to get the government under our control. One of the biggest problems we're facing now is that our people are sharply divided—the haves and the have-nots. And I'm not referring to simply money. It's about title and rank, family and purity of bloodline, social influence, political affiliations, and magical talent. The people are tired of waiting for their voices to be heard and their rights recognized. Many goblins—those in power and those without—have little trust in elven promises. They see any attempt to negotiate a peace with a race they believe wouldn't hesitate to wipe them out as evidence of weakness, regardless of Chigaru's assurances of change. Thanks to Sathrik, many of those occupying government positions are corrupt, self-serving, or both."

"Sounds like what Justinius is dealing with here with the Conclave and the Seat of Twelve," Mychael noted. "Cleaning house has left him with barely enough people to run the island—and he's not even close to being finished."

"The Conclave here, the Khrynsani at home," Imala said.

"Under Sarad's influence, the Khrynsani spread like a cancer until it had worked its way into the entire government body. We could try to remove it all, but the patient might not survive."

I whistled. "In comparison, coming here must be like a vacation."

Tam nodded. "It's early afternoon, and no one has tried to kill me yet. Well, with the exception of our sprint through the Passages. Though by comparison, even that was refreshing."

Imala snorted. "Says you."

"So the Khrynsani have the elven ambassador killed and try to do the same to the director of elven intelligence," I said. "And now we have a monster created by Khrynsani black magic and possibly put inside a mirror tunnel by an elf mage. If that turns out to be the case, the elf and goblin bad guys have stopped trying to kill each other—and are working together to kill us."

"And they're framing us as masterminding the entire thing," Imala replied. "No trust. No treaty. No peace."

7

"Your sister is safe," I told Mychael. *Again. "From everyone.* Including Phaelan. Especially Phaelan."

Short sentences worked better right now. I was yelling. Not because I was mad at Mychael, but because we were airborne.

Having a conversation on a sky dragon was one of life's great challenges. At least this time, I was riding on Kalinpar's saddle behind Mychael, his broad shoulders blocking my views of what I still saw as a quick and messy death, a death I had narrowly avoided the last time I rode on a sky dragon.

I had to admit that clinging to a sky dragon saddle was a highly effective method of waking up. I'd slept last night; that is, if you could call tossing and turning and waking up every hour sleeping.

Tam and Imala had spent the night at the goblin embassy, and would join us at the citadel later to meet with Cuinn Aviniel, the expert mirror mage.

The *Fortune* and *Red Hawk* had been spotted shortly after sunrise five miles off the coast, and Mychael had dispatched two Guardian gunships and four armored sky dragons as escort. He'd also had Ben notify the telepath on the *Fortune* to be expecting them so as to avoid any violent misunderstandings.

Both the *Fortune* and the *Red Hawk* had crews who liked nothing better than a good fight. Taking only one pirate schooner had quelled Phaelan's crew's battle urges about as well as spitting on a bonfire. The boys were spoiling for more, and any ship that got too close had a captain with a death wish.

Mychael wasn't in the mood to take chances, and considering what'd happened to Markus, and had happened—and could have happened—to Mychael's sister, I understood only too well. The closest thing I had to a younger sibling was Piaras, and I knew without thinking about it that I'd have done the same. Not only to protect him, but to warn anyone who had any ideas about harming one curly hair on his head not to even think about it.

The Isle of Mid's harbor had docks and piers for guests and merchants and others reserved for Guardian use only. Mychael landed Kalinpar at the heavily reinforced dragon landing pad at the end of a Guardian pier. A nimble gunboat was waiting there to take us out to the *Fortune*. I half expected Mychael to fly out over Phaelan's ship and drop a rope down to the deck.

I kept that thought to myself. Mychael clearly wasn't in a joking mood. In fact, after my initial reassurances, I didn't say a word all the way out to where the *Fortune* had dropped anchor.

The ships in Mid's harbor were either docked or moored. Smaller vessels with shallower drafts were in slips at the docks, while larger ships anchored toward the middle of the harbor. The *Fortune* and the *Red Hawk* were moored not merely because of their size, but their masters' desire for security as well.

My cousin, Phaelan Benares, was captain of the *Fortune*,

and his father—my uncle, Ryn Benares—commanded the *Red Hawk*. The two vessels shared the honors as flagships of the Benares fleet. However, Phaelan was a captain, while Uncle Ryn was a commodore. Phaelan operated independently of his dad, but if he stepped out of line, my cousin knew who he'd be answering to. Despite being pirates, Uncle Ryn had standards of behavior, and Phaelan crossed that line at his peril. That I knew of, he never had, which was due more to Phaelan being a chip off the old mainmast than any fear of his father. Uncle Ryn had Phaelan's respect, so fear never had to put in an appearance.

This morning, they wanted security. Normally, when a high-profile guest entered the harbor, Guardian gunships would surround the arriving ship, to ensure that no vessel approached unless authorized. The two Guardian gunships Mychael had dispatched were moored nearby, and the sky dragons had returned to the citadel's massive launch pad and stables. If they were needed, they could swoop down from the citadel to the harbor in less than a minute.

Isibel Eiliesor, the new elven ambassador to the Isle of Mid, could not be any safer than she was right now.

Mychael's scowl told me that he still didn't like it. I kept my expression carefully neutral. It wasn't easy since I knew only too well part of the reason for that scowl.

Mychael had shown me a holographic portrait of his younger sister. She was stunning. Phaelan had a keen appreciation for beautiful women. Plus, he'd gotten to rescue this one from pirates. My cousin was like a peacock, he liked showing off for the ladies, and Phaelan had yet to meet a woman who was immune. During the brief conversation we'd had this morning via Ben the telepath, I got the impression that Isibel had been less than impressed, or if she had, she'd kept it to herself.

"Isibel may be on Phaelan's ship," I told Mychael as we dismounted, "but rest assured she's on a pedestal."

His response was a single grunt. I'd learned that translated as he agreed with my opinion, but reserved the right to take action if I was wrong, which in this case meant pounding my cousin into deck wax.

I was looking forward to meeting my future sister-in-law, but I couldn't wait to see Phaelan. I'd know instantly if she'd dropped anchor on his ego.

The ladder was quickly lowered over the side of the Fortune, and Mychael and I climbed on board.

I had to hand it to my cousin, he knew how to control his crew. Of course, knowing that the paladin of the Conclave Guardians' sister was on board, and was to be escorted into Mid's harbor by Guardian gunships and sky dragons, told them how they'd *better* behave when the paladin himself set foot on deck.

Phaelan's crew was as presentable as it was possible to make them with only a few hours' notice, and those not actively involved in anchoring and securing the *Fortune* were standing in nearly straight lines and almost at attention.

It was a stunning achievement.

What I saw next was nothing short of staggering.

Crimson was my cousin's signature color. It said everything about him: fearless and flamboyant.

This morning, Captain Phaelan Benares, pirate most feared, scourge of the Seven Kingdoms' seas, was wearing somber black.

What the hell?

I was sure my expression said that and then some, but the only response I got from Phaelan was a solemn nod. Normally I would be on the receiving end of a rib-crushing hug, deck full of crew or not.

Then my cousin's focus was on Mychael. He crossed the deck to us in a silence so complete, the sharp tap of his boot heels could be clearly heard on the wood. Boots that'd been polished to within an inch of their lives.

I shot a quick glance at Mychael out of the corner of my eye. His scowl was still securely in place, but his eyes were a wee bit wider than usual. I wasn't the only one taken aback at my cousin's sudden display of propriety.

I pressed my lips together against a smile. Mychael had never scared Phaelan before, and I didn't think he'd had a change of heart on that point now. I knew the reason. My cousin's change in heart—and wardrobe—had nothing to do with Mychael, and everything to do with Isibel Eiliesor.

Now I knew why Uncle Ryn hadn't come over from the *Red Hawk*. He didn't trust himself not to laugh his ass off at his smitten son.

Phaelan stopped a respectful distance from Mychael. "If you'll follow me. I thought it best that the ambassador wait below."

As Phaelan turned and we followed, I noticed that he hadn't addressed Mychael either by title or "sir." Apparently my cousin's formality had its limits.

Once in the passageway belowdecks, Phaelan made a beeline for his cabin at the stern of the ship. Mychael had taken my hand to help me down the stairs even though we both knew I didn't need it. My Mychael was a gentleman, and my not needing help for five steps didn't enter into his thinking. He wasn't thinking right now; he was worrying.

Phaelan stopped at the door, and stood aside for us. Mychael reached for the door handle with one hand, the other hand keeping a firm grip on mine.

I pulled my hand away.

That got his attention.

I spoke before he could ask. "You haven't seen her for a few years. You should have time alone. Just open the door when you're ready. I'll be here waiting."

In response, Mychael pulled me to his chest and tightly

held me there as I felt what was probably the first decent breath he'd taken since leaving the citadel. My arms went around his waist and I hugged him tightly and nuzzled beneath his chin.

Phaelan had to be feeling like a third oar, but neither one of us cared.

With a brush of his lips against the top of my head, Mychael released me and went into Phaelan's cabin, closing the door behind him.

I looked at Phaelan. Phaelan looked back at me. I didn't say a word, but simply gave him a quick head-to-toe glance and back, followed by a raised eyebrow. My cousin sighed, rolled his eyes, and unless my eyes deceived me, actually turned a little pink in the face. It wasn't a blush. The second-most-feared pirate would never blush.

I smiled slowly.

"Oh, shut up," he said.

In unspoken agreement, we put a little distance between us and the cabin. Once we did, I was all business, at least until I'd gotten all the facts. Then I'd move on to the fun—a woman finally turning my cousin the pirate into a lovesick cabin boy.

Phaelan wasn't a magic user, so we hadn't been able to talk directly; instead we'd had to rely on the telepath go-between. You could get facts that way, but not details. I wanted details. Mychael would be getting Isibel's side of the story. My job was Phaelan. Mychael and I would be comparing notes later.

"Okay, what happened?" I asked.

"I spotted the *Blue Rose* burning on a shoal about ten miles northwest of Gruen. We got as close as we could to check for survivors. There weren't any. There were two holes blasted in her side below her waterline, and what was left of her mainmast was flying the royal elven standard. We'd just come through the straits, and none of the ships we saw had the guns for that kind of damage. That meant the bastard had run north or west. Since our course was northwest, we held steady and kept close watch. Didn't take us long to spot him. Will Saltman, so-called captain of the *Fancy Devil*." Phaelan's lips narrowed into a thin, angry line. "I knew what cargo Will had been known to carry. As soon as we changed course to intercept, he made a run for it. You don't run unless you've got something to hide."

"Or someone you want to keep."

My cousin nodded grimly. "The *Fancy Devil* was listing a little to starboard. It looked like the *Blue Rose* had managed to get off at least one good shot before she was taken. Then suddenly it was like Will decided to stop running. The sails went slack, and it didn't look as if anyone was at the rudder. I knew something was wrong. Even so, we expected a fight when we got there, not a deck full of dead men."

"Dead?"

"Yep."

"All of them?"

"Every last one, and not a mark on any of them to say what did the killing. From the look on their faces, you'd think they'd been literally scared to death. The captives were locked up below. Whatever took out the crew didn't touch the captives. They said they heard screams that no man should be able to make followed by bodies hitting the deck, then nothing until we arrived."

There were two things Phaelan didn't like: magic and dead bodies that might have been killed by magic. And no man who went to sea wanted to come across a ship full of dead men. Sailors were a superstitious lot, and getting anywhere near a ghost ship was tempting Fate and every last one of her sisters.

"You know I hate to ask this, but did you happen to bring one of those bodies?"

"I brought *two* of them, and I damned near had a mutiny on my hands for hauling those carcasses on board. My men are spooked."

So was Phaelan.

He kept going. "You come across a ship of dead men, you leave them where they fell. But I knew Mychael would want somebody to poke 'n prod the corpses to find out what killed them."

"Who'd you bring?"

"Saltman and his mate, George Pennett." Phaelan shrugged. "Just because it looked like the same thing killed them all, didn't mean it was, so I brought two." He tapped the deck below us with the toe of one boot. "Got them both down in the lowest part of the hold wrapped in an old sail. We hoisted them off their deck and into our hold without anyone touching them; the paladin can get them out the same way." He made a flapping motion with both of his hands. "Hitch one of those flying lizards of his up to a rope or something. Just get them *off my ship*."

"Within the next half hour," I promised him. "Thank you, Phaelan. If we can figure out what got Will Saltman and his crew, it could help lead us to who went after Markus."

"Markus?"

I hit the high points of what had happened.

"Someone's elf hunting," Phaelan surmised. "And it sounds like a goblin."

"We've got a lead on a couple of someones who could be involved."

"To a lot of people, a goblin is a goblin."

I blew out a breath. "I know."

"Are Tam and Imala here?"

"They are."

"Anything attack them?"

"Yes, but it wasn't anyone's fault."

"Huh?"

"They didn't come here by mirror. And the less you know about how they did have to travel, the happier you'll be."

"I've got two dead bodies in my hold, probably killed by magic. So I'll take that happy and raise you a blissfully ignorant."

What would make me happy was to change the subject to Isibel Eiliesor.

"So...You met Mychael's sister."

Phaelan's face went totally blank. It was the face that had won him many a card game. "Yes."

"Oh come on, Phaelan. It's me."

"I know it's you, that's why I'm not telling you anything."

I smiled slowly. "So there's something to tell?"

"I'm not telling that, either."

"I won't tell Mago, I promise."

"That's what you said last time."

"Last time wasn't my future sister-in-law." I stopped. "Wait a minute. You're my cousin, so that would make you and her..."

"Not a problem."

I grinned. "So you've thought about it."

"I'm a man. Of course, I've thought about it." The not-blush was back. "And run numerous scenarios."

"I won't mention your 'scenarios' to Mychael."

"My continued life expectancy would appreciate that."

We hadn't heard a peep from Phaelan's cabin.

Until now.

"Sounds like they've gotten past the reunion part," I noted dryly. "I think it's safe to go in now."

Phaelan snorted. "Safe for who?"

"Not Mychael. But it sounds like he could use reinforcements."

Opening the door didn't stop them. It took several seconds of Phaelan and me simply standing there for there to be a break in hostilities.

Isibel Eiliesor was petite and porcelain-skinned, with hair that was a tumbling mass of fiery curls and eyes the color of violets. The term "fairy princess" had been created just for her.

Women looked like that in storybooks, not in real life.

Yet, there she stood, toe to furious toe with her big brother, the top of her curly head coming only to the center of Mychael's chest.

How she must have hated that.

The fire in Isibel's eyes was only too familiar to me. I'd seen it for years every time I'd looked in the mirror. Being a woman trying to get a start in what was traditionally a man's profession had given me plenty of chances to be enraged at being pushed aside or not taken as seriously as men doing the same work. Infuriated didn't begin to describe the frustration and anger I'd experienced every day.

I saw that in my soon-to-be sister-in-law all too clearly.

Right now I saw that she'd made up her mind that she was where she wanted to be, and no one was going to push her aside again. She was done.

Good for her.

I could also see that Mychael hadn't yet come to that realization, and his big-brother protective urges weren't letting him see what was obvious to me. Yes, her ship had been attacked and she'd been taken captive; and yes, it was a good thing the *Fortune* had come along when she did, but no one person would have been able to prevent her ship being taken or the ambassador's murder, at least not without the help of a certain all-powerful rock of our former acquaintance.

Isibel had a bull's-eye between her eyes and needed protection—the kind that would help her do her job, not the kind that would prevent it getting done.

Mychael wanted to lock his little sister up for safekeeping. I'd been on the receiving end of that impulse, too. Isibel Eiliesor was the elven ambassador, and until Markus Sevelien was on his feet, she was also the senior representative of the elven queen in the peace talks. She couldn't be locked away from anyone.

Isibel had been through hell, and while I wanted nothing more than to give my future sister-in-law the biggest hug I had in me, I couldn't do it. It was what I wanted to do, but it wasn't what Isibel—or Mychael—needed. At least not yet.

Defuse the situation now, repair any damage later.

So I did the best thing for Isibel as the elven ambassador and my future sister-in-law—and for Mychael as my future husband and present paladin. I crossed the cabin to them, extended my right hand to Isibel, and said what both of them needed to hear.

"Ambassador Eiliesor, on behalf of the archmagus, I welcome you to the Isle of Mid." After a thoroughly professional handshake, *then* I gave my new sister a big hug and a bigger smile. "And I'm so glad to meet you!"

Isibel's responding smile lit up her face, and she returned my hug with enthusiasm.

"Are you okay?" I asked.

"Yes, thank you, and thanks to your cousin, Captain Benares."

I turned to Mychael. "See? She's fine. Let's move on."

"We were discussing where Her Excellency will be staying during the negotiations," Mychael said stiffly. He'd put the slightest emphasis on "Her Excellency."

Sounded like he hadn't moved on from that part. Yet. Time for a little nudge in the needed direction.

I gave him a brittle smile. "So I heard—and Phaelan heard and so did every crewman on this end of the ship."

Mychael took a breath and blew it out. "I lost control."

"Yes, you did. And it was understandable. Your sister is in danger. You love her and want to keep her safe."

Isibel was staring daggers at her brother. "By sitting on me like a mother hen."

I paused. That made an interesting visual. "As elven ambassador, Isibel has responsibilities that can't be carried out with you sitting on her."

"Finally a voice of reason," Isibel said.

I turned to her. "At the same time, as paladin, it is Mychael's responsibility to ensure the safety of each and every delegate. Considering the present situation—two murders and a kidnapping—"

Isibel froze. "*Two* murders?"

"Markus Sevelien was attacked by a spider monster inside the mirror tunnel between Silvanlar and here."

"*Inside* a mirror tunnel?"

"Yeah, we're trying to wrap our heads around how that happened, too. Markus was killed, but your brother, the best healer in the kingdoms, brought him back."

"How is—"

"He'll be fine. He's resting now."

Isibel reached back and sat in one of Phaelan's cabin chairs. "I didn't know."

"And until we know who's behind this," Mychael said, "we need to keep as much information to ourselves as possible—and you in secure lodgings."

"You're saying that the elven embassy isn't secure?"

"Oh, it's secure, all right," I told her. "Phaelan and I had a hell of a time escaping from their dungeon a couple of weeks ago."

Isibel blinked. "Dungeon?"

"They probably call it 'security holding cells' or something more polite," I said, "but when you're chained to a wall, dungeon pretty much sums it up."

"I had heard that you were held against your will by Inquisitor Balmorlan."

"And your predecessor, Giles Keril. After that, Markus scrubbed the place clean of cohorts and minions."

"At least as thorough a job as he could with people who change allegiances quicker than the wind changes direction," Phaelan added.

"The best thing we can do now is to get back to the citadel." I held up a hand to stop Isibel's objection. "It's merely a temporary solution until we get the situation under control. Markus has a room in Justinius's tower—for security and medical reasons. Next to Mychael, Dalis is the best healer on the island. She's the old man's personal physician. I know Markus will want to talk to you. And since he won't be leaving his bed for a while, you'll need to be where he is. Agreed?"

Isibel gave me a single nod. "Agreed." She was calm and cool, the embodiment of a diplomat.

I looked to Mychael. "I know this is a big shock, but big shocks are what you handle best." I threw in an encouraging smile. I couldn't tell if it had any effect. Mychael's paladin face was firmly in place: cool and determined. Hurricane-force winds wouldn't faze him. That could be good or very bad. Considering how our day had gone so far, I was going to call it good and leave it at that. I needed one thing in my "win" column today.

"Do Mother and Father know how high you've risen in the foreign service?" he asked his sister.

The calm and cool elf diplomat gave way to a guilty daughter. "Not exactly."

Oh boy.

8

The Red Hawk *had anchored next to the* Fortune—*or as close* as two warships could be and not bump each other to bits when the tide changed. The wakes of other ships passing in the harbor wouldn't be an issue for either vessel—no captains in their right minds would go anywhere near the twin flagships of the Benares fleet.

Mychael took Isibel to the citadel via Kalinpar, and Vegard and I took a launch the short distance from the *Fortune* to the *Red Hawk*. It'd be Isibel's first ride on a sky dragon. I hoped hers would go better than mine had.

Mychael had had his family reunion.

Now it was my turn.

I had just started up the wood and rope boarding ladder when a familiar voice boomed down from the deck above our heads.

"About time. We thought we weren't going to get a decent welcome."

I looked up and it was as if the clouds parted, the sun came out, and choirs of angels sang.

Garadin Wyne. My mother's closest friend and my godfather.

And standing next to him was Tarsilia Rivalin. Former landlady, forever friend, and stand-in mom.

My day instantly went from total crap to absolutely perfect.

Garadin didn't wait for me to reach the top of the ladder. He reached down and hauled me over the top and into his arms. Tears filled my eyes and I squealed in pure joy. Until that moment, it didn't truly set in how badly I'd missed my godfather. I wrapped my arms around his neck, returning the bone-crushing hug I was presently receiving. I knew he'd have come to Mid in an instant if I'd asked him to. I'd only considered it once, then permanently put it out of my mind.

It'd been too dangerous.

I'd been too dangerous.

And you still might be, my little voice whispered.

I pushed that thought out of my head and slammed the door in its face.

No. The Saghred was gone, and so was the danger.

As long as I'd been linked to the Saghred, the men and women who wanted the stone's power hadn't hesitated to threaten those I loved, to force me to hand myself over to them. I wouldn't have brought Garadin and Tarsilia into that regardless of how badly I'd wanted them here with me. I'd endangered enough people, and had refused to add Garadin and Tarsilia to the already too long list.

Garadin was tall and distinguished looking, his eyes intense blue, his short hair ginger, and his beard and mustache immaculately trimmed. That was where immaculate ended. His dark homespun robes swept in virtual tatters behind him. Garadin dressed for himself and comfort, and that was all. None of that had changed since I'd last seen him.

My former landlady cleared her throat loudly. "Leave something for me to hug. You're about to squeeze her stuffing out."

Garadin reluctantly set my feet on the deck. I paused briefly to shout and wave at Uncle Ryn, and then with another squeal, I launched myself at Tarsilia.

Tarsilia was slender, fine-boned, with leaf-green eyes and barely any wrinkles visible in a still flawless complexion. She must have been drop-dead gorgeous in her younger days. She still turned heads of all ages. Her silvery hair swung in a practical braid down the length of her back. Tarsilia had a Conclave background, and she'd spent her younger days on the Isle of Mid. She didn't talk about it, but I knew she didn't learn to fight behind an apothecary's counter.

I knew I was amusing the heck out of Vegard and Uncle Ryn's crew, but I couldn't have cared less.

At least, the crew would have been amused if they hadn't been so busy hauling luggage on deck. I recognized the trunks as Tarsilia's and one as Garadin's. My godfather didn't care at all for fashion, and even though he'd once been a Conclave mage, he didn't have the richly embroidered silk and velvet robes that nearly always went along with the position. When a crewman added four worn duffel bags on top of Garadin's trunk, I knew there was something I didn't know.

I indicated what amounted to all of my godfather's worldly goods. "That's not luggage for a week." The crew brought another trunk up from below and put it with Tarsilia's luggage. My eyes widened. "For either one of you."

They glanced at each other and I knew something was definitely up.

Something potentially wonderful.

I grinned, seriously on the verge of another squeal. "You're staying?"

"For a while," Garadin said.

"Possibly quite a while," Tarsilia added.

"You don't look all that happy about it," I noted. "I'm thrilled, but you're apparently not."

"A favor to an old friend," Tarsilia said.

I knew who that old friend had to be.

Justinius Valerian.

Garadin snorted. "I've only met the man once. I have no idea how I ended up on his short list."

Now I did grin. Things were about to get a lot more sane around here.

"The Seat of Twelve?" I asked, on the verge of jumping up and down.

"You may be looking at two of the new Twelve," Tarsilia said without enthusiasm.

"I didn't think it was possible for me to be any more glad to see you, but I am." I paused and gave them both a sly grin. "Being on the Seat of Twelve's not a full-time job, right?"

"Thankfully no," Tarsilia said.

"In that case, when things calm down a little around here, I have an idea that I'd like to run by the two of you."

Vegard stepped up beside me. His grin was nearly as big as mine. No surprise there. The job of the Guardians was to protect the Conclave, the Seat of Twelve, and the archmagus. A majority of the Seat of Twelve had nearly voted me and Mychael to the execution block and their leader into Justinius's office. The leader was dead, his cronies arrested, and more of those might find themselves without a job if Justinius's investigation into their extracurricular activities bore additional fruit. With the Isle of Mid still under martial law, Justinius had told me he was going to dispense with the usual election process. Now I could see that his appointees to the Seat of Twelve were going to be people who were good at their jobs, not at buying votes.

For the past several years, Vegard and his brother Guardians had been charged with protecting individuals who didn't deserve protecting. While martial law was still in place, Justinius was taking full advantage of the suspension of laws that benefited only the mages who had written them.

The old man was cleaning house with a vengeance.

"Vegard, allow me to introduce Garadin Wyne, retired Conclave mage—"

"Retired. Smart man," Vegard noted.

"And now I'm back, so how smart am I really?"

"And my godfather," I finished.

Vegard shook Garadin's hand. "That's one hell of a job you have, sir."

"From what I hear, you're my goddaughter's bodyguard. I'm a fool and you're a poor, brave bastard. We're quite a pair."

Vegard laughed. "When you get settled we'll have to drown our sorrows and commiserate over a few pints."

"I'd like that. Is the Thirsty Scholar still in business?"

"Yes, sir."

"Bruce Shurik still running it?"

My bodyguard smiled. "They'll have to roll him out in a barrel. We'll start there. Though we'll have to start later. From here, we're supposed to take you to the citadel."

"Justin doesn't want us running loose," Tarsilia said.

Vegard raised a brow. The Guardians knew their ultimate boss by any number of names, many not repeatable—though always meant with affection—but "Justin" wasn't one of them.

"We know each other," Tarsilia told him.

"Yes, ma'am." The very picture of discretion was my Guardian bodyguard.

Tarsilia stuck out her hand. "Tarsilia Rivalin, young man."

"I was about to introduce you," I said.

"I know you were, dear. Just making things easier for you."

"Rivalin?" Vegard asked.

"Piaras's grandmother," I clarified. "Before he came here, he'd been apprenticing with Tarsilia as an apothecary. I lived in the apartment upstairs. Garadin was Piaras's first spellsinging teacher." I paused. "Piaras's big-boy voice came in the first summer after I moved in."

Vegard gave a long whistle.

"Yes, it was fun for the entire neighborhood," Tarsilia agreed.

"No doubt," Vegard said. "I take it you heard what he did his first day here?"

"Oh, yes. The boy's always been an overachiever."

"Since putting half the citadel to sleep and making the Saghred go nighty-night, Piaras has conjured bukas, stopped Magh'Sceadu in their tracks, then he and 'Justin' took down a horde of demons fresh out of Hell." I stopped and thought. "And I've left a lot out. Your grandson's had a busy couple of months. Does he know you'll be here for a while?"

"I'm having dinner with him tonight; I'll be telling him then."

Tarsilia wasn't the only one with a surprise to share, though I didn't know if Piaras planned to tell her about Katelyn yet. I didn't think he knew about his grandmother and Justinius.

Two Rivalins romantically involved with two Valerians. The grandchildren now and the grandparents previously. Though I wouldn't be surprised if the old man had ideas of rekindling some embers.

Tarsilia and Garadin knew what all had happened to me and Piaras since we'd come to Mid—after the fact, of course. If they'd found out any earlier, they would have been on the first ship here. That would have put them in too much danger. Yes, they'd been pissed and told us in no uncertain terms that they could have taken care of themselves, but too many people had suffered for merely knowing us. I had no doubt that Tarsilia would find out *everything* that had happened from Piaras himself. She was relentless. Unfortunately the cadets didn't begin learning interrogation resistance until next semester.

There was a commotion over by the ladder and Phaelan's dark head appeared above the railing. He swung his legs smoothly over the side, grinning like a man about to bust with a secret.

Phaelan's show 'n tell came over the side right behind him. Piaras.

Now it was Tarsilia's turn to squeal. Then she took in the sight of him in his formal Guardian cadet uniform, and her hand flew to her mouth. The squeal stopped and the waterworks started as she closed the distance between her and her only grandchild, enfolding him in a fierce embrace.

The waterworks were contagious.

Tarsilia knew that Piaras had been admitted into the Guardians' cadet corps, but it was one thing to hear about it and quite another to see Piaras standing there, broad-shouldered and proud, in his uniform.

Phaelan, Garadin, Vegard, and I moved away a little to give them as much privacy as we could on the crowded deck of a ship. My cousin looked pleased with himself—and misty.

"The kid was pacing the docks like a lost puppy waiting for her," he said. "So I had him brought over."

"That's a big puppy," Garadin noted.

I wiped my eyes. "He's grown a lot since you saw him last."

"In more ways than he should've had to, and it looks—"

"Yes," I agreed. "And it was my fau—"

My godfather's blue eyes flashed. "It was *not* your fault. Piaras has wanted to be a Guardian all his life. I was going to say that it looks good on him. From what I understand, the boy's made one hell of an impression around here."

"That's an understatement, sir," Vegard told him. "It may have taken my brothers a little time to come around to admitting that it was a *good* impression, but it's not every day they run across a young man who'll probably end up being written into the Guardian histories as a legend." He lowered his voice further. "Don't tell him I said that."

Garadin smiled slightly. "I wouldn't dream of it. Sometimes young men need their confidence boosted, but never their egos."

9

I rode with Garadin and Tarsilia back to the citadel in the carriage Justinius had sent for them. Vegard and Piaras rode with the Guardian escort.

Once there, I got news that had me dashing up the stairs to Justinius's guest rooms.

Markus Sevelien was sitting up in bed. Dalis was by his side, Brina Daesage hovering protectively nearby.

His color was much better. The gray he'd been when Mychael had dragged him out of that mirror was a good color—for a living goblin. For an elf, it meant you were dead.

Fortunately for us, but especially for him, Markus hadn't stayed that way. Mychael reviving him didn't change the fact that he'd been murdered. That said loud and clear that the traitors who'd been caught last month—both elven and goblin—had been merely the tips of some nasty icebergs. There were probably plenty more out there where those had come from. Markus knew it and had been following the bribery and blackmail trail from Mid back to Silvanlar, right up to the day he'd been attacked. The search that had begun in Mid had borne plenty of rotten fruit in the elven capital and beyond.

Maybe one of those bad apples had arranged for Markus's monster spider traveling companion.

Anyone who had been in that mirror room at intelligence headquarters would have been Markus's most trusted. The mage who had prepared that mirror would have been above reproach.

Yet even if the Khrynsani were behind the attack, they would have needed to know the exact moment Markus would step through that mirror in Silvanlar. The Rak'kari hadn't attacked Brina Daesage; it'd come after Markus. For security reasons, Markus's travel schedules—mirror and otherwise— had always been a closely guarded secret. That meant whoever had betrayed Markus had been close to him. Very close. It would have been like Vegard trying to kill me. I would have been devastated. Being the director of elven intelligence, Markus had probably had more than his share of betrayals. In his position, trust had to be nearly impossible to come by.

I wouldn't want to live like that, never knowing who you could truly rely on. Markus Sevelien had never married. I'd always thought it was because he didn't want to endanger someone he loved. It'd never occurred to me that he simply never knew who he could trust, that the person sharing your bed could be a deep undercover assassin tasked with getting close to you and then killing you in your sleep.

That had to be so lonely.

Yet one more reason why I was so lucky—no, blessed— to have found Mychael. Besides rest, all I'd ever gotten from Mychael while asleep had been holding and healing.

It was beyond sad that Markus Sevelien believed—and perhaps rightfully so—that he could never have that. I guess that was what it meant when people said they were married to their work.

Brina Daesage was now a security team of one. Neither she nor Dalis had budged from Markus's side.

Justinius's apartment guards were keeping a very close eye on the elf security captain.

Maybe for good reason.

She'd tapped out a code on the crystal next to the mirror that it was safe for Markus to come through. A crystal that'd been destroyed along with the mirror.

Maybe that wasn't all that she'd signaled.

Markus didn't look uneasy having her sitting that close to him, so he trusted her.

I should trust her, but until I knew more, I couldn't do that, at least not entirely.

Brina looked a little on edge. That was understandable whether or not she was a traitor. I would've been jumpy, too if I'd been locked in a tower guarded by elite, magically and militarily talented knights. Brina didn't know these men, and they didn't know her. Not to mention, she had a new job and her charge had been murdered before he'd even arrived at his destination.

The distrust was so thick in here you could've cut it with a dull knife.

And I'd just added a layer of my own.

Brina was probably just what she said she was—Markus's security chief—and nothing else.

But during the past few months, paranoia and I had become fast friends. More than once, I'd had my new best buddy to thank for my continued survival. I wasn't about to give her the heave-ho now.

I know the Guardians would've preferred to be guarding only Markus. Not him plus a heavily armed and obviously dangerous elven woman. Though after having me around, these guys probably had a whole new definition of "armed and dangerous."

Markus saw me and smiled.

I returned it as best I could. "So, do you keep track of how many times you've dodged death?"

"Stopped doing that long ago. Though Brina tells me that I dodged a little too slowly this time and that I have you and Mychael to thank."

"Me? Mychael was the one who brought you back, not—"

"Brina tells me that thing had me *and* Mychael. You made it let go."

Me and my new color-coded magic.

"Do you remember anything after you stepped through the mirror in Silvanlar?" I asked.

Markus's brow creased as he tried to recall, or merely process what I'd said. "Absolutely nothing."

There were ways to get around that, but Markus wasn't strong enough yet for any of them. Either Mychael or Justinius could magically take a look through his memories in the last few minutes before he stepped into that mirror, and the time he'd spent in between.

His eyes tried to focus on the room behind us. "Where—"

"Justinius Valerian's apartment. You're in the guest room. It's the safest place on the island that's not a vault."

Markus nodded weakly in approval. "Brina?"

The bodyguard immediately came to Markus's bedside, Dalis or no Dalis. "I'm here, sir."

"Tellan Bain?"

"He's been taken into custody for questioning."

I looked from one to the other. "Who is—"

"Our chief mirror mage," Brina said.

"You think he sabotaged his own mirror?"

"Anything's possible, and we operate under that assumption until it's disproven. Tellan Bain was responsible for the preparation and protection of that mirror. He knows the procedure if it's tampered with."

"Brina, I'd like to speak with Raine alone."

"Yes, sir." If she didn't like it, she gave no sign. She simply went and stood on the other side of the room.

He glanced at Dalis and raised one brow. The healer rolled her eyes. "Five minutes. That's all you get. If I see you're getting too tired, it's less."

I smiled, "Thank you, Dalis."

The healer retreated to the other side of the room. If Markus hadn't been dead for several minutes, she would have given us some privacy and left the room. But he had died and Dalis wasn't taking any chances. I was grateful for it. I wasn't taking any chances with Markus, either.

Markus glanced at Dalis. No expression, no raised eyebrow, just a glance. Someone who didn't know Markus wouldn't have read anything into it. I knew Markus. I heard plenty.

"She's Justinius's personal healer. I know and trust her." My mouth formed the words in complete silence. Markus read lips and so did I. Even across the room, Brina would be able to hear even the barest whisper. She was an elf. Our ears weren't just there to look good. Markus said he wanted to speak to me alone, and I was going to maintain his privacy. I sat facing Markus with my back to Brina and Dalis.

Markus blinked in response, took a breath, and let it out. Translation: Good. If you trust her, I trust her.

A man of few words and fewer expressions was Markus.

"And by not actually speaking, you can save even more strength," I continued speaking soundlessly.

One corner of Markus's lips twitched upward. "And Brina can't hear us. I can trust Dalis; you can trust Brina."

"Right now, anyone I don't know, I don't trust. I won't take the chance. Not with you."

He opened his mouth to speak, and I held up a hand, "Brina said there wasn't anything fishy on your end before she came through. Did that change before you stepped in?"

Markus's flat look spoke volumes.

"I know, you'd wouldn't have stepped through if it had. I had to ask. They could have thrown you in. You trusted your mirror mage?"

Markus nodded once.

I told him about what Tam and Imala had said about the Rak'kari and the very strong possibility of Khrynsani involvement. Then I told him about the high probability of elven involvement—and a Khrynsani partnership. Markus was far from peak condition, but he didn't need anything kept from him that could shed light on what had been done to him.

One of the apartment's massive double doors opened as the door sentries admitted Mychael and Isibel. Neither looked pissed. It wasn't exactly sibling harmony, but I'd take it.

Markus pulled himself up in bed, and held his hands out to Isibel.

The new elven ambassador smiled like a delighted little girl and ran to the director of elven intelligence who enfolded her in a hug.

Well, that was something you didn't see every day.

Markus and Isibel were happy. Dalis? Not so much. In her opinion, that was entirely too much activity for her patient, but since Mychael was here, she'd yield that decision to him. They exchanged glances, Mychael nodded, Dalis sighed.

Isibel told Markus what had happened to the *Blue Rose*— and to Ambassador Santis Eldor. I didn't know how well they'd known each other, but the late ambassador had been a lifelong diplomat, a highly educated, well-traveled man of even temper and open mind. I'd been briefed on the delegates I didn't already know and had been looking forward to meeting him.

We let them have a few minutes of quiet reunion. It was Markus who opened up the conversation to include me and Mychael—but especially Mychael.

"You're ready for this," he was telling her. He cut a bemused glance at Mychael. "And don't let anyone tell you otherwise."

Mychael raised his hands defensively. "I never said she

wasn't qualified. I merely would have liked to have known that she'd advanced to first in line for a major ambassadorship."

Isibel patted Markus's hand. "Don't worry. We're past that part. Mychael and I have been talking."

"Not yelling?" I asked.

"Not yelling," she assured me with a smile. "My last promotion coincided with when he was chasing Sarad Nukpana for the Saghred."

"A few days before we tracked him to Mermeia," Mychael added.

"You were most definitely busy," I noted.

"Yes, I was."

"It was a notable promotion, but not worth disturbing my brother while he was fighting the forces of evil," she flashed me a smile, "and attempting to woo my future sister-in-law. Both were infinitely more important than my promotion."

"I can assure you that Isibel is a natural-born diplomat," Markus told Mychael. "As you'll see for yourself in the coming days." He smiled. "You and she share many similarities. I will admit to working behind the scenes to ensure that talent like hers didn't get pushed aside because she is a woman."

If Markus believed in her, that was more than enough for me. For anyone in the elven diplomatic service to even remotely take her seriously, Isibel would have to be twice as smart and work three times as hard as any man.

"When there was an opening on Santis Eldor's senior staff," Markus was saying, "I recommended Isibel, and after meeting her, Ambassador Eldor wholeheartedly agreed with me. I know that he was looking forward to this being her introduction on the world stage." A shadow crossed Markus's face. "He never anticipated that he wouldn't be by her side. I will be."

My friend said those last three words as though they were a solemn oath. I swore an oath to myself that I'd keep him safe so he could fulfill it.

10

It was time to go see another friend. I liked the friend, just not what he did for a living.

Vidor Kalta was a nachtmagus.

Most people thought a necromancer and a nachtmagus were the same thing. To use a snake analogy, necromancers were garden snakes and a nachtmagus was a cobra. Necromancers could only communicate with the dead. They did séances, detected hauntings, and could tell you if you had a frisky poltergeist or an ancestor who simply refused to leave.

A nachtmagus could not only communicate with your dearly departed, he or she could control them or any other dead—in all of their forms. I'd heard that given enough time, money, and motivation, a nachtmagus could raise the dead.

Since coming to Mid, I'd found that there's actually a Conclave college major in necromancy. The college produced both necromancers and nachtmagi. Most of the students with stronger talent became nachtmagi, and the lesser talents were necromancers. There was more money in the former, and if you had the talent, why not go big or go home?

In my opinion, no one majored in either one unless they were just plain weird. In theory, the Conclave college had a way to weed out the weirdos. I don't know what that said about the department's graduates. They wanted to work with dead things, but at the same time, they couldn't be weird. It had to be the college's smallest graduating class.

Vidor Kalta taught graduate-level courses in the necrology department. About a month ago, I'd gotten to experience firsthand just how good he was at his chosen calling. He'd been called to help us discover who or what had killed an elven general—and how. The "how" had been the truly creepy part.

As a seeker, I could pick up impressions from inanimate objects touched by someone I was looking for. I discovered that day that a dead body qualified as the ultimate inanimate object. Thanks to Vidor's expertise, we'd found that after escaping the Saghred, Sarad Nukpana was using a black magic ritual to regenerate his soul into a physical body by taking the lifeforces and memories of selected victims. Nukpana had selected the elven general as one of his victims for his vast knowledge of elven military intelligence. The general had been but one victim. Thanks to Vidor's knowledge, there had only been one subsequent victim, and it was an individual who'd been even more evil than Sarad Nukpana—and yes, it was possible.

Vidor Kalta was tall, thin, and born to wear funereal black. His dark hair was cropped close to his head, probably as a safety precaution. I'd found out the hard way that corpses could get grabby. Kalta's features were sharp, and his face had the pallor one would expect of someone who worked mostly nights. But it was his eyes that gave him away. Black and bright as a raven's, Vidor Kalta's eyes were a reflection of a quick mind, a keen intellect, and an incredible power. Power that was all the more impressive because of his restraint. It was as if the man had Death on a leash and it was following him around like a puppy.

When Phaelan and I came into the room, Vidor was replacing the tarp over one of the bodies.

"We've got to stop meeting like this," I told him.

The nachtmagus smiled in a quick flash of white teeth. "A murder victim in the room doesn't make for a very pleasant social encounter, does it?"

"No, it doesn't. So, it was murder?"

"Of the most dark and evil kind."

Of course, it was.

The last time I'd worked with Vidor, we'd been in a basement room in the citadel. We were still in the citadel, but this room was aboveground and even had a window, which admitted some life-affirming sunshine. If Phaelan's furtive glances were any indication, it also provided a handy escape route. I wondered if the distance to the ground was survivable. I also wondered whether Phaelan cared. The room was also larger, which would give my cousin room for his running jump—or, considering that Mychael and Vegard were here, room to swing and toss a dead body that might not have the decency to stay that way.

I only included Mychael and Vegard among the potential tossers. I knew better than to depend on Phaelan to touch the thing, even if it meant throwing it out a window.

My cousin had stationed himself in the corner closest to the door, and a couple of flying leaps to the window. He liked to keep his escape options open. Phaelan didn't like dead bodies, but he was absolutely terrified of nachtmagi.

Vidor Kalta had asked Phaelan to be here. Vidor had asked; I had insisted. If the nachtmagus thought Phaelan might have seen something helpful on that ship, he'd come ashore and share it with the rest of us if I'd had to drag him by his boots—or send Vegard and a couple of his brother Guardians to do it. Fortunately, Phaelan had come along quietly. But if one of those bodies moved, my cousin wasn't going to stay quiet or still.

To be honest, neither would I.

The room was empty except for two tables with the two bodies—the captain and first mate of the pirate ship that'd attacked the *Blue Rose* and killed Ambassador Eldor. Thankfully, the bodies were covered. Even more thankfully, they weren't moving.

On the floor next to the tables was a sight that stunned me.

The two bags of goblin gold the pirate/assassins had been paid with.

I looked at my cousin in dumbfounded disbelief.

"That's tainted gold," he said. "I don't want anything to do with it, and neither do my men."

"You're a pirate."

"A pirate who doesn't spend money taken off a ghost ship. That's just asking for trouble."

Mychael was pressing his lips together against a smile. "Any idea how they died?" he asked Vidor.

"I have a theory, but I've asked an expert to confirm it."

At that moment, the door opened, and Tam came in.

Vidor stepped forward to shake Tam's hand. "Primaru Nathrach, I'm so glad you could join us."

"A room with you and two dead bodies?" Tam quipped. "How could I resist?"

"Your expert, I take it?" I asked Vidor.

"If I am, it's the nicest thing I've been called today," Tam said. "And this is certainly the most welcome I've felt. I think word has gotten around about who was behind Ambassador Eldor's assassination. Either that, or I'm simply a lot less popular than I thought."

Mychael scowled.

"None of my men have been on shore," Phaelan told him.

"I'm not blaming you or your crew," Mychael said. "The

elven embassy knows what happened. I imagine that's the source of any rumors."

Vidor pulled back the tarp over the first body.

"Will Saltman," Phaelan muttered and quickly looked away.

Phaelan had looked away. I wanted to.

Will Saltman had seen his death. That is, if his death had been delivered in the most horrifying, scare-you-out-of-your-skin way imaginable.

Tam reached down with his thumb and forefinger and opened one of the man's eyes even wider.

Phaelan shifted one step closer to the window.

Tam didn't say a word; he simply replaced the tarp over the face of Captain Saltman and peeled back the one covering his first mate, George Pennett.

Same terror-stricken expression. Tam repeated the same eye exam.

"Death curse," he said, covering the man's face. "Khrynsani."

"Crap," I said.

"To say the least."

"What did you see in their eyes?"

"Broken blood vessels. The curse terrifies, paralyses the major muscles, and constricts the blood vessels. Horrible way to die."

"It's not like there's a good death curse," Phaelan muttered.

"Are you certain there was no living person on the ship other than the captives?" Vidor asked.

"Positive," Phaelan replied. "We looked. My men are professionals. If there's anything worth having on a ship, they'll find it."

"You'd said that there were nineteen dead men on deck and three more belowdecks."

A muscle twitched in my cousin's jaw. "Correct."

"Might your men have—"

"They didn't want to spend one second longer on that ship

than they had to. So I told them they *had* to do a thorough job. I sure as hell wasn't going to go to the trouble to haul two bodies back here and then do a half-assed job in the ship search."

"Of course, forgive me."

"No problem. Just establishing that we looked, and if there'd been anything to find, we'd have found it."

"Your boys typically focus on shiny things," I said. "This wouldn't have been anything they'd want to stick into their pockets and bring home with them."

"Was there any area belowdecks that made you or any of your men want to get out of there?" Tam asked.

"All of them."

Mychael nodded. He knew where we were going with this. "Any area where that impulse was especially strong could indicate a repelling spell. It would cause a more than rational fear of a cabin or a specific area of the ship. That and a veil could have hidden a mirror mounted to a wall."

Phaelan blanched. "Mirror?"

I hated mirrors, but my mirror hatred was nothing compared to Phaelan's feelings. Yes, my cousin was vain about his looks, but the only mirrors he allowed on his ship were for shaving, and it was a near mutiny-level offense if a crewman didn't secure that mirror in a box or duffel after using it.

"After my men searched the ship," Phaelan replied, "I went back over it myself. I'll admit I made quick work of it, but I wasn't sloppy. Five captives held by a crew of dead men is about as spooky as it gets. I didn't like where I was, but I didn't find or feel anything that made me want to run out of there."

"Were there any rats on the ship?" Tam asked quietly.

That question won him the silent and undivided attention of everyone in the room.

Phaelan's forehead creased as he thought. "Come to think of it, there weren't any. And Will Saltman wasn't known for running a clean ship. There should have been rats, most definitely in the hold, but there weren't."

"A Gate," Tam said.

Technically, I knew that a Gate could be torn anywhere, even on a ship under sail. But I'd never heard of a specific instance.

"Rats may be repellent to us," Tam said, "but some of the acts we commit are so abhorrent to rats that they would throw themselves off a ship rather than be anywhere near it."

I suddenly remembered the rats running from the bunker where Sarad Nukpana had hidden while he'd been regenerating his body—and where his soul had temporarily infested Tam's body.

The rats had run like hell from that, and so had we. I'd hated myself for running, but it'd been necessary if we were going to live long enough to get Nukpana's rotten soul out of Tam's body before that infestation became permanent. I'd tried to tell myself that it was a tactical retreat, but that hadn't lessened my guilt one bit. It'd been the rats that had showed us the way out of that underground maze, saving our lives, and, less than an hour later, Tam's as well.

I'd been in a room when a Gate had been torn open. Twice.

If you asked me, the suicidal rats had the right idea.

"Any higher-level Khrynsani mage can open a Gate," Tam said. "Evil is more needed than strength."

Gate fuel included terror, torture, and death. The more that was produced, the larger and more stable the Gate.

"One mage?" I asked Tam.

"Maybe a temple guard or two with him, but one mage could have done it alone. He wouldn't have needed much time to do what he did. One mage and one word."

Killing with a single word sounded impossible, but it wasn't. I'd seen it done. Once.

Tam had done it.

One mage had ripped a Gate onto the *Fancy Devil,* scared every rat into jumping overboard, struck the crew dead with a single word, and left the way he'd arrived.

"He left the captives alive as witnesses," I said. "And the gold to frame the goblin government for all of it."

Mychael nodded. "It was worth more to the Khrynsani that those two bags of gold with the Mal'Salin royal seal be found. We know the Khrynsani and the goblin government are no longer the same."

Tam's expression hardened. "We're the only ones who do."

When we left the morgue, I almost had to run to keep up with Phaelan.

"Death curse?" he blurted. *"Death curse?"*

"Yeah, so? You said yourself Will Saltman and his crew were bottom-feeding scum that deserved anything they got, including a death curse."

"They did. I don't."

I was officially confused. "What?"

"I brought two bodies that'd been struck dead by a Khrynsani death curse on board my ship."

"They're dead. They can't hurt anybody. Death curses aren't contagious."

"Try telling that to my crew."

"You don't need to."

"I don't *have* to. Enough of my men knew it was dark, heebie-jeebie magic that killed them. I've got to clean the *Fortune*. Now."

Somehow I couldn't visualize my cousin swabbing decks. At least not anymore. While Phaelan and his brothers had been growing up, the decks of Uncle Ryn's ships had been clean enough to eat off of. Whenever any of his boys got out of line, he'd put a mop in their hands. Those boys had done a lot of deck swabbing.

Phaelan stopped just short of rolling his eyes. "Not scrubbing. Blessing. I need a priest." He frowned. "More than one. I need a priest from every religion on this island."

"Aren't you overreacting?"

"No!"

"Your crew won't care—"

"My crew will be going over the side like those rats if they get wind of this. And they will find out. They always have." He stopped, a puzzled look on his face. "I've never figured out how. It's not like they're very smart." He took off again. "But they've got superstition in spades. They're a good crew, and I'm not about to lose any of them."

Phaelan ran out the citadel's front doors.

"What's gotten into him?" Mychael asked.

"Temporary religion."

11

Markus Sevelien was one of the most determined people I'd ever met, but even he had to admit, late in the afternoon, that when the peace talks officially started tomorrow morning, he wasn't going to be sitting at the elven delegation's table.

The elven delegation had originally consisted of Ambassador Santis Eldor, Isibel, and Markus. The ambassador's assassination and Markus's thwarted murder left Isibel as the sole representative of the elven queen. Markus had said she was good, but few people were that good.

The injuries to Markus's body would be keeping him in bed, but his mind had been working furiously on a solution. That solution arrived along with the last of my relatives who would be attending my and Mychael's wedding.

My cousin Mago Benares, aka Mago Peronne, aka anyone else he needed to be.

The eldest son of my Uncle Ryn, Mago had determined long ago that the best way to make money was to manage it for other people. He'd kept his first name but changed his last, because needless to say, most people wouldn't trust their money and investments to the son of the most notorious pirate in the Seven Kingdoms. He could change his name, but nothing could alter his instincts. Mago was a vice president at the First Bank of D'Mai in Brenir. My cousin may have had the instincts of a pirate, but he lacked the stomach of one. For Mago, to set foot on a deck was to feed the fishes. The last time he'd come to Mid had been by ship. It'd taken him the better part of a day to recover from the experience. This afternoon he'd arrived from Brenir, dashingly attired in flying leathers, on a chauffeur-flown sky dragon.

Sailing made him sick; flying only messed up his hair, and that was from the helmet.

Go figure.

Mago was your basic tall, dark, and handsome elf. Phaelan had always claimed that Mago had stolen all of the height so there'd be none left for him. If that'd been possible, Mago would have been the one to have done it. He was well educated, well traveled, and well heeled—the very personification of a gentleman adventurer. He could change identities and professions at a whim.

It was that skill that'd led to Markus attempting to lure my cousin away from his lucrative banking career and into intelligence. His efforts hadn't borne fruit after his initial effort; however, he seemed to be having better luck this time, at least temporarily.

Mago had agreed to assume yet another identity, this time in service to his queen.

He and Isibel had been meeting with Markus for the better part of the late afternoon and early evening, plotting strategy. Dalis had hovered protectively, ensuring her patient didn't exhaust himself.

My cousin would be playing the role of a diplomat. It'd

been said that he could rob a man blind and have that same man thank him for his good work. It'd be interesting to watch him work his magic at the negotiating table.

Mago was born to sit at a negotiating table—or as he was doing right now, schmoozing at a reception.

Today had been exhausting enough, but tonight had proven that there could always be something worse.

A cocktail party.

To get the delegates talking to each other before the peace talks officially started tomorrow morning, Justinius Valerian was hosting a reception in the citadel.

I'd never liked fancy parties. Fortunately, I'd never been invited to that many, but I knew I wouldn't like them.

I was right.

I'd never been one for small talk. If you didn't have anything to say, or there wasn't anyone you particularly wanted to talk to, then why go to the trouble? It didn't help matters any that Mychael wasn't here yet. He was in down in the communications room. Ben had contacted the ship carrying Mychael's parents to make sure the Guardian escorts were with them. They were expected tomorrow on the evening tide.

I wanted to meet my in-laws. I was also terrified to meet my in-laws.

Mychael had been assuring me that once they met and got to know me, they'd love me.

I wasn't holding my breath on that one.

That sense of impending doom wasn't doing a thing to help how I felt right now. I felt like a major diplomatic blunder waiting to happen. Not only was I a fish out of water, I was flopping around on the dock.

Mago, on the other hand, couldn't have been more in his element. To look at him you'd never know that he hadn't spent his entire career in the foreign service. He and Isibel looked stunning together. Mychael's sister didn't strike me as the type to have her head turned by a handsome face, but Mago also had wit, charm, and intelligence in spades, as did Isibel. The two of them were working the room like the professionals they were.

I almost felt sorry for the other delegates.

Almost.

For the role of elven diplomatic attaché, Mago had assumed yet another alias—Mago Nuallan. It helped that he'd recently grown a dashing, meticulously trimmed beard. It went well with his new identity.

Mago Peronne was the personal banker of the goblin king Chigaru Mal'Salin, not exactly a shining example of elven impartiality. Mago Nuallan was a brilliant up-and-coming, hotshot member of the elven foreign service. Rumors had been carefully and strategically placed so that Mago would be touted as Markus Sevelien's secret protégé—and secret weapon.

Markus's absence had been noticed and asked about. Mago and Isibel had gone with a version of the truth—always best when the absolute truth would cause a panicked stampede. Markus was recuperating from an illness, and hopefully would be well enough to attend the talks in the next day or two.

If it were anyone else, I'd have said fat chance of convincing the best diplomats in the kingdoms, but this was Mago we were talking about. He was all of that and things they wouldn't know until it hit them at the negotiation table.

I'd spoken with Mago and Isibel twice so far this evening. Now Mago, making his way toward me through the crowd while Isibel was chatting with the Caesolian ambassador, signaled he was stopping by for chat number three. As far as the delegates were concerned, we'd only recently been introduced, not grown up together.

Everyone knew only too well who and what I was, and they were steering clear. Once Mychael arrived that would change, but until then, it was as if I was an ill-tempered sky dragon. Steer clear and you wouldn't get fried.

"At least they're acting like they're enjoying themselves," I noted to Mago when he got close enough.

"These are career diplomats, Raine. Not only do they enjoy this kind of thing, it provides them with valuable insight to their fellow delegates, or as we say in the financial sector—fresh meat." My cousin inclined his head to a Majafan delegate with a smile a barracuda would've been proud of.

"You're having the time of your life."

Mago took a deep, satisfied breath. "It is a refreshing change of pace."

"Markus wants to steal you from your banking job."

More smiling and nodding. "I know. We're presently in the courtship phase of negotiations." He glanced over at where Tam, Imala, and Dakarai Enric were acting like they were enjoying drinks and light conversation. Tam wasn't even wearing leather. Imala had dimples. Dakarai Enric was a sweet old man. None of it helped. Every last one of the other delegates was giving them a wide berth, like feeder fish around sharks.

Maybe it'd help if goblins wore a color other than black.

"They're not going to make friends like that," I muttered. "Though if Tam and Imala walked up to any of the other delegates, they'd pee themselves, faint, or have a heart attack."

No one had weapons. That was a good thing. No chance of panic-related accidents. Though apparently word had gotten around about Tam's abilities. Unless you were suicidal, no one wanted to talk to a man who could kill you with a single word. The whole death curse thing worked against you, especially in social settings. Even more unfortunate was that the Nebian ambassador had met Tam before. It hadn't gone well. Tam didn't like the Nebian, either. It was the only thing they'd ever agreed on.

Mago grinned devilishly and set his drink on a passing tray. "I don't think this will cause heart attacks, but let's see if I can stun the room into complete silence by introducing Mago Nuallan, elven diplomatic attaché, to the goblin delegation."

I bit my bottom lip against a snort. Oh, I wanted to see that.

"And me with a front-row seat," I murmured.

Mago straightened his doublet. "Prepare to be dazzled."

As my cousin crossed the room, Isibel gave him a breathtaking smile and joined him—and you could have heard a cocktail fork drop as the two elves gave a warm greeting to the three goblins.

"Isibel and Mago seem to be enjoying themselves."

The voice came from right behind me, and I damned near jumped out of my skin. If recognition hadn't overridden my survival instinct, I could've stabbed my own fiancé.

"Don't do that," I said around a smile for the benefit of the Brenirian attaché, who was venturing closer, now that Mychael was by my side.

Mychael put his big hand around my waist. It was warm and comforting. I breathed out a little sigh and felt myself relax. A little.

"You really don't like these things, do you?"

"No, I don't. If I knew—and liked—these people, it'd be different. But I don't, so it isn't. Are there a lot of receptions that the paladin is required to attend?"

"Unfortunately, yes. Some are Conclave related, others for the college and faculty."

"I know some of the faculty, and like them. That might not be too bad. Conclave mages…" I didn't finish that sentence, and knew I didn't need to. Mychael knew how I felt. Though if Garadin and Tarsilia signed on as two of the Seat of Twelve, I would have no problem attending any function on this island. I told Mychael about their arrival and the potentially amazing news.

He smiled and nodded in approval.

"Words can't describe how wonderful that would be," I said.

"If Justinius is self-appointing replacements, he'd better

do it quick and get them invested and sworn in even quicker," Mychael said. "In times of crisis, an archmagus has made personal appointments, but that was for the sudden death of one or two of the Seat of Twelve."

"Two would die at the same time?"

"About two hundred years ago, one challenged another to a duel. Let's just say they were too evenly matched."

"That could do it."

"It could and did."

"Has he told you the names of any of the other candidates he's considering?"

Mychael shook his head. "He has his work; I have mine. If I need to know or he needs my help, he'll tell me."

I just looked at him.

"Yes, I know. You couldn't do that."

"Aren't you in the least bit curious?"

"He has his work—"

"And you have yours. Yes, I got that. But—"

"I had no doubt that he'll make fine choices, and I'll enjoy hearing them when he tells me."

I looked over to where Justinius was listening while the Caesolian ambassador, Duke Something-or-other, talked the old man's ears off, probably about their northern border with Rheskilia and the goblins. The Caesolian delegation had a near obsession with it. The Caesolians were concerned that once the goblins made nice with the elves, they'd turn their military might loose on their southern neighbor. I had two bits of news for the duke. One, the goblins' military might was in disarray right now, and quite frankly had always been larger in rumor than reality. Two, goblins had absolutely zero interest in acquiring anything south of the Straits of Mourning. Well, unless it was Caesolian red wine. Goblins loved their Caesolian red. But as far as I knew, no kingdom had ever gone to war with another over fermented grape juice.

Though from the way Justinius Valerian's fingers clenched his wineglass, he'd probably like a bottle of it right now to break over His Grace's head to get him to stop talking.

"I think he prefers 'traitor mage housecleaning' to diplomacy," I observed.

Mychael took a healthy swig of his own wine. "Don't we all? It's certainly easier to know when you're making progress."

12

"Another day, another room I hate," I muttered.

Vegard grunted in agreement. "I don't think anything good has ever happened in here."

It was early the next morning, and we were standing in the meeting room of the Seat of Twelve.

The last time we'd been in here, there'd been a raised dais with twelve throne-like chairs. It had looked less like a meeting room and more like a star chamber for passing judgment.

I'd been summoned once to a meeting of the Seat of Twelve, though it had felt more like an ambush. The Khrynsani had claimed I'd stolen the Saghred from the goblin people and wanted me turned over to them for prosecution. Inquisitor Taltek Balmorlan of elven intelligence had wanted to lock me away for everyone's safety. That was what he'd said. What he'd really wanted was to use me and the Saghred as a weapon to wipe out the goblins. Carnades Silvanus, an actual member of the Seat of Twelve, had merely wanted my head on an executioner's block, the sooner, the better.

None of that had scared me. Well, not too much. What had terrified me was Carnades's and Balmorlan's claim that through my contact with the Saghred, I'd contaminated Piaras. They wanted to take him into "protective custody." Taltek Balmorlan was later exposed as an arms dealer, except that the weapons he dealt in were magically gifted people, people who had talents that made them powerful and deadly weapons. Like Piaras's spellsinging ability. He'd later had Piaras kidnapped, and Phaelan and I had barely been able to rescue him before Balmorlan would have taken him off the island on his private yacht.

So this room had absolutely zero fond memories for me.

Over the next few days, if we managed to get a peace treaty agreed upon and signed, I'd reevaluate my opinion, but not until then.

The room was of a size to contain the twelve thrones and any poor sot or sots who got called in to answer for their actions.

For now, a circular table had been installed with twenty-one chairs around it. There were Seven Kingdoms, and no more than three delegates per kingdom were being allowed at the negotiating table or in the room.

That didn't mean the delegations couldn't have ridiculously large support staffs. But Justinius had declared—and Mychael would enforce—that only three of the staffers could be in the citadel during the talks. If one of the delegates needed anything, that request would be relayed through one of the three Guardians assigned to each delegation. That meant one Guardian per delegate from the time they entered the citadel until they left. Outside the citadel's walls, the delegates' safety was the responsibility of their own security people. Armed Guardian escorts were available to escort delegates back to their embassies, if requested.

So far, no one had asked for it, but Justinius kept the offer on the table. He didn't want to waste valuable Guardian time and resources playing chaperone to any delegates who decided to have a night on the town. If they got themselves into trouble blowing off steam or releasing tension from spending a day at the negotiating table, their own people would have to haul them out of whatever they landed in.

However, if that trouble ended behind bars, it would be Mychael's job to go down to the city watch station, smooth down any ruffled diplomatic feathers, bail them out, and escort them under guard back to their embassy.

Justinius had made sure that each delegation knew the rules before they set foot on the island. He was too busy to babysit people representing their kingdoms who didn't have the good manners and enough sense to act like it.

Mychael and Sedge Rinker, the chief watcher, were fully prepared to make an example of the first one who tried. Or, if the arrestable offense was serious enough, the offending diplomat could cool his or her heels in a cell overnight before being escorted back to their embassy and forced to remain there for the duration of the talks, so-called diplomatic immunity be damned.

The Myloran delegation had just arrived. There were only three of them, but they were huge. Two rough-looking men and one seriously imposing woman, all of them taller than Vegard. They wore furs and leather, and if any of the delegates were going to get in trouble, get arrested, and get thrown in jail, chances were good it'd be these people. For them it wouldn't be breaking the law, it'd be a night on the town.

I rather liked them.

Vegard definitely liked them. My Myloran bodyguard was grinning.

"You know any of them?"

"By reputation only."

"What kind of reputation?"

"It ain't for their diplomacy."

"I got that impression."

"With my people, what you see is what you get. We prefer blunt talk to diplomacy."

My family was much the same way. Phaelan's idea of diplomacy involved firing cannon shot across your bow rather than through your waterline.

"From the looks of this group, their idea of blunt talk includes blunt force trauma. Good thing weapons aren't allowed in here."

Vegard chuckled. "Only if who they're negotiating with likes hearing themselves talk and takes too long getting to the point."

I thought of the Nebian ambassador. Imala had told me that "weasel" was about the best thing Aeron Corantine could be called, and that was being exceedingly generous. One weasel versus three massive Mylorans with no patience for oily maneuvering and evasive talk. This was gonna get real ugly, real fast. Though at least it meant it wouldn't be boring.

"Do you know who's been assigned to babysit them?" I asked.

"Herrick, Arman, Drud, and Jarvis."

"Those names sound familiar."

"They're the Guardians who were assigned to babysit Piaras when Sarad Nukpana was trying to take over his mind."

"Big guys, magic heavyweights, don't take any crap."

"That would be them."

"Wait, I thought it was one Guardian per delegate."

Vegard grinned. "The paladin thought it'd be prudent to give the Myloran delegation an extra."

"Good idea."

"They know when to stand back, and when to step in. They'll let the Mylorans enjoy themselves while minimizing the bloodshed."

"What section of town would be their idea of fun?"

"They usually stay close to the waterfront. We're a sea-faring people."

I winced. "That's what I thought. I'd better warn Phaelan to keep his boys on a short leash. Their idea of fun involves bloodshed, too."

Vegard glanced around at the new décor. "At least they've taken out the thrones."

"I see I'm not the only one who thought that's what they looked like."

"That's one more thing I'm going to change," came Justinius Valerian's voice from behind us. "Plain, comfortable chairs. Not too comfortable, though. Decisiveness and quick action need to be taken in this room, not naps—and certainly not self-glorification."

I went and stood next to him. "Has anyone told you today that they love you?"

The old man grinned impishly. "Not a one."

I leaned over and gave him a peck on the cheek. "Well, I love you."

Unless my eyes deceived me—and they didn't—Justinius Valerian blushed just ever so slightly.

Mychael came over. He'd heard the exchange. "Sir, are you trying to steal my fiancée?"

The old man shrugged. "I'm cursed with too much charm for one man."

"He's magnetic," I said. "Irresistible. If only someone would have warned me before it was too late."

"If I can trust you two alone with each other, I need to go down to the communications room. I've just gotten word that there are responses coming in to the queries I sent out."

I was confused. "Queries?"

Mychael turned his back to the delegates, who were beginning to take their seats around the table, to prevent anyone from reading his lips. As an added precaution, he also lowered his voice. "I sent messages to people I trust with access to both government and private mirrors. We need to know if what happened here is isolated or not. Meanwhile, Cuinn is down in our mirror room working on how a Rak'kari was able to get inside the elven mirror."

"Here's hoping for isolated." I glanced around the room full of diplomats. "Seeing that this is the last place where I belong, I'll go with you."

"Let me know as soon as you hear," Justinius told us. He sighed. "I'll be right here getting these children started on their classwork."

13

Yesterday I'd been in a room for permanently dead bodies.
It was early afternoon, and I was back in the place where
Markus Sevelien had become one temporarily. Though I'd
hardly call the citadel's mirror room an improvement on the
creepy scale. If I had to pick something to attack me, I'd take
a reanimated corpse over a heart-stopping, black-webbed,
Khrynsani-spawned spider monster any day.

Professor Cuinn Aviniel, the Conclave's expert in the
science behind mirror travel, had sent word that he knew how
a Rak'kari had been able to ambush Markus Sevelien in the
seconds between Silvanlar and the Isle of Mid, and he wanted
to tell me and Mychael all about it.

In the mirror room.

I really hoped there weren't going to be any demonstrations.

Tam and Imala were here with us. For obvious reasons,
they were interested in having their education broadened about
what the Khrynsani might now be capable of, too. When the

delegates had taken a lunch break, Tam and Imala had joined us here. Goblin ambassador Dakarai Enric had assured them that he had the negotiations well in hand, and that getting to the bottom of this was just as important as a peace treaty.

As much as I wanted to know how someone—and evidence was emphatically pointing at the Khrynsani—sent a Rak'kari to assassinate the director of elven intelligence, I'd really hoped it'd been a one-time crime, impossible to be replicated.

The moment I saw Cuinn, I knew that the mirror magic professor was way too excited to have run across a mere anomaly. He'd made a major, world-changing discovery, which probably meant what had happened to Markus could happen again. To anyone.

The only mirror mage I'd ever known had been Carnades Silvanus. You could say we'd been on a first-name basis, though we preferred more descriptive epithets to call each other.

It helped that Cuinn Aviniel didn't look a thing like Carnades. For one, he was younger than I was. He was a little taller, red-haired, freckle-faced, with big blue eyes. He was an elf, so he had upswept ears. There were freckles on those, too. Cuinn was just about as cute as he could be.

Carnades had considered himself the pinnacle of elven aristocratic breeding. From what I was learning of his family, he was the result of elven aristocratic inbreeding. There were only four families the Silvanuses would marry into. Those four families had been going round and round for the past hundred years or so. It was no wonder Carnades had been nuts.

One of those families had the last name Balmorlan.

Like I said, the height of elven inbreeding.

According to Mychael, Cuinn had been a child prodigy who had quickly become the top expert on mirror magic and the science behind why they could do what they did. He'd been offered the job of department chair of what was actually called dimensional studies, but he'd turned it down because he didn't want to run a department; he wanted to teach and do research.

Mychael introduced him to us. "Chancellor Nathrach and Director Kalis have a vested interest in hearing any information you may have found to explain what happened here."

"Sheer genius was what happened here," Cuinn said with unabashed admiration. "Unspeakably evil and scary genius, but still genius." His words then came in an eager torrent. "There have been theories floating around the intra-dim research community for years that Void manipulation could actually confirm the existence of an extra—"

I raised my hand. "Professor Aviniel?"

His face lit with a boyishly enthusiastic grin. "Cuinn, please."

I couldn't help but smile back. This kid couldn't have been more different from Carnades. Wherever his rotten soul had ended up, he had to be clenching his ghostly patrician jaw at the thought of his position as reigning mirror expert being usurped by someone this perpetually cheerful.

"Cuinn. Some of us…okay, probably just me, didn't understand a thing you just started to say. I'm just a mirror user, and only then if you throw me through the thing. Most of the interactions I've had with mirrors have been bad, as in near-fatal bad. I need the remedial explanation."

That made him stop and think—probably how to dumb it down far enough.

"Actually, in all likelihood, you've experienced precisely what I'm about to explain." He gave an apologetic wince and smile. "Though the comparison could be even more unpleasant than your mirror experiences."

"Just say it."

"I understand that you've been inside the Saghred."

"Unfortunately, more than once."

"Rumors spread pretty quickly around here."

"Take anything you heard from Carnades Silvanus with a grain of salt, a boulder-sized one."

All signs of perky instantly vanished. "I always did. Not to speak ill of the dead, but I was really glad to hear Carnades wasn't coming back." He paused, his freckled brow creased in concern. "Though is it true that his body was never recovered?"

Looked like I wasn't the only one who believed that if a body wasn't found, the person might not be dead.

"Sarad Nukpana stabbed and killed Carnades Silvanus," I assured him. "I was standing right next to him when it happened, and I saw him die. I've seen dead bodies before, and I know dead when I see it. That being said, I didn't see what happened to his body afterward, but more than one highly reliable source in the goblin court said they saw a sea dragon eat him."

"Oh, good." Cuinn winced. "That didn't come out right."

"I think it came out perfectly. In fact, I couldn't agree more."

"Unofficially," Imala chimed in, "Chancellor Nathrach and I couldn't have been more thrilled."

Mychael didn't say a word. His expression was carefully neutral, but his eyes were smiling.

Yeah, we'd all been happy there hadn't been enough left of Carnades Silvanus to bring back home with us.

Still, Cuinn lowered his voice. I guess when you lived and worked in a place where secrets were merely rumors that hadn't been spread yet, old habits died hard. "I overheard Carnades telling another member of the Seat of Twelve what he had seen when he touched you with that questing spell. A detestable act, by the way, well deserving of being eaten by a sea dragon. Until that time, I didn't think I could have had less respect for Carnades, or disliked him any more than I already did. I don't make a habit of eavesdropping, but when one's professional survival is at stake, you do what you have to do. For some reason known only to him, Carnades wanted me gone."

"Then you're lucky to still be alive," Tam muttered.

"Hmm, let's see," I mused. "You were half his age, and probably double his talent."

Cuinn blushed. "I don't think I'd go that far, but I do believe he felt threatened by my being in the department. Regardless, any information that would give me an advantage or future ammunition...Well, I'm not ashamed to have done what was necessary to protect myself and my department."

"I take it that working conditions have improved?" Mychael asked.

The smile was back. "Paladin, I think we're the happiest department in the entire college. And we're not the only ones in the college who look forward to coming to work every day. The next time you see Archmagus Valerian, thank him for us. Yes, we have to do more work with fewer people, but those who are left are here for the right reasons. We want to teach the next generation, not play political one-upmanship."

"I'll be sure to let him know."

"We appreciate what he's done for us, and for the students. Whatever political fallout happens from all this, tell him the faculty—at least I can speak for my department—will stand with him no matter what."

"He'll be really glad to hear that his efforts are appreciated," I told him. "The Saghred is far from my favorite topic, but if it'll help us understand what happened to Markus, feel free to use it as an example."

"When viewed from the outside, the Saghred was small enough to hold in your hand."

I swallowed, more of a gulp actually. That cued the flashback to the Khrynsani temple, of Sarad Nukpana forcing my hand down onto the Saghred's surface, and the stone essentially fusing my skin to it.

"Uh-huh, you could hold it in your hand." I hoped my voice didn't sound as reedy as it felt. I don't think Cuinn noticed.

"What is a contained and finite space when viewed from the outside is much larger on the inside, infinite even when viewed by those inside. The area where mirror travels occurs is a seemingly empty space, which is why it's called the Void. When two mirrors are linked, a tunnel of sorts forms, providing safe—well, previously safe—travel from one destination to another. Nothing lives in the Void, and certainly not a creature that doesn't exist without being conjured. From what I understand from Chancellor Nathrach, the tips of a Rak'kari's legs are sharp, but mirror tunnels cannot be punctured. It was deliberately placed there. And considering who was traveling through that tunnel, and his importance to the elven peace talk delegation, I believe that Director Sevelien was the intended victim."

"So what would it take to make a hole in a mirror tunnel?" Mychael asked.

Cuinn looked perplexed. "Perhaps I misspoke, Paladin Eiliesor. I don't believe the structural integrity of the tunnel was compromised." He indicated the now-empty frame of Markus's shattered mirror. "When the tunnel formed around the mirror, it was already inside, waiting for Director Sevelien to arrive."

We all looked to the nearly two dozen mirrors down the long length of the room's wall—ending at the mirror linked to the Mal'Salin palace in Regor.

I had to resist a strong urge to take a step back.

"If all the Khrynsani wanted to do was kill Director Sevelien, they would have booby-trapped only that mirror. If they'd wanted Primaru Nathrach and Director Kalis as well, they would have set a Rak'kari on the mirror from Regor. Or if they wanted to kill Director Sevelien *and* make the Guardians look bad, nothing would have stopped them from booby-trapping every single mirror in this room—or beyond."

My body involuntarily swayed a little in the direction of the door, my feet threatening to follow.

"What did you hear from your queries?" I asked Mychael.

"I got five responses. Four had no problems." He paused. "One traveler, a Caesolian merchant, didn't arrive at his destination. However, both of those mirrors were older and didn't have a signaling pad."

"So...He could have missed the boat, so to speak."

"So to speak."

"You don't sound too confident."

"No, I'm not. There could easily be other victims. Those that responded are but a small fraction of the operational mirrors in the Seven Kingdoms." He turned to Cuinn. "If there had been a Rak'kari on the other side of our mirror, our mages would have known it."

Tam swore.

"What?"

"A containment box."

Yet another unwanted comparison to the Saghred. The rock had had one. The box had done a crappy job of containing it, but the Saghred had come into my life complete with its own Carrying Case of Evil.

"Though a better comparison would be a cage," Tam continued. "The Rak'kari is inside. The lock is deactivated when a predetermined action takes place, such as the intended victim entering the room it's concealed in. Such boxes are often hidden by a veiling spell to make them blend with a wall, or even look like a mundane object in the room. It's an entirely plausible explanation, considering that Rak'kari are killing machines. To get one to stay put, it'd have to be confined."

"So either Markus stepping through that mirror in Silvanlar triggered the Rak'kari's release," Mychael said, "or it happened when our mirror mage activated the mirror on this end."

"Or when Brina Daesage sent the message back to Silvanlar that the coast was clear for Markus to come through." That earned me a look from my betrothed. "I'm not saying she's involved."

Cuinn spoke. "It *is* protocol for a senior official's guard to come through a mirror first and signal that it's safe."

"And whoever planted that thing could've easily known that," I said.

"While we obviously need to know who's behind this," Tam said, "equally important is *how* it was done. A Rak'kari can live anywhere, including the Void, but nothing else can. So how did a Khrynsani put a containment box—if that theory is correct—on the other side of that mirror frame?"

"Mirrors are not the only way to travel through the Void," Cuinn reminded us. "And ours is not the only dimension."

While we all knew that, none of us wanted to hear it—or think about what it could imply. Tam's mom was a mortekal. The fact that she'd lost the trail of her prey was unheard of.

Unless Sandrina Ghalfari wasn't in our dimension any longer.

Her son had been carried into the Lower Hells by a horned demon—and all of her evil hopes and dreams had been taken away along with him.

I glanced at Tam. He looked like he was having similar thoughts.

"Think Sandrina and some Khrynsani went to Hell after Sarad Nukpana?" I asked.

"Worse things have happened."

I blinked. "They have?"

Tam seemed to be having second thoughts. "Probably not."

"Have you cleaned the uniform you were wearing when the Rak'kari attacked you?" Cuinn asked Mychael.

"No, it's still in my quarters. With all the residue, the tunic's probably beyond saving."

The mirror mage's eyes lit with barely disguised glee. "What kind of residue?"

"Web slime mostly."

"Good. I need that tunic, and any clothing Director Sevelien was wearing that might have come in contact with the Rak'kari. Each of the known dimensions that are accessible from our own has a distinct environment. If the Rak'kari was conjured elsewhere, there's a good chance it could have had residue from its dimension of origin."

Tam nodded in agreement. "Let's figure out where it came from. Finding those Khrynsani and making them stop is imperative."

From his fierce expression, Tam wanted to be at the front of the "make the Khrynsani stop" line. And I didn't think he intended to leave anything for the rest of us.

"That settles it," Tam said. "I need to look inside that mirror."

14

No one liked Tam going into the mirror, but being a dark mage, he'd had experience dealing with elementals. He'd never personally created a Rak'kari, but by being a perpetual thorn in Sarad Nukpana and the Khrynsani's collective side almost all of his life, he'd had experience staying alive on the numerous occasions when an elemental had been sent to kill him, which made him the most qualified to dangle himself as bait—most qualified in that he was the most likely to survive should what grabbed Markus grab him.

There was also the possibility of a Rak'kari having been put inside the citadel's goblin mirror specifically to attack Tam. If that was the case, anyone else stepping inside wouldn't trigger an attack.

Yep, that was the actual plan, believe it or not.

Trigger an attack with Tam as bait.

Imala wasn't seeing the logic—or sanity—in Tam's plan.

As little as any of us wanted to follow through with this,

it was necessary. We had to know if the attack on Markus had been isolated, or part of a Khrynsani evil master plan. If it wasn't isolated, our next step would be to determine whether only the citadel's mirrors were affected, or whether the infiltration extended to the rest of Mid—or God help us, beyond.

Tam had sent a message via Ben down in the contact room to the royal mirror chamber in the Mal'Salin palace in Regor. Tam's teachers, Kesyn Badru and A'Zahra Nuru, were now waiting on that end along with some of Tam's dark mage school buddies, now royal guards. Cuinn Aviniel would activate the mirror here. Once the tunnel had formed, Tam would step through. The goal wasn't to travel the hundreds of miles back to Regor, it was to trigger the Rak'kari attack that Tam had avoided yesterday by coming to Mid via the Passages. However, we'd made sure that both destinations were prepared for what might happen.

Tam was wearing one of Mychael's suits of battle armor. This particular suit provided complete head-to-toe-coverage, including the face, with narrow lenses for the eyes. Like Mychael's other suits of armor, this one fit like a second skin; and since Tam and Mychael were pretty much the same size, it fit the same way on Tam. Set into the center of the armor's chestplate was a spy gem. Time was different inside the Void. To Tam, a second of time would pass. In the Void, he would be there much longer. The gem would record what really happened.

That was the other big reason for Tam turning himself into bait—to get a look inside the tunnel that formed, and hopefully a hazy look out into the Void. According to Cuinn, the walls of a mirror tunnel were mostly opaque. However, occasional transparent sections provided glimpses out into the Void.

"I have to say, if you're going to die, we'll be dragging a fine-looking corpse back through that mirror," Imala noted. Her arms were crossed, her dark eyes set on glare, and she was most decidedly not happy.

"The armor will provide ample protection," Tam told her.

"You've done this before." It wasn't a question.

"No."

"So your survival is mere theory."

"Technically, yes."

Imala went with more glaring.

Tam's expression softened and he stepped forward and put his hands around her shoulders. Brave man, playing monster spider bait *and* getting within fist and knee range of Imala Kalis. Either brave or suicidal. Since Tam was a goblin, there was a good chance it could be both.

"If the Khrynsani are behind this, once the other delegates find out—and they will—they'll think Chigaru ordered it."

"And you getting yourself killed will prove them wrong. Brilliant plan."

"Imala, would anyone else stand a better chance of survival?"

Silence. Silence that said Tam was right and Imala didn't want him to be. None of us did.

"I'll only be gone for a few seconds."

"In our time. In Void time, it'll be like leisurely dragging a baited hook through shark-infested waters."

"Imala, I haven't survived all that I have for as long as I have to be killed by a spider regardless of how big it is. I'd die of embarrassment first."

In addition to the armor, Tam would be covered in his best shielding spells. And to ensure Mychael didn't have to go flailing around in a mirror again with an unprotected arm, Tam was also wearing a steel harness attached to a steel cable. Attached to the other end of the cable were four huge Guardians wearing armored gauntlets. If something snatched Tam in there, they'd snatch him right back here.

Ben and his scrying bowl had set up shop in a room just down the hall, with a Guardian stationed at the closed door to relay any message. Regular noise didn't bother Ben, but the yelling and cursing that could occur if we had to get Tam out of that mirror fast would be distracting to say the least.

All the precautions that could be taken had been taken.

Mychael put on a pair of gauntlets and added himself as the fifth Guardian manning that cable. Naturally, he went to the front of the line, so if they caught anything they couldn't handle on their Tam-baited line, Mychael would be the first one to get yanked in. Mychael, being Mychael, wasn't about to allow any of his men to do anything he wouldn't do himself.

I gave him a look that, while not at an Imala level of glare, let him know that I took a dim view of his amendment to Tam's plan.

The crystal signal pad set into the frame of the goblin mirror turned green.

"Regor's ready, gentlemen," Cuinn said. "Are we?"

Tam took a breath and lowered the visor on his helmet. "As much as I'm going to be."

"Knights?" Mychael asked.

"They're ready, sir." Vegard was standing by with a pair of now glowing short swords, hoping that should he need to use them, they'd work against either spider or web.

"Have a nice trip," I said before I could stop myself.

Tam stepped through.

Moments passed.

Cuinn's control of the mirror never wavered.

Then the cable jerked. Hard.

Mychael pulled. "Get him out! Now!"

I was strong for my size, but I'd just be in the way, and I hated it. But my hating it didn't change the fact that the best thing I could do to help Tam would be to stay out of the way.

The cable snapped, and an instant later Mychael and his Guardians were piled on the floor. Before any of them could get to their feet, Tam fell out of the mirror, armor smoking from what looked like acid burns covering his entire body.

Tam wrenched the helmet off and threw it aside.

He stripped off what he could reach, and Mychael and his Guardians scrambled to their feet and all but tore off the rest. Beneath the armor, Tam wore a quilted arming jacket and trousers. The pieces were laced on and buckled. The cloth and padding inside were melting.

Imala instantly had a dagger in her hand and was slicing through leather straps and laces, and the linen undergarments beneath.

In moments, Tam was as naked as the day he'd been born.

There wasn't a burn mark on him.

And there wasn't anything else wrong with him, either.

I'd never seen Tam naked, and from the borderline embarrassed expression on Imala's face, this was a first-timer for her, too.

"Do I really want to know what just happened here?" Justinius Valerian stood in the open doorway, surveying the nudity, dissolving armor, and generalized chaos.

"Apparently Rak'kari venom isn't limited to dissolving flesh," Tam noted, making no move to cover anything.

Justinius nodded. "Uh-huh."

Mychael quickly detached the spy gem from the still bubbling chestplate lying on the floor. The gem and the area around it appeared to be undamaged. "This will show us what happened inside the mirror tunnel."

He started telling Justinius what had resulted in Tam's unclothed state when the goblin mirror flashed a bright, acid green.

Cuinn got his hands back up and pushed back. "What the hell is—"

A massive spider leapt through the mirror straight at Tam and Imala.

I didn't think. I reacted.

I dove between it and the two goblins, instinctively putting my hands in front of me, either to protect myself or will the thing to stop.

Both were stupid. Neither worked.

My world turned crimson and I screamed.

I also must have squeezed my eyes shut against my impending messy death.

When my skin didn't start melting from spider spit, I took a quick peek.

The Rak'kari's head—complete with fangs dripping skin-dissolving venom—was right in front of my face. And I do mean right in front of. The spider was the size of a werehound. But it couldn't get any closer. The reason why was just as terrifying as the spider itself.

I kept my now trembling hands out in front of me, fingers spread, mere inches from the exterior of what looked like a Rak'kari-sized sphere.

A deep red sphere.

It looked like a big Saghred, except that I could clearly see what was inside, and what was inside could see me, and it was pissed.

I echoed Cuinn's sentiment, albeit a couple of octaves higher. "What the hell?"

"You did it, girl," Justinius said.

"I know I did it. Again, what the hell?"

"I'm starting to have a theory," was all he said.

Oh, that didn't sound good.

The red glow began to fade, leaving a clear sphere floating in midair, giving us all an even better look at what I'd somehow managed to contain. Venom was frothing around the Rak'kari's fangs, dripping down the insides of the sphere, and pooling at the bottom.

I was trying not to hyperventilate, and not doing a good job.

"How long will it hold?" Cuinn asked.

"How am I supposed to know?"

"You made it."

"And I don't know how."

"We need to get it into a containment room," Mychael said, his voice perfectly calm.

Glad one of us was.

"How are we gonna do that? Roll it down the hall?"

"Do you think you can walk it there?" Justinius asked. "You don't look like you're going to be dropping it anytime soon."

"If that venom eats through the bottom, that's exactly what I'll be doing, followed by running."

"No, you won't."

"I won't?"

The old man shook his head.

I growled. "You're right. I'll stand my ground like an idiot and try to redo what I did right up until it bites me and sucks my brains out."

"I can push and guide it," Mychael said, still the epitome of calm.

Justinius pushed up his voluminous sleeves. "And I'll back you up, if you need it." He flashed what he probably meant to be an encouraging smile. "Just hold it steady, girl. We'll do the steering."

15

Most of the citadel's containment rooms had air vents. This one didn't. The Rak'kari didn't need air, and none of us that did would be going in the room with it.

The room did have an observation window. The glass wasn't really glass, and could withstand any known corrosive, as could the coating and spells on the stone walls.

I didn't trust either one.

The sphere containing the Rak'kari was inside a magically enhanced steel cage. I didn't trust that, either.

I definitely didn't trust the sphere.

Or where I was starting to suspect it'd come from.

The first time it had manifested, my new magic had dissolved a strand of Rak'kari web around Mychael's throat, which at the time had looked and felt less like web and more like rope. Now, I'd caught and contained an actual Rak'kari, a monster Tam had said were rarely conjured because they couldn't be controlled, even by the most powerful Khrynsani dark mages.

The time for worrying about what was happening to me had passed.

The time for finding out what it was had arrived under full sail.

Mychael was arranging security for the Rak'kari. Justinius was standing to my right, Imala and a now-clothed Tam on my left. We were all looking through the observation window at what had attacked Tam and what I had unwittingly caught.

"Sir, you said you had a theory." I never took my eyes from the eight-legged captive. "What is it?"

"It's just a theory. Your papa might have a better idea."

"Your theories are sounder than most mage's facts. What is it?"

"For one, I don't think that beastie is going anywhere until you let it out."

"I don't plan on doing that anytime soon. Not to mention, I don't know how."

"I wasn't suggesting that you let it out. Just saying that if that orb's made out of what I think it is, that thing's in there for good."

Suddenly I felt like I was the one in the airtight room. "You said orb."

"I did. You and Mychael told me what happened when you destroyed the Saghred. You stabbed it with the Scythe of Nen, the souls left, Reapers were standing by to take the souls."

He turned away from the window and toward me. I stayed right where I was, staring at the spider. I wasn't ready to look into those intense blue eyes. Not yet. I didn't want to see what the knot in my gut was telling me was the truth.

"Your hand was fused to the Saghred the entire time," he said.

Justinius really didn't expect an answer. I needed to give him one, to say it out loud. Some things were less terrifying if you gave them voice.

"Yes."

"When the Saghred was empty, it wasn't red any longer, but your hand was still locked to it."

"Yes."

"Then you removed the Scythe of Nen, reversed it, bringing the pommel down on the Saghred and destroying it. But until that instant, you still couldn't pull your hand away."

"No, I couldn't."

Silence filled the hallway.

"But the souls that powered it were gone," Tam said. "Kesyn said it was almost clear enough to see through."

"Just because you can see through something doesn't mean it's empty," Justinius said.

I didn't like hearing that, or what it implied.

The Saghred hadn't asked me what I wanted when it bonded itself to me. And it sure hadn't asked me what I'd wanted when I'd been trying to destroy it.

"In those last seconds, it was afraid," I heard myself say. "It was trying to save itself—any way it could. When I stabbed it with the Scythe, it was like driving that dagger into my own guts."

Tam glanced behind me. Mychael was there. He'd been there long enough to have heard enough.

"You were standing next to her that night," Tam said to him. "Did you see anything? Or sense?"

"Nothing."

I could see my fiancé and our friends reflected in the glass in front of me. My eyes were directed at the spider, but I wasn't seeing it. I was seeing myself, seeing what I now knew I was. When words made it out, they were quiet and even. "You're saying that whatever gave the Saghred its power, its core, whatever made it what it was, is now inside of me." It wasn't a question. There was no use asking a question when you already knew the answer. "Basically, I destroyed the Saghred's body. I have what's left of the Saghred's soul. To save itself, the last soul the Saghred took through me was its own."

"The Saghred was neither good nor evil," Mychael said to reassure me. "It was power. It was the Khrynsani who used that power for evil. We've talked about this. You're not evil and you never will be."

"The Saghred has always needed to be fed," I said.

"Feeling an urge to slurp souls?" Justinius asked.

I finally turned and looked at him, at all of them. "No, I don't."

"Then you're not going to slurp souls."

The old man was rational thought personified. I wished I could have been calm and rational about what was happening to me. I was treading new ground—historically, monumentally new ground.

"Yes, you are." His hand reached down and took mine, his thin fingers closing around my fingers, surprisingly warm, and even more surprisingly comforting.

He smiled as I started finding air to breathe again.

"So the reason why my magic's unreliable is that I have some unknown power in residence and it's still getting settled into its new home."

Vegard's voice came from behind us all. He sounded proud, not afraid. "Ma'am, Piaras isn't the only one who's going to end up in the Guardian histories as a legend."

In addition to his scrying bowl, Ben had brought a crystal ball up from the communication room. Now we gathered around to watch what had been captured on the spy gem Tam had worn.

We were down the hall from the citadel mirror room. The goblin mirror had been closed, locked, and completely secured. Depending on what we saw in that crystal ball, those actions might be extended to every other mirror in the citadel—at the very least.

Having set up the crystal ball for us, Ben turned to leave.

Justinius stopped him with a raised hand. "Hold on a minute, Ben. If we end up shutting down mirror travel on this island or anywhere else, you and your boys are going to be busy. You have every right to see what we're dealing with."

Ben gave a solemn nod. "Whatever I see won't leave this room until you tell me otherwise."

"Good man."

"I try, sir."

Mychael set the spy gem next to the crystal ball and murmured a few words.

A nightmare unfolded before our eyes.

"I didn't see any of this when I was in there," Tam breathed in disbelief.

"That does it," I said. "I'm never setting foot in a mirror again."

I'd seen masses of cobwebs and spiders before. Those had been spiders you could crush under your boot heel.

I swallowed with an audible gulp. "Are all those the same size as Gargantua down in the containment room?"

"I don't see why they wouldn't be," Tam replied. "All of the Rak'kari I've ever heard of being conjured have been the same size."

The wall of the mirror tunnel Tam had been inside of was virtually translucent. It was as if the Rak'kari wanted to show off their building skills.

We could see out into the Void. I had no idea how far it extended, though I imagine it was called the Void for a reason. Regardless, as far as our eyes could see were webs and Rak'kari, scuttling back and forth into the distance on what we knew to be rope-sized strands of web like a highway.

"Ladies and gentlemen, we have a problem," Justinius said.

"There must be hundreds," Imala managed. "There aren't that many mirrors on the island."

"No, ma'am, there aren't," Cuinn replied.

We watched in the crystal ball as a mass of web shot toward Tam like a net, engulfing him, yanking him violently forward.

Toward a mass of glistening, sticky black web.

Almost immediately, Tam was pulled again, this time from behind. That would have been Mychael and his Guardians trying to get him out.

The Rak'kari wasn't giving up its prize that easily.

Another round of tug-of-war followed, ending with the cable snapping and Tam falling out of the citadel mirror.

The spy gem continued playing what had happened when we'd gotten Tam back. It stopped when Tam's chestplate had been ripped off and had landed on the floor.

The room filled with stunned silence.

Mychael stepped up to the crystal ball, murmured a few words, and the action went in reverse as Tam was being captured and pulled forward by a Rak'kari web. Mychael held the tips of his fingers close together, then slowly spread them out, zooming in on what was blocking the goblin mirror's exit in Regor.

"Cuinn, is that…cocoon, for lack of a better word, being built where the mirrors are?"

The young elf stood utterly still. "Yes, sir."

"They're elementals," I said. "Conjured from magic. Can they reproduce?"

"I've never heard of elementals reproducing, but…" Tam's words trailed off as Mychael moved his index finger to the next cocoon, repeating the same motion to zoom in on it.

Cuinn made a strangled sound.

There was a foot and part of an arm sticking out of the cocoon. From the color of the skin, it was human or elf.

Mychael froze. "I think I know what happened to that Caesolian merchant."

I spat my favorite four-letter word, the one I reserved for life-or-death situations I couldn't do a thing to prevent.

Mychael zeroed in on three more cocoons. One was empty—at least of a dead body. The other two had a body each, and one of those bodies was goblin.

Mychael hadn't wanted to cause a needless panic by telling the delegates what had happened to Markus until we had more facts.

What we'd just witnessed was about as factual as it got.

Now it was time to panic.

16

Every telepath in the citadel's communication room was working overtime. There was already a list of contacts and procedures in place for relaying vital messages during catastrophic emergencies.

What we had on our hands qualified on every level.

Justinius and Mychael composed a message to be sent out immediately to every ruler, government agency, merchant guild, and higher academic institution in the Seven Kingdoms. The message included the order to continue spreading it, via messenger on horseback, if necessary.

Stop all mirror travel immediately. Lock, cover, and secure all mirrors now.

The message included what was infesting the Void, the fact that it was indestructible, and what would happen to anyone attempting to travel through a mirror. It also promised that we were doing everything in our power to come up with a solution.

Somehow I didn't think that was going to make anyone feel better. I knew it wasn't doing much for me, considering that I was one of the people trying to find that solution.

Those familiar with dark magic elementals would be able to do the math and determine that the Khrynsani were responsible, but until we knew that for a fact, Justinius didn't want to include it, at least not yet.

We all knew why.

The peace talks.

Or what would be left of them, once the delegates were told what had happened.

Justinius was making arrangements to tell them within the hour. In person. And once he did, the peace talks would go straight down the crapper before they had a chance to make any progress, and any hope we might have had of getting the delegates' signatures on a nonaggression treaty would be gone. The goal of the talks wasn't just peace, it was getting agreement that magical objects of power like the Saghred shouldn't and wouldn't be sought out and used against another kingdom. We'd known that the main objection would be self-defense and protection, whether they intended to use whatever they found for that reason or not.

But now, with swarms of indestructible Rak'kari infesting the Void, if I was a ruler, I'd want whatever I could get my hands on to protect my people, and damn the consequences.

The blame for those swarms would fall squarely on the goblins—any and all goblins. The delegates would claim that the goblins had declared war on the Seven Kingdoms by sending their monsters to shut down all mirror travel, thus paralyzing commerce and government, sending them back to the dark ages of traveling by horse.

The Mal'Salin family had a history of being linked to the Khrynsani, and no one would believe that any monarch with the last name Mal'Salin would have broken with tradition now. Chigaru had been on the goblin throne for less than a month. He was unknown and untried. Yes, he had ordered the Khrynsani disbanded, hunted down, and either arrested or killed if they resisted. Chigaru could claim that he despised everything they stood for until he was blue in the face. No one would believe a Mal'Salin wanted to live in peace.

But right here and right now, Tam and Imala would take the brunt of the blame. Considering Tam's death-curse reputation, those accusations probably wouldn't be said within his hearing, but the damage would be done regardless.

"Some people are going to step through a mirror anyway," I said.

"Those are the people no one's really going to miss," Justinius said. "A little less stupid in the world right now would be nice. Cutting themselves from the herd would do the rest of us a favor."

"If filling the Void with Rak'kari is the Khrynsani's doing, what are they trying to accomplish?" I asked. "The attack on the elven delegation's ship and Ambassador Eldor's murder was timed close to the Rak'kari attack on Markus. Mal'Salin gold was used to pay the pirates. Now the Rak'kari are killing anything that steps through a mirror. What do the Khrynsani want, other than to stop the peace talks by essentially holding the Seven Kingdoms hostage? I mean, is there going to be a ransom note at some point? Or was it some kind of accident?"

"That's a big accident," Cuinn muttered.

"There were less than three hundred Khrynsani in the temple at any given time," Imala said. "Perhaps that could have been increased by another hundred once Sarad Nukpana had the Saghred to protect. We arrested one hundred and forty-two."

"That leaves a lot unaccounted for," Mychael said.

"The sea dragons ate some," I reminded them.

"True, but what could a hundred Khrynsani do?"

"Set a plan in motion that had been put in place when the Khrynsani were at full strength," Tam said quietly.

Justinius sat up straighter. "You've got my attention."

"Sarad was building that massive Gate outside of Regor to instantly deploy hundreds of troops at a time to anywhere in the Seven Kingdoms," Tam said. "To simultaneously unleash a worldwide Rak'kari infestation and render every mirror unusable would be the most effective way to isolate the kingdoms from each other, *then* they could launch attacks through that Gate using the goblin army. Communication would be limited to telepaths—and then only the very best ones who could keep their emotions in check would be able to function. Even that wouldn't do them any good if there wasn't a telepath at the other end still alive to receive a message." He indicated the frozen tableau shown in the crystal ball. "To set up sabotage on this scale would take the Khrynsani at their full power. To conjure even a single Rak'kari takes a level of skill that only Sarad Nukpana's inner circle would have possessed. What we're seeing here is the result of *years* of work."

"Why haven't we seen any until now?" I asked.

"A Rak'kari can easily survive without air. As I've said, when they're created, they're immediately contained. Their digestive systems don't finish developing until they've fed for the first time, so they can be stored for a couple of years in containers and survive perfectly well."

Justinius spoke. "The Khrynsani have been making and stockpiling those things until they needed them."

"That appears to be the case, sir."

"Sons of bitches."

"Another true statement, especially when it comes to Sarad Nukpana and his inner circle. Sarad has never taken defeat well. He referred to it as a 'temporary inconvenience.' He always had a backup plan."

"He's in Hell," I reminded Tam.

"That doesn't mean that there wasn't a plan in place, just that he wouldn't be there to execute it. There were survivors, highly placed and magically talented survivors—like Sandrina

Ghalfari. Only half of his inner circle perished the night the Saghred was destroyed…" Tam winced. "Sorry, Raine."

"Quite all right. As far as I'm concerned, you can keep right on saying that. The Saghred was destroyed. That's the story we're going to be sticking with, so let's get good at telling it."

"We captured two of Sarad's inner circle that night," Imala said, smiling. "I think Grandmother should have a chat with them."

A'Zahra Nuru was Imala's grandmother. She had also been Tam's teacher and black magic rehabilitator, and was presently Chigaru's moral compass. In my opinion, she was also an all-around nice lady. So her having what Imala as the director of the goblin secret service would call a successful "chat" to obtain information was a startling revelation.

"Your grandmother tortures people?"

"She can question a person and read their thoughts, see their memories. The more specific the questioning, the better chance to bypass any thought defenses they may have." She glanced at the crystal ball with its image of a Void full of monster spiders. "Even if neither of those two men were directly involved in conjuring the Rak'kari, chances are they would at least know about the plan, which would give us confirmation that the Khrynsani are behind it. Ben, would you contact my grandmother and tell her what we need?"

Ben looked to Justinius. "Sir?"

"Move it to the top of your list. We need that information. As soon as we're finished here, contact her."

"Consider it done, sir."

"I think I'm seeing a bigger picture here," Tam mused. "The Khrynsani no longer have the goblin king and army backing them up, there's no Saghred to speak of, and Sarad is gone. There can be only about a hundred Khrynsani left. And they're setting up the new goblin government to take the blame." He shrugged. "No one's ever trusted the goblins anyway. The elves are the only kingdom equipped to go to war over it—and from what I understand, after the fallout from Carnades's treason, their government is in nearly as much disarray as ours. That would only leave the Conclave and Guardians capable of doing anything about it."

Justinius snorted.

"I take it that means you're not going to be declaring war on us."

"Don't be ridiculous."

"Good. Glad to hear it. The Khrynsani don't waste resources, so what they've done in the Void can't be just a monumental waste of perfectly good monsters—"

Mychael blinked. "Perfectly good?"

"Sorry, but you know what I mean. You have to admit they couldn't have picked a better way to stop mirror travel—Rak'kari get the job done and they're terrifying while they're at it. If all the Khrynsani wanted to achieve was no peace treaty and no trust for goblins…We've never had either one. A few Rak'kari in the Void would have sufficed to stop mirror travel, or at least slowed it down." He tilted his head toward the crystal ball. "That nightmare ensures no one's going to travel by mirror anytime soon."

"If ever," Cuinn added. "They're indestructible, right?"

"If they can be destroyed, the Khrynsani never found out how."

Mychael leaned forward thoughtfully. "The governments of the two strongest kingdoms can barely field armies, and the other five don't trust either one enough to sign a peace treaty. And when the delegates learn about the Void, what little trust there might have been will be gone." He paused meaningfully. "The Seven Kingdoms have never been more vulnerable to attack than they are right now."

"But from who?"

"Unknown. If we're lucky, it's only a few desperate and spiteful Khrynsani."

17

Being a believer that a picture was worth a thousand words, Justinius hauled the crystal ball and spy gem into the room where the delegates had been asked to gather, set them on a table, activated them, and told the delegates to watch.

When the recording had finished playing, he told the horrified assemblage what they'd seen. Then to ensure they understood the seriousness of the situation, he backed up the recording and zoomed in on the remains of the poor unfortunates who had made the life-ending choice to travel by mirror in the last day or two.

The delegates did exactly what we thought they'd do—panic and adamantly refuse to give up anything they thought might give them an advantage in what they believed was an imminent goblin/Khrynsani attack.

The claim that the present goblin government wasn't involved was met with derision from the Nebian ambassador and wide-eyed terror from the Caesolian contingency, who had steadfastly refused to accept that all goblins had ever wanted from the Caesolians was their wine. Justinius wisely hadn't mentioned that Sarad Nukpana always had a backup plan. All we had now were monster spiders and no mirror travel. While it was starting to look like the first step of a colossal and evil master plan, until it was known and confirmed, any discussion was mere speculation.

"Well, at least the delegates are predictable," I murmured to Mychael.

"I think I can do something to change their minds."

"Good luck."

"Hopefully I won't need it."

He stepped forward with what looked like another spy gem. "Ladies and gentlemen, Chancellor Nathrach risked his life to obtain what you just watched. As you saw, even armor provided minimal protection against these creatures." He held up the orb in his hand. "One of these is mounted above the door to the citadel mirror room at all times to record everything that happens whenever a mirror is activated. You need to see it." Mychael didn't direct that last part to the Nebian ambassador; he didn't need to, we all knew.

Mychael looked to Tam. "With your permission?"

Why would he ask? Oh yeah, the naked part.

Next to me, Imala bit her bottom lip against a smile.

Next to her, Tam sighed and waved his hand in acquiescence.

It played and the delegates watched. No one looked away, no one could. And like any good story, it had a surprise ending. No one expected full frontal nudity.

I'd bet the delegates would talk to Tam now—at least the ladies would.

I leaned toward Imala. "If that's not an icebreaker, I don't know what is."

I didn't know which had made more of an impression: monster spiders or naked Tam.

Not only did Tam not slink down in his chair, he cast an

arch glance at the Nebian ambassador, Aeron Corantine. The Nebian pretended not to notice.

Point Tam.

"Well, I guess we know who won *that* competition," Imala noted dryly.

Dakarai Enric stood, raised his palsied hand for silence, and surprisingly got it.

Dakarai was a goblin, but he looked like a kindly grandfather, which was quite an achievement, considering his fangs. His long hair was white against his dark blue robes, and his eyes a warm dark brown instead of the usual goblin black.

"Honored colleagues, may I speak?" It was a question, but the goblin elder statesman wasn't asking for permission. He had something to say, and no one was going to stop him from saying it.

"The histories of each of our kingdoms contain individuals who had a twisted desire for absolute power. They found others who shared their ideology and established organizations whose goal was to force the societies that they contaminated to accept and adopt their distorted vision." He paused meaningfully. "I need not name the organizations or their infamous leaders. *Each* of our kingdoms has had them, dark and shameful times in our respective histories. Yet *none* of us has ever failed to struggle against them; and eventually, we have all prevailed and gained our freedom. What permitted such groups to grow and even flourish were our own base—and baseless—fears and prejudices. Racial differences bred fear, which twisted into distrust, then turned into hatred. Others gained holds with religious persecution, or a need to subvert, conquer, and enslave. The causes were many. Unfortunately, our defenses against them were far fewer. Once these sects gained sufficient power, to defy them was death—but defy them we did, fighting them secretly, then resisting openly, many paying with their lives. The Khrynsani were nothing less than a cancer on goblin society. The events of the past few months—

of which you are all aware—have cut that cancer from us. The wounds are still fresh, but the healing has begun. There is no longer a foothold for the Khrynsani in Rheskilia. Their temple has been destroyed, their leaders have either perished or been arrested. Yes, some have escaped, and what we have just seen is a final, desperate effort to incite terror and prevent what we are here to accomplish—peace through unity, cooperation, and nonaggression. Chigaru Mal'Salin may share Sathrik's name, but he could not be more different from his late brother. Our new king has no intention or desire to attack or declare war on anyone. I have known Director Kalis and Chancellor Nathrach since they were children. Tamnais—"

"Was taught alongside Sarad Nukpana—the infamous leader of the Khrynsani—by the same teacher," Aeron Corantine said. "Mages are the product of those who teach them."

Imala's hand locked Tam in place. He could have moved, but he didn't. And I knew it was taking every bit of self-control he had not to go for the Nebian's throat—or give him a long-overdue death curse demonstration.

"If you are referring to Kesyn Badru," Dakarai said into the suddenly silent room, "he is an honorable man—as is Tamnais Nathrach."

"Who openly conspired to bring down the goblin government and replace it with his puppet, Chigaru Mal'Salin. He even conspired and manipulated Chigaru into declaring him his heir until the king and his queen produce one. It is well known who controls the new goblin king and the goblin people—Tamnais Nathrach, a known dark mage and master of black magic."

"Malicious lies and baseless innuendo have no place in these proceedings," Mychael said coldly.

Aeron Corantine smiled and spread his hands. "I am not claiming these opinions as my own. I am merely relaying what I have heard said." He paused. "Often."

"A wise man only gives voice to words he believes in

his heart and knows to be true," said an amused, deep voice from the back of the room. The Myloran ambassador, Herryk Geirleif. "A foolish man repeats whatever he hears." He crossed his massive arms over his even larger chest. "I do not know Chancellor Nathrach personally, but there are those I count as friends who do. They tell of a mage of the highest honor, a warrior without peer, and man who would give his life for his friends and his people. I would gladly welcome such a man into my longhouse and share with him the warmth of my fire and bounty of my hunt." The Myloran gave the Nebian a brittle smile. "Liars and slanderers are left outside with the wolves."

Justinius had dismissed the delegates. Predictably, the Nebian delegation immediately returned to their embassy. Others remained and spoke to one another in small groups and quiet voices.

Dakarai Enric's words had accomplished what an elder statesman/kindly grandfather did best—calmed everyone down and restored some semblance of sanity to the proceedings.

The Myloran ambassador's words had made the Nebian ambassador look like an idiot.

I didn't know which one I appreciated more.

"At least they haven't found out why Markus isn't here," I murmured to Mago, "and whose gold paid for Eldor's assassination. Khrynsani monster spiders in the Void are bad enough."

"Aeron Corantine is lucky that Chancellor Nathrach can control his temper. Were he not, at least we wouldn't have to endure that man any longer. I feel a need for a bath every time I have to speak with him."

"That happening often?"

"Just because Pengor and Nebia share a small portion of border south of the Hart Forest, Aeron is determined that we should be as close as brothers."

"Wouldn't it be fun for him to actually meet your brothers?"

Mago closed his eyes and inhaled as if I'd just held a snifter of fine cognac under his nose. "That much enjoyment is illegal in five out of the Seven Kingdoms. Even worse, I'm not the only one who has been beset by our Nebian neighbor. Dear Isibel has been a paragon of self-control."

"The next time he tries to kiss my hand, he'll be getting my fist."

Isibel stepped out from behind my cousin. There were definite advantages to being petite; you could eavesdrop from virtually anywhere.

"If anyone could get away with decking that one," I told her, "it would be you. You'd inflict pain and embarrassment with one punch."

"I've been told that I have a mean right hook," she said with a tiny smile. "Ask my brother."

I laughed. "Oh, I will. Before I leave this room I'll ask. I deserve some fun."

Mago lowered his voice. "Mychael said you caught one."

My cousin didn't say what "one" he was talking about and he didn't need to. My skin tried to crawl away and hide. "Yeah, I did. I don't know how, and I'd rather not think about what would have happened if my magic hadn't flared up when it did."

"Do you think your magic might be able to help with that?" He inclined his head toward the crystal ball.

"Mago, I wouldn't begin to know how."

"Do you think you might receive enlightenment before we start waking up wrapped in black web bedsheets?"

"I don't think I could be floundering any more than I am right now, but I'm hopeful that I'll figure out something." Justinius had just finished speaking with Dakarai Enric and was within earshot. "However, a very wise man of my acquaintance once said: 'I just had this dumped on me. Brilliance takes time.'"

Justinius beamed. "It's so encouraging when young

people listen to and learn from their elders. The Brenirian ambassador was asking me a similar question. Whether Raine Benares the Saghred slayer could go into the Void with a big fly swatter and take care of business."

I glanced at the Brenirian ambassador out of the corner of my eye. He was bespectacled and solemn. I was nearly certain his face would break if he smiled. Come to think of it, I'd never seen him assume an expression of any kind. "He said that?"

Justinius shrugged. "My words, not his. But it was what he meant."

"I'm certain he isn't the only one," Mago ventured. "You have quite the martial reputation."

"Let's hope there's a more reliable solution, because my magic isn't."

"I have the chairman of our cryptozoology department working on the problem," Justinius told us. "He and his faculty are creative thinkers."

"I hope they're also fast thinkers. The Nebian ambassador may have been the only one who said it, but the rest of them believe it, or at least suspect it. And, bottom line, it's true, at least in part. They don't trust Tam because they don't know him, and they don't know him because they're scared to be in the same room with him. To them, there's not much, if any, difference between Tam and Sarad Nukpana. The Nebian did his homework; he knows Tam and Sarad Nukpana had the same teacher and that both went to the dark side, though it was after both had left Kesyn's classroom. Nukpana stayed on the dark side. Tam didn't. But there is no proof of that, at least no proof that they'd believe. If Tam walking into a Rak'kari nest doesn't change their minds, I don't know what will."

Once the delegates began returning to their embassies, Justinius asked to speak with the goblin ambassador. While

Dakarai waited for the Majafan delegation to finish peppering the archmagus with questions, we talked. Ever the grand courtier, Dakarai linked my arm through his and we strolled down the corridor outside of the meeting chamber, talking about Aeron Corantine's accusations taking hold with the other delegates.

"I have served the Mal'Salins all my life." Dakarai's dark eyes twinkled. "Though I openly admit some times were with more enthusiasm than others."

"So what do you think about Chigaru?"

"He's still young and relatively inexperienced, but he is receptive to advice from those he trusts. His exile has made his trust a difficult thing to earn. Such caution will serve him well." He glanced fondly over at Tam and Imala. "As will those he surrounds himself with."

"How did it ever come to this?" I asked him.

"The same way it always has and—to our great misfortune—probably always will. With fierce hate harbored by a few and complacency displayed by the rest. All it takes for evil to take hold and flourish is for men and women of conscience to do nothing."

"We're doing something—at least we're trying."

"Yes, we are."

"But will it be enough?"

Dakarai Enric smiled very slightly. "What are we, my dear?"

"Pardon?"

"What are we, you and I?"

It took me a moment, but I got it. My small smile was a match for his. "We're an elf and a goblin."

"Taking a lovely stroll together, arm in arm. And where are we?"

What Dakarai was getting at really sank in, and my tension faded ever so slightly. "In the citadel of the Conclave Guardians—an organization neither of our people has ever really trusted, whose mission it is to protect a group nobody really likes."

The old goblin stopped and turned to me, taking one of my hands in both of his. "Regardless of what happens or does not happen with these peace talks, we've already won. The rest will come."

If the next Khrynsani surprise didn't come first.

18

The sun was beginning to set when Mychael and I took another trip to the harbor, this time by coach, to do something that was even scarier than flying there on Kalinpar—or looking a Rak'kari right in its multi-eyed face.

Mychael's parents had arrived.

It was time to meet my future in-laws.

The Eiliesors were an old and respected elven family. They were minor nobility and had no ambitions past that, which was unusual for elven aristocrats. They had overseen the same lands and vassals for centuries and were content to keep doing it. They married into appropriate families and had appropriate children.

Change was unwelcome.

I was the walking and talking embodiment of change, and my family couldn't be more inappropriate if they tried.

Mychael's family was landed gentry from aristocratic stock. My family were pirates; though if you wanted to look at it that way, they were pirate royalty. When you were the most notorious criminal family in the Seven Kingdoms, people weren't lining up to tell you what you couldn't call yourselves.

Elven nobility meeting people you'd invite to dinner only if you had to, and when they left, you'd count the silver.

I sighed.

I was doomed.

A Benares wouldn't care what anyone else thought. We did what we wanted where we wanted, and would never try to be anything we weren't for anyone.

Mychael agreed with my family's credo. He told me to just be myself and his parents would love me.

I sighed again.

I was still doomed.

I glanced up. Mychael was looking at me.

"My parents will love you," he told me. "How many times do I have to tell you that?"

"Until I believe it."

"When will that be?"

"When I see it." I shifted uncomfortably on the coach seat. "Last time I was this nervous, I was being pushed down an aisle toward a sacrificial altar."

"My last time was watching you being pushed down that aisle."

"So you *are* nervous about them meeting me."

"No, I'm nervous about them coming here, especially now. Two days ago, the closest danger to them was the possibility of more Khrynsani-paid assassins in our waters. I thought they'd be safer here."

"Well, we didn't know, and your parents aren't going to be anywhere near a travel mirror. Though we're going to be occupied trying to exterminate some spiders. What did your parents do for entertainment the last time they were here?"

"They've never been here before."

That earned some silence.

"Unlike your sister," I ventured, "you have told them what you do for a living, haven't you?"

"Yes, but not until I had to."

"What is it with your family and secrets?"

"We don't tell what's likely to be disapproved of."

"You told them about me." I let out a short laugh. "Though it wasn't like you had much of a choice."

"I told them about you because I'm proud of you. I'm prouder still that in a few days, I'll be able to introduce you as my wife."

I didn't know what to say to that, so I just let the goofy, love-besotted grin happen again.

"Why would they disapprove of your job?" I asked. "You're the Paladin of the Conclave Guardians, for crying out loud."

"It's not overseeing the family estates."

"No, it's saving the world as we know it on a daily basis, so other people can stay home and mind *their* family estates. You doing your job means those families will survive and those estates will stay theirs."

"Tell my mother that."

"If she brings it up, I will. That's a ridiculous opinion. Though I won't say it quite that way."

"It'd probably be best." Mychael grinned. "Though the look on Mother's face would be worth it."

"I'll consider it an opportunity to practice diplomacy. As the paladin's wife, I'm trying to learn."

"That'll be fun to watch, too."

"Speaking of fun to watch, I could see you running the family estate."

"You could?"

"Sure, you'd be good at it. I just couldn't see you being happy."

"Nice that it's obvious to you."

"Considering that I'm marrying you, that's a good thing."

"My parents have accepted it; they just don't understand it."

"What about your sister? Any chance Isibel will eventually

want to go home and tend farms?" I snorted as soon as the words were out of my mouth. I waved a hand, "Never mind; stupid question. So when you and Isibel inherit, what are you going to do with all of it?"

"What should have been done long ago: give the farms to the families who have worked that land for generations. They've more than paid for those farms. They should legally own them."

I whistled.

Mychael gave me a strange look.

"I don't disagree. The whistle was for what your parents will think. Do they know?"

"They do."

"And?"

"Well, at least they've given up trying to talk me out of it."

"They have?"

Mychael shrugged. "Either that or it's merely a temporary retreat to reevaluate their tactics."

"My money's on that one. Your head for strategy had to come from somewhere."

"Mom."

"Really?"

"Um-hum. She never gives up."

Wonderful.

Mychael favored both of his parents, at least in appearance, and Isibel was most definitely her mother's daughter. Whether they—like their son—could ignore what my family did for a living had yet to be determined. Well, what my extended family did for a living. My mother hadn't been a pirate; she'd been a sorceress of marginal ability, like myself. My father was one of the original Conclave Guardians—original as in over nine hundred years ago. With his soul now residing in the body of a young Guardian who had been murdered by the

Demon Queen, my dad was going to be walking me down the aisle in a few days, along with my godfather, Garadin Wyne.

One side of my family were pirates; the other side was merely complicated.

A wagon was standing by to take Brant and Edythe Eiliesor's luggage to a citadel guest apartment. My soon-to-be-in-laws would be riding back in the coach with us.

Awkward wouldn't even begin to describe it.

As I said before, I didn't do small talk. I either had something to say or I didn't. Though chances were good there'd be more along the lines of awkward silences. Neither parent would be saying: "So, tell me about yourself." Mychael had already told them. Everything. Well, at least everything he thought they should know and could handle. If that was the case, it meant he hadn't told them much of anything. My last name was more than enough.

I'd changed into a gown for the occasion. I was going to be enough of a shock; I didn't want to push them completely over the edge. Though I had to admit, there were advantages to wearing a gown. With the situation on the island being what it was, I had a small arsenal of bladed weapons within easy reach.

When Mychael met them at the base of the gangplank, I was right there with him, hoping my smile didn't look like a terrified rictus.

The Eiliesors' smiles were neither terrified nor a rictus. They were beyond thrilled to see their son. There were enthusiastic hugs all around. We were surrounded by a Guardian security detachment, and once again, Mychael couldn't have cared less who was watching.

I was standing a little off to the side. The Eiliesors hadn't noticed me yet, and I was completely good with that.

Then suddenly I was the center of attention. I took a deep breath, and smiled as best I could.

Mychael turned and held out his hand to me. I concentrated on not letting any of my weapons clank as I walked over to them.

"Mom, Dad, this is my fiancée, Raine Benares. Raine, these are my parents, Brant and Edythe Eiliesor."

I paused in a fluttering moment of panic. I had no idea what was the proper way to greet elven aristocrat in-laws. A curtsey was out of the question. One, I think they were reserved for kings and queens and the like. Two, I'd never done one in my life and didn't know how. Three, there was the distinct possibility my blades would throw me off balance and I'd end up in a clanking pile at their feet. So I simply went with what I knew. A handshake. Fortunately Mychael's dad was closest, and a handshake with a man wasn't a social faux pas—at least I didn't think so.

He took my hand and didn't give it back. "We'll have none of that." He pulled me in for a hug. "Welcome to the family, Raine."

It was a genuine hug, warm and accepting—and it couldn't have been further from what I'd been expecting. As a result, when he released me and I turned to face Mychael's mother, I was too dazed to know what to do next.

Edythe Eiliesor stepped forward, put her hands around my upper arms, regarded me for a few intensely uncomfortable moments, and then did the double-cheek-kissing thing.

I didn't know if I'd just passed a test, or she was reserving judgment for later. Then again, there was a section of southern Majaf where a double-cheek kiss was a challenge to a duel to the death. While I hoped it was the former, my instincts said she was reserving judgment. There was nothing wrong with that. I did it all the time.

I had a feeling it was going to be a long ride back to the citadel.

"Mychael said the two of you have had quite the eventful three months," his dad said when we were bounced into silence

after the Guardian coachman succeeded in hitting yet another hole in Mid's cobblestone streets.

"Yes, yes we have."

Another bump, another few moments of silence.

"They know everything," Mychael told me.

"Saghred?"

"Saghred. And Sarad Nukpana, Rudra Muralin, Carnades Silvanus, Taltek Balmorlan, and the Demon Queen."

"Wow, you *did* tell them everything."

"While we have sorcerers on both sides of our family," Brant continued, "neither Edythe nor myself have any magic, nor does Isibel."

"Trust me, it's way overrated," I told him.

"Has Isibel arrived?" Edythe asked.

"Yes, she has," Mychael told her. "Yesterday morning."

He'd told his parents all about me, but wasn't volunteering any information about his little sister. My trouble had come and gone. Isibel was still up to her neck in it. Mychael was treading carefully and running interference for his sister. I wholeheartedly approved of both.

The hooves of multiple horses clattered on the cobbles directly behind us. Our coachman pulled to a stop. My hand instinctively went for the pocket in my gown, a pocket with a big slit in it that let me reach the daggers in my thigh sheath.

Guardians.

I relaxed my grip.

Edythe Eiliesor noticed.

"I believe in being prepared, ma'am."

"An admirable trait."

Again, the words said one thing but could imply another. My future mother-in-law would have made a fine goblin, though even I had enough sense not to tell her that.

Mychael climbed out of the coach to speak with one of his senior knights. There were grim faces all around. I tried unsuccessfully to eavesdrop, but the late-afternoon city sounds all around us made it impossible. After about two minutes, Mychael came back to the coach, but made no effort to get back in.

That didn't imply anything good.

"Raine, I need for you to take my parents on to the citadel. Something's come up."

He didn't elaborate, and I didn't ask. I knew he would've told me had his parents not been there; at least I would've hoped so.

One of the junior knights gave Mychael his horse, and within seconds they were headed back the way we'd come. I turned and looked out of the coach's back window. At the next block, they took a left.

Toward the center city, home of the Conclave government buildings, college campus—and the embassies.

Nope, none of that was good.

I turned back to my soon-to-be-in-laws, my expression saying that nothing out of ordinary had happened.

I looked from one to the other and back again. "So, tell me about yourselves."

A Guardian messenger was waiting in the citadel's courtyard.

"Ma'am, where's the paladin? I have a message from the archmagus."

Crap.

Trouble was coming from every direction.

Justinius believed in handling his own problems. If for some never-good reason, he needed help, he'd call in Mychael. A crisis in the central city *and* here. That didn't bode well for anyone's evening.

"One of your brothers beat you to him," I said. "Intercepted our coach just south of the central city. It looked like that's where he was headed."

"Good." He handed me the envelope. "This is for both of you. The archmagus said he needs you there as well."

I broke the seal and read the message.

It was the old man's chicken scrawl all right.

The Mylorans have an uninvited guest and need an exterminator.

Oh crap.

I turned to where my future father-in-law was assisting my mother-in-law out of the coach. They'd heard the exchange.

"Don't concern yourself with us," Brant said. "We'd like nothing more than a quiet meal in our rooms. It's been a long day."

A small squadron of servants stood ready to see to the Eiliesors' every wish.

My presence was clearly not needed.

Nothing could have made me happier.

Still, I couldn't let it go that easily. "Are you sure that—"

"I need to speak with my parents, Raine, and now is as good a time as any."

Isibel.

She stood dwarfed by the citadel's massive doors, looking somewhere between a daughter about to be reunited with her parents and a prisoner on her way to the executioner's block.

Isibel was taking one for the team.

She had a lot to tell her parents, and I didn't blame her for wanting as few people as possible in the room while she did it.

Still, with my only other option being pest control at the Myloran embassy, staying here and baring my soul to my future in-laws might be more enjoyable.

19

Mychael wasn't at the Myloran embassy.

That meant and confirmed that we had two emergencies.

My escort waited outside and Vegard came in with me.

I'd been in the elf and goblin embassies and, quite frankly, never wanted to set foot in either one ever again. Both were cold, formal, and imposing—and that was before I'd come close to being tortured in one and dying in the other.

Mylorans were a different kind of people altogether.

They didn't share a border with any of the other six kingdoms, they didn't want anything anyone else had, and they could not have cared less what the other people and races thought of them.

Two guards opened the doors for us. That they were out here and not inside said that it couldn't be too bad, at least not yet.

Mylorans were big, and they lived large and loud. Their

embassy was furnished for their taste and comfort—with stone, wood, leather, and fur. But what I liked most about the Myloran people was that it took a lot to rattle their collective cage.

Including me.

They knew who I was, they knew what I was, and when they'd first arrived last week and we'd been introduced, they'd looked happy to meet me. Though to put it in perspective, these were people who wrestled polar bears for fun.

Vegard and I stepped into their front reception hall and were met by the completely unexpected.

There was no bloodshed, battle cries, or hacking blades. And no Rak'kari.

Mylorans and Brenirians were in the front hall, drinking horns in hand. Tables groaned with food. I recognized the Brenirian delegation—and the Caesolian delegation.

It was a party.

I was confused.

"Little nephew!" boomed an impossibly tall and broad, leather-clad man. He was bearded, blue-eyed, and thrilled to see whoever it was he was bellowing at.

Vegard stopped. "Wybjorn?"

I gaped. "You're *little*?"

"Compared to that."

What followed more closely resembled my bodyguard being mauled by a bear than a family reunion.

Vegard managed to pull some air into his lungs. "What are you doing here?"

The man set Vegard on his feet and slapped him on the back. "Keeping our delegation out of trouble."

"They haven't been arrested yet; you must be doing a fine job."

"I thought it would be a good idea to keep the drinking in the embassy."

"An even better idea." Vegard turned to me. "Ma'am, this is my Uncle Wybjorn Rolfgar."

"So I gathered."

"Uncle Wybjorn, this is—"

Wybjorn waved a massive paw, and the air it displaced snuffed out a nearby rack of candles. "I know who she is." He proceeded to engulf both of my hands in one of his. "I'd heard she was a tiny thing, but I didn't expect—"

I grinned up at him. "Looks are deceiving."

The huge Myloran barked a laugh. "We've heard that, too."

"I know your people get along with the Brenirians, being neighbors and all, but how did you get the Caesolians here? Now *that's* diplomacy."

"One of the Caesolian delegates has a cousin who is a friend of the Brenirian ambassador's brother." Wybjorn nodded solemnly. "The Caesolians are shy. They go from the citadel back to their embassy, nowhere else. So, we invite them to share our food and drink." He glanced over to where the almost smiling Caesolian ambassador was draining his drinking horn. "Our mead makes them not shy."

"We're doing this all wrong," I said. "We should be serving mead at the talks."

"The quicker they sign this treaty, the quicker we get home," Wybjorn said. "The hunting season is ending, and a certain saber-toothed ice cave bear has been spotted near the Magnild Glacier. I don't want to miss a chance at Old Hugi."

I fought back a smile. "So you'd rather go hunting than put up with a bunch of bickering diplomats."

Wybjorn half winced. "Peace is important. Though a good war can be a fine thing. I didn't mean that—"

I did some hand-waving of my own. "No, no. I understand completely. If everyone would agree to play nice, not steal anyone else's toys, and keep their hands and armies to themselves, none of us would have to be here—and I could get married in peace."

The Myloran's teeth flashed in a grin. Jeez, even his teeth were big.

"I've congratulated Paladin Eiliesor on his good fortune in taking such a fierce battlemaid for a wife."

"Uh, thank you."

The sound of cheers came from beyond a closed doorway at the end of the vast main hall.

"Come," Wybjorn told us. "We are missing the fun."

The Myloran embassy staff's idea of fun had apparently involved luring a Rak'kari out of the embassy mirror—and when it got here, giving it a hearty welcome.

The men and women in the embassy's mirror room were armed with an assortment of swords, axes, and clubs—more than half of them glowing with magic—and appeared eager to use any and all of them.

The mirror stood in the corner, a crack running from top to bottom. That spider wasn't going out the way it'd come in.

In the center of the room, the Rak'kari was perched on top of what looked like a stone totem pole that was carved with Myloran gods, though I didn't think you could call something a pole that was as big around as Wybjorn and three times as tall.

The Rak'kari was making no move to come down off of that totem.

Smart spider.

"This is fun?" I asked Wybjorn without taking my eyes from the Rak'kari.

"We do not use our mirror. We prefer to travel by ship the way our gods intended."

"So do I," I said fervently.

"Since the mirror is not used, we did not know that it was unlocked. This one came in. We have contained it in this room. Our Caesolian and Brenirian guests are not hunters, and would not understand the sport."

"No, they definitely would not," Vegard agreed.

I snorted. "And I can do without hearing the Caesolian ambassador scream."

On the floor next to the room's massive fireplace was a side of beef with a big chain looped around it.

"We attempted to lure it down with food," Wybjorn explained. "It seems to prefer its food alive."

And not surrounded by gigantic, axe-wielding Mylorans.

Like I said, smart spider.

"We sent a messenger to Archmagus Valerian," Wybjorn said. "Our people do not wish to stand here all night."

"Not when there's a party out there."

Wybjorn smiled. "Yes! You understand."

"More than you know." I needed a horn of mead right now, too.

"We thought the Saghred slayer would be able to help."

I just looked at him. "Saghred slayer?"

"You have to admit, ma'am, it has a ring to it," Vegard said.

My bodyguard was hoping I could do something about all this. So was I. My first Rak'kari encounter had been only a web strand around Mychael's neck. I'd acted in rage to protect the man I loved. This afternoon, I'd been staring death and a lunging Rak'kari right in the face. That was self-preservation and protection of Tam and Imala.

I didn't know if my new magic was something I could simply call up. But I did know that I didn't want to find out—and possibly fail—here in front of a room full of Myloran embassy staff.

I looked up at the giant spider. The giant spider looked down at me. At least I think it was looking at me. The thing had eight eyes, so who knew?

"I don't suppose you'd want to come down and just go back where you came from?" I muttered in its general direction.

The Rak'kari responded by turning its back and firing two webs out of its spinnerets and down at me.

The three of us dove out of the way. The webs struck the floor like black steel cables, and faster than I could get back to my feet, the Rak'kari slid down the webs.

I rolled just as the spider slammed into the stone floor where I'd been seconds before.

The ten Mylorans instantly had it surrounded and were doing a dart, distract, attack combination that wouldn't have been out of place with an enraged ice cave bear. Vegard and Wybjorn joined them.

A dozen Mylorans versus one giant spider.

My money was on the Mylorans.

The Rak'kari's thorax was armored, but apparently its face, or whatever it was on the front of its head, was not. A couple of axe and club hits at least made it stagger. I was impressed. I was even more impressed by the Mylorans' bravery and tenacity. They weren't about to give up or even think about retreating.

I was concentrating with everything I had to summon some Saghred-spawned, dark red magic.

It wasn't happening.

Vegard darted around the spider and away from the Mylorans for an attack.

The Rak'kari saw its chance and took it.

Time slowed to the speed that gives you time to figure out how not to die horribly.

Or how to save the life of your bodyguard and friend.

The Rak'kari used the tip of one of its legs and swept Vegard's legs out from under him. Vegard hit the floor, and the spider attacked.

So did I.

Instinct took over. The instinct that told me what should be done to a poisonous spider.

I glanced up at my target. The Mylorans were out of its range. Vegard was too, just barely.

I reached out with my mind, my will, and my magic…

…and yanked that totem pole down.

The entire embassy shook, the floor cracked, and dust fell from the ceiling when several tons of rock squashed the Rak'kari flat.

Vegard staggered over to me, coughing from the dust. "We'll have to tell the Chancellor." He nearly had to yell over the Mylorans' cheering.

I was still dazed from the thought of what I'd just done. "What?"

"He said Rak'kari are indestructible." Vegard looked at the squashed spider and gave me a huge grin. "I'd say you just destructed one."

I couldn't help but smile. Not too shabby for an itty-bitty battlemaid in a dress.

Mychael looked down at my handiwork. He'd been at the goblin embassy two buildings down when he'd actually heard the boom of the stone totem hitting the floor.

He'd had a feeling I was involved.

There hadn't been a giant spider at the goblin embassy, but there had been news Imala wanted Mychael to know immediately. News he didn't want to tell me until we'd left the Myloran embassy.

Walls had ears. I understood that.

I gazed out over the room full of broken rock. "It seemed like the right thing to do at the time," I told him. "It did make one heck of a mess."

Though describing a monster spider squashed under a massive, toppled totem as a heck of a mess was the ultimate understatement.

He wrapped an arm around my shoulders, pulled me close, and kissed me on top of my dusty head.

"It's beautiful and so are you," he told me.

The door was closed, and the party continued virtually

uninterrupted on the other side. Wybjorn had announced that one of the staff—the one who'd wielded a giant club, the largest human I'd ever seen in my life—had accidentally knocked over the totem. He'd poured plenty of mead around it to appease the gods, and as a result, divine retribution would not be forthcoming. There were more cheers at that, and the party had continued.

Gotta love Mylorans.

"I tried to do what I did before," I told Mychael. "You know, with the red sphere, but it didn't work."

"Sounds like you weren't scared enough."

"I had a spider bigger than I was sliding down a web at me faster than I could get out of the way. Trust me, I was scared. It didn't work. I was just as scared when I threw myself between that spider and Tam and Imala. It worked then."

"That was instinct. Instinct is the source of a lot of the more powerful magics. They manifest during stressful situations and strong emotion, like protective instincts. Later they can be consciously summoned."

"But when it went after Vegard…"

"Your magic came and you did what needed to be done." Mychael kissed my head again. "You proved once again that you care more for others than you do yourself. You're going to make a fine Guardian."

I pulled away, but only a little. "We've had this talk. I haven't earned the title or—"

"Okay, Guardian-*affiliated*—"

The door opened.

"Fierce battlemaid, Saghred slayer, and destroyer of stone gods!" Wybjorn boomed. "I bring you drink!"

Mychael chuckled. "Those work. What do you think?"

I grinned and elbowed him in the ribs.

20

The next morning, we'd just finished having breakfast with Mychael's parents and were waiting for our horses to be saddled. Isibel had excused herself from breakfast, citing a need to prepare for the resumption of the peace talks in another two hours. As far as I was concerned, Isibel could have used any excuse. She'd had dinner with her parents last night. She'd earned it.

Mychael's dad was just as charming as his son. We hit it off. Mychael's mom? I couldn't tell how she felt about me. She was still cool and collected. Either she'd decided what she felt and was being polite, or she was still reserving judgment, or she simply wasn't the type to show emotion one way or another. I could usually read people. Not Edythe Eiliesor.

Even Mychael had noticed, but he hadn't said anything. Diplomacy ran in the family. Maybe he was still giving her a chance to come around. Maybe he knew it was a lost cause. Maybe I couldn't stand it anymore and had to ask.

"Does your mother like me, not like me, has no clue what to think about me?"

"Mother is reserved," Mychael said.

"No kidding."

"She has to know someone a long time before she shows her emotions."

I sighed.

"She likes you."

"No, she doesn't."

"She doesn't know you yet."

"And she doesn't want to."

"Dad adores you."

I grinned. "He's great. I could fall for him pretty quick, too. Like I did his son."

"Give Mother a chance."

"I'm giving her a chance. It'd just be nice if she'd give me one."

Mychael's hands tightened around my waist, his expression solemn. "I don't care what my mother thinks, and you shouldn't either."

I opened my mouth to retort.

"I said you shouldn't care, but I know you do. And that's just another reason why I love you and want you to be my wife." He suddenly grinned like a little boy. "Wife. I love saying that."

I snuggled against him, my chin resting on his chest, looking up at him. "And I love hearing it, Husband." I stood on tiptoe and gave him a quick kiss on the lips. "Well, your mom's going to like me—or not. I only know how to be myself, and if she doesn't like that, then…" I threw my hands up in the air.

"That's my girl."

* * *

Mychael had been at the goblin embassy last night because A'Zahra's questioning of the member of Sarad Nukpana's inner circle had borne fruit. The Khrynsani did have a plan in place to regroup should they ever suffer a catastrophic defeat. The Saghred had been their reason for existing for the past thousand years. In one night, the Saghred had been destroyed—at least, the rock it'd lived in had been smashed—sea dragons had gutted their temple, and their leader had been carried off into the Lower Hells.

I'd call that a catastrophic defeat, and apparently the Khrynsani agreed.

The Khrynsani prisoner had known the name of the dimension/world where they were to regroup.

Ferok.

The goblin name for iron.

Unfortunately, neither Imala, Tam, nor Dakarai had recognized the name as anything other than that. Mychael had forwarded the information to Cuinn last night.

During breakfast with Mychael's parents, we got a response from Cuinn. He had an answer for us.

I didn't know what to expect on the inside of a building that housed the Conclave college's department of dimensional study, but what I saw wasn't it.

It was the middle of the semester, early in the day, and apparently between classes. Students filled the halls, the crowd punctuated by an occasional dark-robed mage professor. Most of the kids and all of the professors wore what looked like medallion-sized lockets on chains around their necks.

I knew that inside those lockets were mirrors.

Thankfully, none of them were large enough to get anything into—or for anything to get out of. It was more a badge of their field of study than anything else. But hopefully, the kids had enough sense to keep their fingers to themselves and out of their mirrors.

They were talking excitedly in small groups, talk that turned to absolute silence when they saw me and Mychael walk through the front doors. Vegard was with us as well as four other Guardians, but I knew who the silence was for.

I half turned to Mychael and tried to speak without moving my lips.

"One day I'd like to walk into a room and have no one notice."

"Today's not that day, ma'am," Vegard said from behind us.

Some would have recognized me as the wielder of the Saghred. Others would have also known that I'd been responsible for bringing down Carnades Silvanus, resulting in him being sent to Regor and his death at the hands of Sarad Nukpana.

The silence from the students and professors was followed by smiles, which turned into applause, and then cheers.

Not one of them was afraid of me.

They knew who I was, what I was, what I'd done, and they were giving me a—dare I say it—hero's welcome.

Words could not describe how badly I needed that.

I suddenly had a lump in my throat.

"Thank you." I said the words, and they couldn't hear me over the cheers and whistles, but they had to know how much I appreciated it.

I kind of wished we'd brought Mychael's mom. I might have earned a few points.

Mychael threw his arm around my shoulders and gave me a squeeze. "I've told you there are good people here."

Cuinn Aviniel waved to get our attention from behind a group of cheering students. He good-naturedly shooed them out of the way and motioned for us to follow him. We did and quickly arrived at his laboratory. Cuinn closed the door, cutting off the sound of the students, but that was fine. I'd heard it once, and would never forget it.

Two of the Guardians remained outside of the lab, the other two and Vegard came in with us.

"Sorry it took us so long to get here," Mychael told Cuinn. "We were having breakfast with my parents."

Cuinn turned to me and blanched, an impressive feat for somebody already that pale. "I interrupted you meeting your in-laws for the first time?"

"Technically, I met them last night, but—"

"I am *so* sorry."

"Don't be."

"But I'm sure they—"

"Were still tired from their trip and didn't mind in the least," Mychael assured him.

Cuinn took a breath, and blew it out with a wince. "Good. Because I have a lot to tell you."

"I didn't accept the department chair position, but I accepted Carnades's lab space," Cuinn said, turning up the lights in the high-ceilinged room he'd led us to.

I stopped, suddenly creeped.

Surprisingly, there were only four mirrors in the entire lab. All were set in heavy wooden frames mounted on wheeled stands. They were in what I'd learned was locked mode. It was a spell that distorted whatever the mirror reflected, making the surface look like an undulating wave, its pattern constantly changing. Yet another reason why I never would have made a good mirror mage, or even a bad mirror mage—every time I looked at an undulating mirror, my stomach would do the same thing.

The elf mage gave me a quick smile. "Don't worry, those are mine. Everything that belonged to Carnades is in storage, though the archmagus had his investigators go through all of it for evidence first. And after all the equipment was gone, I had the place scrubbed, magically and otherwise. I was tempted to have a priest cleanse it, but a friend from the necrology department came over and declared it clean. He'd known Carnades Silvanus and assured me that his ghost wasn't here."

I smiled. "That friend wouldn't be Vidor Kalta, by any chance?"

"Yes, it is."

"He's a good friend to have, and he definitely knew Carnades. If Vidor said Carnades isn't here, he isn't."

Cuinn gave us a big smile. "Always good to have a result confirmed. It's good science *and* good for my nerves. We moved in two weeks ago and haven't had any disturbances."

"If Carnades was going to 'disturb' you, he would have done it by now."

I couldn't help but gawk at what filled the ceiling area above our heads.

Moving slowly in circles were what looked like clouds of various sizes, sparkling from within with twinkling lights, as well as spheres in a combination of colors and sizes. Both the clouds and spheres were strung like jewels on narrow metal rings. Some of the rings were small, others large, all interwoven, and slowly orbiting. I didn't see a power source, but there had to be one.

I couldn't imagine Carnades building something this beautiful.

"Did this belong to Carnades? It looks like it's been here a while."

"No, that's all mine," Cuinn said with a hint of pride. "I've spent a lot of sleepless nights lately getting it set up. This is the first time I've had a laboratory large enough to display it. It's a work in progress. We're discovering new dimensions and worlds all the time. The clouds represent dimensions, and the spheres are worlds." He pointed up. "See the green and blue one there?"

"Yes."

"That's our world."

I suddenly felt incredibly tiny.

"And all these others?" I asked.

"These are the worlds and dimensions that are close enough to our own—not in proximity, but through portals and rifts—for access year-round. There are other worlds and dimensions that can be reached from our own, but they only occasionally come into contact with the edges of our orbit. Once every million years, every hundred years, twenty years, twenty months. Those aren't represented here. There's not enough room."

"Wow."

Cuinn gazed up at the smoothly orbiting planets and dimensions like a kid with the best toy ever. "Yes, wow."

"There's another blue and green world on the other side of the room." I pointed it out. "What's that one?"

"Its inhabitants call it Earth. It's very similar to our own world. While we can travel there year-round, it's easiest twice a year at what they call their 'equinox.'"

"Access to Earth is highly controlled," Mychael told me. "The inhabitants are rather advanced; however, they don't believe any of us exist. They have elves and goblins in their mythology, but they think we're simply that, myths."

I snorted. "That's gonna be a rude awakening one of these days."

"The goal is to not have that happen anytime soon. The population is strictly human. Those that go there must wear full-time glamours to disguise what they are. It's odd for a civilization to be that advanced, yet so adamant that they are the only life in the universe."

"They have buildings that are framed in steel and are over a hundred stories tall," Cuinn said with quiet awe.

My eyes went wide at the thought of being that far above the ground. And I knew steel was light, but to build with it? "No. Just no."

"They also have hollow metal machines that fly through the air like sky dragons. People sit inside to travel great distances."

"Okay, that's just horrifying."

Cuinn nodded in agreement. "I would love to see the buildings, but I have no desire to fly inside of a metal sky dragon."

"I don't want to fly, period."

"Is all of this yours?" Mychael asked him.

"I felt guilty taking this large of a space for myself," Cuinn replied. "So I'm sharing it with several colleagues—friends, actually—who are interested in the same kind of research as I am. Research that, thanks to the soil residue I found on Director Sevelien's clothing and Chancellor Nathrach's armor, has just moved from theoretical to having real-world applications." He paused. "I know where the Rak'kari came from."

"Was the information I sent last night of any help?" Mychael asked.

"It's the goblin word for iron," Cuinn said, "but I didn't recognize Ferok as either a dimension or a world."

"We were thinking it must have been a Khrynsani code name."

"That would be my guess, as well." He flashed a little grin. "However, discovering that it's the goblin word for iron confirmed what I did find. Rak'kari don't need air and could have been stored anywhere. But if the Khrynsani planned to regroup there, they'd need air to breathe. The soil residue on the clothing and armor was identical. The Rak'kari's legs must have come in contact with the ground before they were driven through an unlinked mirror and into the Void. Of all the known worlds or dimensions that can be accessed from our own, only one has soil containing such a high quantity of iron as well as a breathable atmosphere similar to our own. Timurus." He pointed up to a small, dark red planet slowly orbiting near our own world.

Mychael frowned. "I've never heard of it."

"Not many have, outside of academic circles," Cuinn

told him. "Which is probably one of the reasons why the Khrynsani selected it. They needed a storehouse for their Rak'kari that would remain undiscovered. And they remained undiscovered because no one lives on Timurus—at least, they haven't for a very long time. There are still animals there, plenty of animals. Timurus had a thriving civilization—one that was rather similar to our own—that was suddenly wiped out about seven hundred years ago, leaving an archeological treasure trove."

"By who or what?" I asked.

"Still unknown. They came, they killed or took the people, and they left."

"Killed or *took*?"

"Astava, the city most easily accessed from our own world, didn't contain nearly enough remains to account for the population." Cuinn shrugged. "And we assumed that the invaders left since no one's there any longer to ask."

"So the Khrynsani have this world—or at least a portion of it—to themselves," Mychael said.

"We assume so."

"And they sent the Rak'kari into the Void from there?"

Cuinn nodded. "They would need an unlinked mirror and a mage who had the talent and strength to hold it open." He saw my confused expression and backtracked. "When a mirror is linked to another, it forms a tunnel inside the Void from one place to another, a destination. Tunnels are what give mirrors their stability and enable travel. When an unlinked mirror opens directly into the Void, the Void itself is the destination."

"But nothing—well, other than Rak'kari—can live there," I said.

"Exactly. And in the hands of anyone other than a master mirror mage, such an opening would instantly turn into a vortex. Everything in its pull would be sucked into the Void. If the mage completely lost control of the mirror, theoretically there's no limit to what would be pulled inside."

I whistled. "That would be bad."

"Very."

"But if the mirror mage was strong enough to hold and stabilize an unlinked mirror," I ventured, "you're saying that it would give them direct access to the inside of the Void itself."

"Correct."

"And they could essentially toss in the spiders and 'slam the door,' so to speak."

"Precisely."

"You're the strongest mirror mage on the island right now, which makes you one of the strongest in the Seven Kingdoms."

"Well, that's open for debate, and—"

"Yes or no."

"Yes."

"Are you strong enough to hold an unlinked mirror?"

"I believe so, yes. However, I'm not stupid, desperate, or insane enough to try."

I turned to Mychael. "If an elf mirror mage allied with the Khrynsani, that'd qualify them as insane, or at the very least arrogant enough to believe they'd survive dealing with Sarad Nukpana's inner circle and an unlinked mirror."

"Are you thinking of a member of Carnades's family?" Cuinn asked quietly.

Silence.

"We are," Mychael admitted. "His older sister is reputed to be—"

Cuinn was shaking his head. "His mother." His lips curled in a humorless smile. "Another advantage to eavesdropping. I heard Carnades telling one of his…" He paused as if searching for the right word.

"Minions?" I offered helpfully. "Cronies? Bootlickers?"

"All of the above, and some you politely didn't mention. He bragged that he inherited all of his skill from his mother. According to Carnades, Methena Silvanus is considered to be the most powerful mirror mage the Silvanus family has ever produced."

Mychael and I exchanged a glance.

"I'd say that bumps her up the list to our prime suspect," I told him. "And what do you want to bet she blames all of us for her son's death."

"Can you pinpoint exactly where on Timurus the Rak'kari were released into the Void?" Mychael asked Cuinn.

"There are only six places on Timurus—at least that are documented by explorers—that are accessible from our own. Of those, there is one plateau where the soil is so permeated with iron that it's the color of rust. The plateau overlooks the city of Astava, or at least what's left of it after the war."

"Could you open a rift at or near that location?" Mychael asked.

"Uh, yes," Cuinn replied uneasily, "but I don't think…"

"I don't want to do it, either, but we need to get a look through that rift."

"You said the population of Timurus was wiped out about seven hundred years ago?" I asked Cuinn.

"Seven hundred forty-seven, to be precise."

"Before we risk taking a look, why don't we talk to someone who was alive then and traveled—a lot."

21

My father, Eamaliel Anguis, was nine hundred thirty-four years old, and had spent most of those years on the run from the Khrynsani and everyone else who wanted to have the Saghred for their very own. It was simply good logic that if you needed to avoid someone, you needed to know all of the places where they could possibly be. Depending on how long the Khrynsani had used Timurus as their secret hideout, my father might have more than a passing acquaintance with it.

Cuinn Aviniel said that it would take him and two of his colleagues the rest of today and possibly most of tonight to calibrate a rift to open onto Timurus's Table of Iron. That gave us a little time to figure out how to do this without any unfortunate and deadly consequences.

My father's soul was presently living in the body of a twenty-year-old Guardian. When Sarad Nukpana had escaped from the Saghred, so had my father. That escape had coincided with the death of a young Guardian named Arlyn Ravide at the hands of the Demon Queen. Arlyn's death had given my father's soul a home.

Arlyn Ravide had been a good disguise and one that my father had needed, because apparently there wasn't a statute of limitations on Saghred-stealing. About nine hundred years ago, he had led the team that had gone to Rheskilia and recovered the Saghred from King Omari Mal'Salin and his chief mage, Rudra Muralin. Once he'd brought the stone back to the Isle of Mid, the survivors of that team and a few of the most magically powerful Guardians tried to destroy the Saghred and failed. It didn't take long for word of what the Saghred was capable of to spread around the island and through the Conclave. The more powerful the mage, the more they wanted to get their hands on that rock.

To keep it out of the hands of anyone who would abuse its power, Eamaliel fled from Mid, taking the Saghred with him. While he occasionally managed to stop running and live like a normal person, most of those hundreds of years were spent on the run. The Saghred bonded itself to him and, as a result, kept him alive and prevented him from aging. During one of those stops, he'd met my mother, Maranda Benares. They'd fallen in love and I'd been born. They'd remained together during most of my first year. But eventually, as always, the Khrynsani had picked up his trail. Dad had left us, drawing his pursuers with him. But not all of them followed. Mom had been only a marginal sorceress. She didn't stand a chance against Khrynsani bounty hunters. Garadin Wyne had been my mother's best friend and had taken me in.

Now that the Saghred's orb had been destroyed, my father didn't know whether he would age normally in the young Guardian's body that his soul was living in or whether the antiaging qualities the Saghred had given him would continue in his new body. Either way, an elven mage and Guardian with nine hundred thirty-four years of experience couldn't be expected to live the life of a twenty-year-old novice knight. As a result, "Arlyn Ravide" had resigned his commission, and had supposedly returned home.

Eamaliel was presently using a glamour to reassume his own appearance. Those like Carnades Silvanus would have demanded his execution as a traitor, even though his supposed "crime" of taking the Saghred away from the Isle of Mid to prevent it from falling into the wrong hands had been committed nine hundred years ago. Those men and women hadn't cared about time, only persecution and—if they got their way—execution. They had been the real criminals and traitors. They were gone, either permanently by death, or for long enough by imprisonment.

My father was now the safest he had ever been in his entire long life.

Justinius had provided him with an apartment in the citadel, though Eamaliel was spending most of his time in the Scriptorium. He was a scholar at heart, and had been happily spending his days, and much of his nights, reading and researching.

The peace talks were due to pause for lunch in another few minutes, and Mychael was waiting to tell Justinius, Tam, and Imala about Timurus and determine our next steps.

I was knocking on my father's apartment door, hoping he was at home and not in the Scriptorium. After my run-in with Chief Librarian Lucan Kalta soon after I'd arrived on the island, I knew I wouldn't be welcome on his turf ever again.

"Come in, Raine," Eamaliel said.

I didn't know how he knew it was me, but he'd done it often enough that I chalked it up to nine hundred years of experience on the run.

I opened the door and froze.

Eamaliel Anguis's original body had been that of a silver-haired, gray-eyed, pure-blooded high elf. That's what he looked like right now...

…sitting across the table across from my godfather, Garadin Wyne.

The smile stayed plastered on my face as I just stood there in the doorway looking from one to the other.

Eamaliel was my biological father, and my mother had been the love of his life. To save her and me, he'd led the Khrynsani away from us. I'd heard that story from him and Sarad Nukpana. For my father, it was a source of shame; for Nukpana, a source of gloating. I accepted it as truth.

I didn't know what Garadin believed.

All he knew as fact was that my mother had been murdered and I'd been left behind. Did Garadin believe that Eamaliel had left to draw his enemies away, or that he had run to save his own skin?

That the two of them were sitting there alive, fully conscious, and without apparent injuries implied that they'd smoothed over any awkwardness and uncertainties, and had moved on like two mature—and in my father's case, *very* mature—adults would do.

As to who would be walking me down the aisle, I wanted both of them to, but I hadn't actually asked either one of them yet.

Yes, I was a coward.

"I see you two have met," I eventually said.

"The way you're running around here," Garadin said, "if we waited for the three of us to be in the same room together, it'd be in the middle of your wedding." My godfather smiled, an actual, real, and honest smile. "We're big boys, Raine. We can do this ourselves."

"This" covered a lot of ground—from taking care of their own introductions, to mending any misconceptions, and unless my instincts deceived me, becoming friends. Then I noticed a glass in front of each of them and a bottle of Brenirian whisky in between.

Friends *and* drinking buddies.

I blew out a double-lungful of air and let my shoulders sag in relief.

"Let's hear it for good news," I told them both. "I sure can use some."

They exchanged a conspiratorial glance.

"Should we tell her?" my father asked Garadin.

"You heard the girl. She wants good news. She'll like this." My godfather's blue eyes were bright with mischief. "At least I think she will."

Eamaliel spoke. "Justinius asked me and Garadin if we would serve on the Seat of Twelve."

"Tarsilia, too," Garadin added.

I took a deep breath. "And?"

"And we all accepted," Eamaliel said.

"Yes!" Tears welled up in my eyes. I brushed them away and hugged them both. Hard. "There are three more spots. Do you know who else he's asking? And yes, I understand this is top secret."

"Well, I imagine you could tell Mychael," my father said.

"Good, because I would be."

"There have never been goblins on the Seat of Twelve. Justinius wants to change that. He'll be asking A'Zahra Nuru and Kesyn Badru."

I clapped my hands and squealed like a little girl.

"We didn't get that reaction," Garadin noted.

"She cried when we told her," Eamaliel said.

I ignored them both and reached between them for the bottle. "Do you have another glass, or can I just toast this news out of the bottle?"

Eamaliel stood. "I think I can find you one."

"Good, because after the toasting, I need another drink for fortification."

"That bad?" Garadin asked.

"And getting worse. Though we're hoping you'll be able to help."

I told them everything, beginning with Markus's attack, and ending with Cuinn's findings.

Garadin's response was a long whistle.

"Thoughts?" I asked.

"Besides we're going to need another bottle?" my father asked.

"That doesn't sound optimistic. I take it you've been to Timurus?"

"I have."

"And?"

"I went there soon after leaving Mid with the Saghred. I had a friend on the east coast of Brenir who was a dark mage and a good man. Mirror travel didn't exist then, but the Passages did. He knew of a stable entrance to the Passages, and the location there of a rift that would take me to a little, out-of-the-way world where I should be safe for a while."

"Timurus."

Dad nodded. "I came out of the rift near a fairly large city. Being noticed was the last thing I needed, so I always tried to stay in cities. A new face in a village is gossip for a year. I glamoured my ears and fit right in. The Saghred and I stayed there for…let's see, about fifty-two years. Long enough to realize that I wasn't aging, and whose fault it was."

"What was the name of the city?"

"Phirai."

"That wouldn't happen to be near Astava, would it?"

Eamaliel raised one of his perfect eyebrows. "Just to the south. Why?"

"That's where Cuinn Aviniel thinks the Rak'kari came from, a plateau that overlooks Astava."

My father swore. I'd never heard him do that before, at least not that word.

"The Table of Iron, the locals called it. It overlooked everything within a hundred miles. I had to leave Timurus because the Khrynsani had found it. I don't know if they had been there before, or simply tracked me there. I sensed them as soon as they arrived—through a rift on the Table of Iron."

"Crap. Well, that confirms Cuinn's theories."

"They had seekers with them, good ones. When we were in Rheskilia getting the Saghred back, our camp was attacked one night. We survived, but we couldn't go back to retrieve our gear. As a result, there was a possibility that the Khrynsani obtained some of my personal possessions, magical implements that I used that would hold traces of me and my magic indefinitely. If that were the case, they could find me. Phirai was only ten miles south of Astava. The goblins knew what questions to ask, and the time period that I had arrived there. Between that and the seekers, I knew it'd only be a matter of time until they found me. My Brenirian friend had given me a map he'd made of the Passages. I knew how to open a rift. I left the same day I'd sensed the Khrynsani and returned here."

"Here as in Mid or our world?"

"Our world." He gave me a rueful smile. "I'd heard Mylora was lovely in the spring."

I hesitated. "Cuinn said that all of the people were either killed or taken about seven hundred years ago."

My father's eyes grew haunted. "A little less than two hundred years after my first visit, I went there again. I had been traveling around the Seven Kingdoms, and reasoned that the Khrynsani and other rogue mages who wanted the Saghred would believe that I was still there. I went to Timurus again. Astava was under siege, surrounded by one of the largest armies I'd ever seen or heard of. They had battle dragons, huge brutes. I'd lived on Timurus for fifty-two years. I'm a scholar at heart, and make it a point to learn about the places I've traveled. There were no dragons of any kind on Timurus."

"An off-world invader," Garadin said quietly.

Eamaliel's short laugh was humorless. "Like myself, except I came in peace. The people of Timurus had mages and magic, not to our level, but impressive in its own way. The magic I felt from that besieging army was different from anything I'd ever felt before. Needless to say, I left immediately. I did go back five years later to look. What Astava looked like then is what this Cuinn Aviniel says it looks like now—no human life. His description of 'wiped out' is entirely too accurate."

I took a breath and blew it out. "I really hate to ask this, but we're since going to need to get a look through that rift on the Table of Iron, by any chance did you hang on to that Passages map to Timurus?" I hesitated. "Just in case we need to have a backdoor way in?"

My father and godfather looked at me like I'd lost my mind.

I completely agreed with them both.

22

Mychael knew where I was going next. He could reach me if anything worse happened, but I really hoped for at least one or two uneventful hours. I was going to a place I wanted to be, to be pampered and happy for a little while, and not have to worry about the Khrynsani, their motives, their monster spiders, or my mother-in-law.

I was having my final wedding gown fitting.

Alixine Toril was a friend, a sorceress, one of the finest mage robe designers in the Seven Kingdoms, and in two days, she would be my maid of honor.

Alix was using the shop of a fellow robe designer here on the Isle of Mid. The proprietor was a friend of Alix's, and had given her the full use of his shop, workroom, and staff. She'd offered to come to the citadel for my fittings, but I'd turned her down. And now I was especially glad that I had. During times like these, a girl just needs to get out of the fortress.

When I'd told Alix that Mychael and I were getting

married, Alix had been thrilled for two reasons. One, her best friend had landed herself a seriously hot catch. Two, that seriously hot catch was the paladin of the Conclave Guardians, sacred protector of the archmagus and the Seat of Twelve, and the top lawman in the Seven Kingdoms, meaning that my wedding—and my gown—would be the talk of said Seven Kingdoms.

I had hated to disappoint her, but the ceremony was going to be small—okay, smallish. Last month, I'd worn a white gown and been pushed down the aisle of a massive temple toward a sacrificial altar. Been there, experienced that, had the trauma. A big wedding was out of the question, though not only for the aforementioned reason. Mychael and I simply weren't "big wedding" people. The most important thing about our wedding would be the two of us being married. In our minds, it wasn't about anything else.

Mychael would be wearing his formal uniform for our wedding. Normally, I hated wearing gowns, not because I didn't like them, but because I liked being able to fight for and preserve my life more. This was the one time when I actually wanted to wear one. However, just in case there was a possibility that I'd need to fight for my life—and lately that'd been most of the time—I had insisted on something light, not a brocaded, encrusted edifice that weighed more than I did.

As always, Alix had come through for me. Having experienced firsthand the kind of trouble I'd attracted during the time we'd known each other, she knew I was serious about needing a wedding dress that wouldn't get me killed. The resulting confection had a skirt consisting of three layers of the lightest Pengorian silk. The bodice was of matching Pengorian silk, and both had a gossamer overlay painstakingly stitched with crystal beading and dainty pearls.

I loved it, and I loved Alix for making it for me.

I was admiring the gown by looking down at it, not by seeing my reflection in a full-length mirror.

Even though I'd told Alix that I loved the gown, she knew that I couldn't get the full effect without a mirror. She didn't like that I couldn't see it properly, and quite frankly, neither did I. A final wedding gown fitting was something I was only going to experience once, and I wanted the full treatment.

"Any good news on the mirror front?" she asked around a mouthful of pins. While nowhere near Justinius Valerian's league when it came to mindreading, Alix had a smidgen of that particular gift, plus she knew me only too well.

I told her what happened last night at the Myloran embassy, this morning with Mychael's parents, and an hour ago with Cuinn Aviniel. Alix had come by the citadel yesterday with my shoes, and knew that my wedding week wasn't quite shaping up as I'd hoped or planned, which really hadn't been a shock to either one of us.

"You can't worry about what Mychael's mother thinks or doesn't think of you."

"You're right."

"Of course, I am."

"I'm letting my feelings get in the way."

"Yes, you are. Unfounded and paranoid feelings."

"Huh?"

Alix spit out the last two pins, and sat back on her heels. "Raine, I've seen the way Mychael looks at you. That poor man's got it bad. And from everything you told me about what happened with the Saghred, that man put himself through hell—and taking on the Queen of Demons nearly makes that one literal—and risked everything, including his life, for little ol' you. That's love. Pure, unconditional, and permanent. That's the kind of man who doesn't care what his mother thinks about the woman he loves and has decided to spend the rest of his life with."

My shoulders sagged in relief and realization that my best friend was right, I was wrong, and Edythe Eiliesor was going to be however she'd decided to be. I couldn't change it, and it didn't make any difference to the man who loved me more than his own life.

"Yes, I'm right again," Alix said, getting back to work. "Now stand up straight."

I did. "Sorry. How did I get so crazy?"

"Let's see…impending wedding, peace talks where peace is the last thing they're talking about, Khrynsani spider monsters shutting down all mirror travel in the Seven Kingdoms, the Khrynsani wanting who knows what, all that business with your new magic, and your future mother-in-law doesn't like you. Maybe."

"That'd do it. Oh, and speaking of Edythe, if we girls still get to go out tonight, Tarsilia thinks we should invite her."

Alix stopped pinning and looked up at me in disbelief. "Has Tarsi been sampling some of her own apothecary brews?"

"Yeah, I'd kind of wondered that myself. But I ran into Sora Niabi late yesterday, and she agrees. They think that if Edythe and I could get into more of a relaxed social setting— without Mychael—that she could get to know me better. Hence, going out with us."

"It doesn't sound like she's the social type," Alix said.

"And I don't think she's ever been relaxed."

"Though she and Brant did manage to make two children," Alix pointed out.

"You don't have to be relaxed for that."

"What do Isibel and Imala think?" Alix asked.

"I haven't had a chance to ask either one of them."

"After being locked in the peace talks all day, both of them will need to let their hair down. But I can't see Isibel doing that with her mother there."

"I can't see either one of us doing that."

"You like Mychael's dad, right?"

"Definitely."

"Does he love her?"

"It looks that way. And she loves him—and Mychael."

"She's a mother, Raine. She just wants what's best for her son."

"And she doesn't think that I'm it."

"Has she said that?"

"Not directly."

"Well, I think you should directly ask her—after the wedding, of course. We don't want to possibly mess *that* up. What did Mychael say?"

"That she'll like me once she gets to know me."

Alix rolled her eyes. "Doesn't know that much about women, does he?"

"Knows enough to make me happy."

"That's not the kind of knowing I'm talking about."

"I like it."

"I'm sure you do. The thing is there's nothing you can do that you haven't already done to get her to like you. You're not the problem; she is. Has Mychael had a chat with her yet?"

"I don't think so. We've been kind of busy."

"For your happiness—and sanity—I would suggest that he make the time. He loves both of you, both of you are unhappy, and it's about him. You've done everything you can. She's done everything she's willing to. It's time for Mychael to tell his mother exactly how it is and how it's going to be."

"And if he doesn't think that's necessary?"

Alix gave me a wicked smile. "Then it'll be up to your bridesmaids."

23

Sending out an order to lock all mirrors and cease all mirror travel had proven beneficial in two ways: people weren't traveling to their dooms and becoming spider food, and the spiders were becoming hungry.

Very hungry.

According to Tam, once a Rak'kari had fed for the first time, they had to keep eating. After all mirror travel had been suspended, the spiders got hungry, then agitated, then desperately started trying to consume each other. I was surprised how little time it'd taken. Within three days, they were in a frenzy to feed. If anyone in the Seven Kingdoms decided to live dangerously and try to go somewhere in a mirror, they wouldn't be living for long, dangerously or otherwise. Since Rak'kari need living food with warm blood and liquefiable internal organs, trying to dine on each other wasn't going well, as Rak'kari had none of those things.

The result was spider monsters that weren't picky eaters.

Justinius Valerian's claim that the faculty in the cryptozoology department were creative thinkers had borne fruit. One of the professors, a believer that the more minds put to work on a problem, the more potential solutions you could get, had been particularly successful. She'd told her graduate students the problem, offered them a big chunk of extra credit, stepped back, and watched the magic happen. Literally.

The winning plan was a team effort of an enterprising young couple: the girl was a cryptozoology grad student, her boyfriend was one of Cuinn's lab assistants.

It was early afternoon, and I was back in Cuinn Aviniel's laboratory. Me and a lot of other people. Good thing it was a big room.

"Use one monster to kill another," I noted with approval. "I like it."

The salvation of the Seven Kingdoms' mirror travel came in the form of Majafan sandworms. They were the length and width of your forearm, their skin was puncturable, and their blood warm enough for a starving spider.

Blood that was deadly if ingested—at least for normal creatures. We didn't know if it applied to a Rak'kari, but Cuinn had a plan to find out.

Best of all, the cryptozoology lab had hundreds of sandworms, thousands during their mating season, which apparently was often. The kids in the lower level crypto courses dissected them in a lab course. When sandworms were less than two months old, they were still just as large, but were nonpoisonous, and were fed to Guardian sky dragons like hay.

A plentiful and quickly renewable resource.

There might not be enough sandworms to kill every Rak'kari in the Void, but it would put one heck of a dint in their numbers. The chairman of the cryptozoology department was having more shipped in from a small magic school in Brenir that should be enough to finish off the rest of the Rak'kari.

"They wiggle," the department chairman was telling us. She was brisk and businesslike with a wry sense of humor and reminded me a lot of Sora Niabi, the chairman of the demonology department. I was sure they knew each other, and were probably friends.

"The spiders should like the wiggling," she continued. "The sandworms are fat, juicy, and highly poisonous." She gave us a quick, borderline evil grin. "And if the poison doesn't kill them, the explosion will."

I perked up at that. "Explosion?" Now she was talking my family's language.

"Once the poison's ingested, it turns to a gas." She put her hands together, then spread them apart. "Boom."

"Will that do it?" Mychael asked Tam.

"I don't see why not. Given enough pressure buildup, even an armored Rak'kari should explode."

"Which brings up your students' next project," I said. "How to clean up *that* mess?"

"Would the Void be damaged by any of this?" Mychael asked Cuinn.

The elf mage thought. "Theoretically, it shouldn't." He sounded fairly confident, then he flashed a boyish grin. "But then no one's ever blown up Rak'kari inside the Void using Majafan sandworms before. I don't know about you, but I can't wait to see this."

Taking a peek through a rift and getting visual confirmation of the Khrynsani on Timurus was important. Knowing where they were was the first step to finishing what was started that night in the Khrynsani temple. Tam, in particular, couldn't wait to get started on that project.

But exterminating the Rak'kari infesting the Void took precedence. If the Khrynsani had anything up their collective black sleeves, getting mirror travel reestablished was critical.

Tam had said the Khrynsani didn't waste resources. They wouldn't have conjured hundreds of Rak'kari simply to inconvenience mirror travel in Seven Kingdoms. They had cut us off from each other for a reason, and with the Khrynsani, that reason would never be good.

Cuinn Aviniel put calibrating a rift to Timurus aside in favor of doing what he had told me and Mychael that a mirror mage would have to be insane to try—opening an unlinked mirror.

To get the Majafan sandworms into the Void, we couldn't link two mirrors. That would form a tunnel, and that would deny the vast majority of the Rak'kari the feast we'd prepared for them. I hadn't known many mirror mages, but those whom I had known and heard about would have been too arrogant to accept help opening a mirror, linked or unlinked. Thankfully, Cuinn wasn't most mirror mages; he had half a dozen colleagues in his lab to help with the heavy lifting, or in this case, the heavy holding. Cuinn wouldn't be merely opening an unlinked mirror; he had to ward it to prevent any Rak'kari from coming through, or any sandworms from coming back. Both outcomes would be extremely undesirable.

As to how we were going to see the results of our hopefully successful experiment, we couldn't simply open a mirror or a rift and look inside. You had to step through to see through. Tam had done that once; neither he nor anyone else was doing that again. And we couldn't simply strap a spy gem to a sandworm. We needed to be able to get the spy gem back, and we really wanted to do it without a starving Rak'kari attached.

We were going with the cable method, a double-strength one this time. Instead of Tam attached to the end, Cuinn had rigged up a sturdy mount for the spy gem, kind of like a steel frame with the gem inside. That way, the gem could record from all directions, and give us a good look at the Rak'kari hopefully enjoying their meal. The vortex that would be formed when the unlinked mirror was opened would take care of sucking the cable and spy gem inside. Getting it out could be a challenge, but that was one of the reasons why we had plenty of armored-gloved Guardians standing by.

As a test, half a dozen sandworms were tossed into the Void along with a spy gem attached to a cable to record what happened. The results were intensely gratifying. The Rak'kari raced to get to the sandworms, they drank their insides, and then those that had consumed the tasty morsels went boom.

After the successful test run, some cryptozoology faculty and grad students delivered six large, shoulder-high crates. I could see through the wooden slats what was squirming inside, and thought about offering to help ward that mirror. We did *not* want any of those things coming back through that mirror once they were dumped inside.

While I wasn't keen to be around while any of the above was happening, my newly discovered special skill set required me to be. Since much of my new power was unknown, I didn't know how I'd be able to help, but if the situation suddenly went to the Lower Hells in a handbasket—which had been the only direction situations had gone lately—I strongly suspected my magic would be there when or if I needed it. While I didn't like where the magic was probably coming from, I had to admit I was glad it was there if needed. I mean, how bad could something be that kept you alive?

One thing definitely made me feel better—twenty things, actually. Mychael, Vegard, and eighteen other Guardians. The boys would have my back. Though at the moment, I had theirs. Mychael didn't want me anywhere near that mirror when Cuinn opened it, so my view was presently through the space between Mychael and Vegard's broad shoulders. That didn't bother me. Should the situation go to crap, I had no doubt of my ability to shove them out of my way, especially if anything, be it spider or worm, attacked either one of them.

Tam and Imala were at the talks and couldn't be here, but I'd promised to tell them all the gory details of Rak'kari death and destruction later.

Cuinn and company had the largest mirror in his lab warmed up and in stand-by mode, meaning it was glowing and pulsing at a speed that was disturbingly similar to a heartbeat. At least the color wasn't red, more of a pale blue light.

I'd had enough of red glows to last me a lifetime—a normal one, not what my father had endured.

Four Guardians pushed the first crate up to the mirror, stopping less than a foot from the pulsing surface. Two backed away, and the other two stood to the side of the crate, but outside of the mirror's frame, ready to slide open the crate's wooden door.

Cuinn looked to Mychael. "Are we ready?"

"Whenever you are."

The elf mage turned to face the mirror, about to do what he'd said a mirror mage would have to be nuts to attempt. His next words were for his four colleagues. "Ladies and gentlemen, you know what to do."

One of the men laughed nervously. "Piss my robes?"

"You can do whatever you want *after* we serve lunch." Cuinn fully extended his arms, fingers spread wide and glowing with what started as blue, then intensified as a white so bright I couldn't look directly at it. "Now."

That was it. No shouted commands, just one word. And at that one word, the three men and two women opened an unlinked mirror, something that simply wasn't done because of the danger. For us, right here and right now, the danger was greater if we didn't do it.

The two Guardians pulled the first crate's wooden sliding door aside, and the vortex created with the formation of the unlinked mirror did the rest, sucking the contents of a shoulder-high crate full of Majafan sandworms into the Void, then taking the empty crate along with it.

I wasn't sure they meant for that to happen, but no one was opposed to a flying crate smashing a spider or three.

Crate after crate was pushed into position, opened, and the contents sucked into the Void. Cuinn and his mirror mage colleagues held that huge mirror under perfect control the entire time. Brows were sweating, arm and hand muscles tensing, and breathing was growing harsh, but the men and women of the dimensional studies department held their own.

Between the first and second crates, the spy gem secured to a steel cable was thrown in. When the last crate had been emptied, Cuinn and his friends held the mirror open for another minute while the Guardians reeled in the cable with the spy gem attached—and a Rak'kari thankfully not attached. Their work done, Cuinn and company closed the mirror, secured it, and promptly collapsed into the closest chairs.

We had a large crystal ball in place and ready for viewing. When the spy gem was hooked up...I could describe what I saw, but suffice it to say that the sandworms performed as promised. The Rak'kari found them irresistible, scuttling and surging over one another in their eagerness to reach the bounty first. After the first couple of dozen spiders exploded in splats of black blood and viscera. Mychael said he'd need to look back in later; but for now, we'd let the Rak'kari dine in peace—and then explode into pieces.

24

Mychael wasn't anywhere near ready to declare the Void clear of Rak'kari and safe for travel. That would have to wait until the sandworms had done their work, and after we'd looked into the Void again and didn't find it full of a new Rak'kari infestation. Tam had said that what we'd seen in the Void had been the result of years of Khrynsani work. Now we could only hope that they hadn't been overachievers and held a couple of hundred Rak'kari back just in case their first infestation hadn't gone as planned.

The peace talks were on a brief break. From what I could see, they needed it. I imagined that most of the delegates weren't exactly used to seeing hundreds of giant spiders and the people they'd consumed. That experience was a first time for me as well, but during the past few months I'd seen many things that I'd never seen before and really hoped to never see again. Come to think of it, I hadn't seen any of those things again; I was getting a dose of new horrors.

I was standing just outside of the two massive doors leading into the Seat of Twelve's place of judgment. Even though Justinius had done a fine job cleaning the traitors out of the Seat of Twelve and had succeeded in talking Garadin, Tarsilia, and my father into serving as three of the new Twelve, I still had no desire to set foot in there again. Still, with a new Twelve being assembled, including the goblins possibly being represented by A'Zahra Nuru and Kesyn Badru, I'd have to change the way I thought about this place. Instead of a place of judgment, it'd be more like the Hall of Happiness and Rational Thought.

Isibel saw me and came out into the hall. From her expression, I'd better hold off on that renaming. She wasn't happy, and chances were good that there hadn't been any kind of rational thought going on during the past few hours. No rational speech, either.

"Are we still going out tonight?" she asked.

"That's the plan."

"Good."

"Need it?"

"Desperately."

Sorry, Tarsilia and Sora, I thought. I would not be asking Edythe to go with us. Isibel did not need that. If they asked why, I'd tell them it was for the good of peace in the Seven Kingdoms. Isibel was the elven ambassador, and the elven ambassador needed to unwind. She couldn't do that under the disapproving looks of her mother.

"Anything good happening?" I asked.

"The only two delegations getting along are the elves and goblins. Most of the other delegations get along with us, but not each other."

I glanced past her into the chamber. Aeron Corantine looked even less happy than he had last time it'd been my misfortune to see him. Plus, he was one of those people who perpetually looked to be up to no good. Every person who had ever given me that impression had proven me right.

"Has anyone punched Aeron Corantine yet?"

"No, but during the last break, the Myloran ambassador was expressing a most fervent desire to toss him in the harbor."

"I've heard he can't swim."

"I believe that was the point." Isibel blew out her breath in an exasperated sigh. "Markus wants to join the talks tomorrow. At least for a while."

"What does Dalis have to say about that?"

"She said that she'll be coming with him, and she defies anyone to attempt to prevent her."

Cuinn had wanted to see Rak'kari eat sandworms and explode. Isibel looked like she wanted to see Aeron Corantine try to have Dalis tossed out of the talks. Her delicate jaw was clenched, and so were the dainty fists by her side. The Nebian ambassador didn't know it yet, but he would rather be tossed in the harbor by the Mylorans than get what Dalis would be dishing out if he tried to separate her from her patient.

"Mago and I have been meeting with Markus every evening," Isibel was saying while glaring at the Nebian, "and he has been giving us invaluable advice, but…"

"I know. There's just no substitution for him being there," I said. "Mago's amazing at reading people, but Markus is the master. Especially since he knows all of the delegates personally." He had something else Mago and Isibel did not—decades of experience doing just this. Mago knew only too well that a person could say one thing and mean another. Markus knew the person, too.

Imala Kalis spotted me and came over to join us.

Tam was in heated debate with the Caesolian ambassador. The Caesolian was a head shorter than Tam, but he wasn't letting that stop him. Dakarai Enric stood nearby, scowling.

That scene wasn't the most shocking thing I'd seen today, but it came close.

"The Caesolian ambassador found his spine?" I asked Imala once she was close enough. I had the sudden image of a tiny lap dog antagonizing a very angry werehound. This could get messy, and fast. Though at least it'd be over quickly, except for the cleanup.

She glanced back at the scene. "And Tam's about to rip it out for him."

"It looks like Dakarai wants to help. Two days ago the Caesolian wouldn't stand on the same side of the room as Tam, and now he's in his face. Should we stop him from committing suicide by Tam?"

"I'm not going to stop him," Imala said in the Caesolian's general direction. "He deserves whatever he gets." She took a deep breath to calm herself. It didn't work. "It's progress, but not the kind we'd hoped to have. As you can see, we are all growing increasingly frustrated."

"Did finding out about the spiders in the Void do this much damage?"

"It certainly didn't help," Isibel said. "All of the delegates knew why they were coming here, and they agreed that it needed to be done—no one needed to have a weapon like the Saghred. But almost as soon as they got here, it's as if they've changed their minds. It's not merely the Rak'kari and the possibility of the Khrynsani being behind it or something larger. It's as if every kingdom believes every other kingdom is out to get them. Paranoia is running rampant around here."

"And Tam does look ready to snap," I noted. "Getting a bunch of humans to cooperate and sign a piece of paper is frustrating, but it's nowhere near the level of stress Tam wakes up to every day. This isn't like him at all. And it certainly isn't like Dakarai. I've never seen him angry."

Imala stood utterly still. Only her eyes moved—quickly taking in everyone in the room, darting from delegate to delegate.

I froze, too. Something was wrong. Imala knew what it was. I didn't. And considering how intent the little goblin woman was, I didn't think I was going to like it when I found out.

"What is it?" I said without moving my lips.

"You said it yourself—the people we know are behaving uncharacteristically, and those we don't know aren't acting as they should." She hissed a curse in Goblin. "I may have been affected as well. As an agent, I'm trained to pick up on tampering; yet I didn't see what was right before my eyes until you pointed it out."

"Tampered?"

"With the delegates' minds. Either by spell or drug. Tam would have detected a spell long before it got this far. That means we're being drugged."

"How could that happen?" I raised my hands defensively. "Don't take this the wrong way, but are you sure you're not just tired?"

"There's only one way to find out."

Tarsilia Rivalin was an expert on poisons, drugs, and other mind- or mood-altering substances. Basically anything that could be concocted to heal or harm, she knew all about it.

Imala probably knew nearly as much as Tarsilia did about the drugs and poisons, but since she was one of the victims, she yielded that part of the investigation to Tarsilia. Still, it didn't mean she wasn't looking over Tarsilia's shoulder in the hastily assembled lab Justinius had ordered set up for her.

Imala being drugged along with the other delegates might have been the best thing that could have happened. She knew every symptom of every known substance used to alter behavior. While she probably could've diagnosed herself, Tarsilia's guiding questions and keen observations would help get to the bottom of this a lot faster. Before long the two of them would be talking shop and sharing recipes.

Mago was not amused when I told him someone had been messing with his emotions. And as I talked to my cousin, it became obvious to me that there had to be a drug involved. Nothing got under Mago's skin, and if it did, he dealt with it in a calm and rational way. My cousin was presently neither calm nor rational.

In the meantime, Mychael and Justinius agreed not to tell the other delegates anything until we knew for sure what had happened—and depending on what we found out, maybe not even then. Tarsilia said that if we found the source, we could remove it and everyone should return to normal fairly quickly, or at least not get any worse. Of course, how long that took depended on what the substance was that seemingly all of the delegates had ingested or come in contact with.

Justinius was ultimately in charge of the peace talks, so he could—and did—call an early stop to that day's deliberations, citing what he called a need to step away from the table, regain your composure, and remember that you're adults and representatives of your kingdoms. He didn't quite word it like that, but I knew the old man; he wanted to.

Whatever the drug was, it had to have been introduced when all of the delegates were together, which meant inside the citadel chamber. It would've been impossible to get to all of the delegates otherwise. That conclusion made Mychael just as angry as the delegates, since it implied that one or more of his Guardians was involved. Mychael refused to assign any blame to his men until he had irrefutable proof.

"The room is guarded day and night," Mychael said. "At the end of each day's deliberations, it's locked and secured. And should a delegate need to retrieve paperwork after hours, they are guarded and watched."

He ordered an immediate review of the surveillance gems mounted in each corner of the room to record the talks. The gems recorded all night as well for security purposes, and our review began after the talks concluded late yesterday afternoon. The elven and goblin delegates said they had begun to feel particularly short-tempered by mid-morning today, pointing to the drug being introduced into the room overnight.

Each day's procedure in the chamber was the same. At the end of the day, everything was left exactly as it was with the exception of the trash, which was emptied and burned in the citadel's incinerator, and the refilling of the inkwells and paper supply at each delegate's place. We watched as around nine o'clock last night an elderly, black-robed man went to each place and refilled the wells, replaced the pens, and replenished the paper.

"Those robes look familiar," I said.

"He's a Scriptorium employee," Mychael told me. "Niall Reeves has been on the staff for nearly forty years. He keeps the entire citadel stocked with ink and paper."

I didn't say what I was thinking; I let my arched eyebrow do it for me.

"And no, he can't be bribed or blackmailed. Drugs or mind-tampering could be possible, but he's not adding anything other than ink to the wells. Niall isn't involved in making the ink; he only delivers it."

"We've all been taking notes and passing messages," Tam said. He showed us two of the fingertips on his right hand. They were stained with black ink. "And the pens are leaking. I noticed it this morning." He scowled. "Yet one more thing to piss me off."

Mago, Isibel, Dakarai, and Imala looked down at their own hands. All of them had ink stains on at least one of their fingers.

"It's the ink," Imala said with absolute certainty and no small measure of rage. "And he replaced the pens with ones that leak. They didn't leak before this morning."

I'd never heard her so angry. Part of it was obviously directed at the culprit, but she had to be furious with herself. Detecting poison was part of her job. One didn't get to be director of the goblin secret service without being an expert on drugs, poisons, and their uses.

"You were drugged, too, Imala." I told her. "If it was the ink, you couldn't have known."

"I should have known. More to the point, I was expecting an attempt, vigilant against it, and yet it still happened. To me."

"The Khrynsani dumped hundreds of monster spiders into the Void and completely shut down mirror travel. Between that and trying to talk sense into people like Aeron Corantine on a daily basis, how were you to know your anger came from being drugged?"

"Raine, you have to understand that we take every precaution against poisons or drugs," Tam said. "Daily, lifelong precaution."

"Daily *and* lifelong?"

Tam shrugged. "We're goblins, surrounded by other goblins. It's necessary." He half grinned and lowered his voice even though Imala was standing right there. "When we find who did this, may I suggest giving them to Imala for five minutes in a closed room? She'll find out everything we need to know."

Imala smacked him.

"Where does the ink come from?" Dakarai asked Mychael.

"The Scriptorium, as does the paper."

"Where do they get it?"

"The Scriptorium has a staff that makes all of the Isle of Mid's paper and ink. With the college being here as well as the Conclave, we go through a lot of both. It'd cost too much to have it shipped in. We make our own."

"A few centuries ago," Imala said, "a court noble attempted to kill the goblin queen's secretary with poisoned ink. The noble was found out before the poison reached fatal doses in the secretary's body. The secretary swore off ink." Imala slowly smiled in a show of fangs. "He used blood instead—

collected from the noble who had attempted to poison him. We goblins adore irony."

Jeez. Tam was wrong. It wouldn't take five minutes for Imala to extract a confession from the culprit. She could do it in less than one.

25

I was going to the Scriptorium. I had a letter from the archmagus giving me permission to search anything and everything I thought necessary to find out who had done this and how, and to make them stop by arresting them and taking them back to the citadel with me. Though "letter" was a misnomer. Justinius had written it more as a formal order and handwritten command, complete with the midnight blue seal of the archmagus giving me complete access to the Scriptorium and all of its employees.

The letter might get me inside without question, but I wasn't going to hold my breath on it.

The Scriptorium's chief librarian, Lucan Kalta, hated my guts. Professionally and personally (he believed in being thorough). The last time I'd walked in here with a permission note—a letter giving me access to certain books—Lucan Kalta had found a legal loophole as a way around it. Like I said, thorough.

Which was why I was taking his older brother, Vidor, with me.

I'd had an up-close and unpleasant encounter with Lucan Kalta within days of arriving on the Isle of Mid. He didn't like me then, and I thought it highly unlikely that he'd warmed to me since. His fiefdom was the Scriptorium, a massive repository of nearly every magic-related book, scroll, or stone slab. He didn't like me because I'd defied his authority in front of his staff. The rule I broke was stupid to begin with, so I'd seen nothing wrong with going around it.

Now I was walking into his territory with six armed Guardians—seven, counting Vegard—wanting to question the members of his staff. The Guardians were mainly security for me, but they'd be prepared to step in if needed if we located our suspect and either he or she tried to make a run for it or fight back using magic. My magic wasn't exactly what you could call dependable; it could also be deadly, neither of which we wanted to advertise right now.

For the icing on the cake, I couldn't tell Lucan Kalta anything more than that a crime had been committed and that one of his staff may have been involved.

Oh, that was going to go over well.

Vegard was acting in Mychael's stead. The letter covered that, too. Cuinn had needed to see Mychael about an issue with the rift to Timurus, and Justinius was smoothing ruffled feathers with the Caesolian and Nebian delegations.

I was the last person who wanted to go into the Scriptorium and kick what I was sure was going to be a hornet's nest. I didn't do diplomacy and neither did Lucan Kalta.

But as a seeker, I had to go.

With my pre-Saghred seeker skill set, I had to touch an object either belonging to or recently touched by a person to be able to track them. Or know a person really well.

Now, I could find out more, with less.

The ink had been made in the Scriptorium, and Tarsilia had

confirmed that there were substances that could be introduced into the bloodstream through the skin to cause the symptoms that the elven and goblin delegates were exhibiting.

All of those substances were goblin.

Yet another attempt to sabotage the peace talks and frame the goblins.

The Conclave Scriptorium was located at the center of the college campus, a massive granite building rising four stories above ground and descending I had no clue how many stories under it. In addition to being the largest and most complete collection of books, scrolls, tablets, and anything else you could write, scratch, or engrave words on in the Seven Kingdoms, it stank to high heaven, magic-wise. Before my first trip inside, I'd been told that spending too long in the company of the Scriptorium's contents could send a sensitive into magic overload that'd make your worst hangover pale in comparison. Nontalents did most of the book retrieval in the stacks. The reading rooms were separate. Only certain mages were allowed to spend time in the stacks themselves.

I'd met one of those mages for the first time in the Scriptorium's stacks, also referred to as The Vault because that was what it felt like being in there.

The mage had been Carnades Silvanus.

It'd been entirely appropriate to have met Carnades in a place with such a name, considering he'd wanted me executed from the moment he'd met me until the instant of his death. He'd been tenacious, I'd give him that.

Beyond the massive, iron-banded doors was a cavernous, cool interior lit by lightglobes recessed into the walls. The counter at the far end was a wall-to-wall monolith of black marble manned by librarians who looked less like academics and more like a robed line of defense for the precious books that lay beyond. There was a single opening in the center to allow mere mortals to pass into what Lucan Kalta considered his personal inner sanctum. As I had learned, nearly the hard way, attempting to leave with a book he didn't want you to have had immediate and unpleasant consequences.

I glanced up.

No kid stuck to the ceiling this time.

Lucan Kalta and his senior staff used the vaulted ceiling in the entrance hall as detention. Break a rule—like trying to take a book without checking it out—and you'd find yourself floating up to the ceiling. How long you were kept there depended on the severity of your transgression.

Certain books weren't to be checked out, others were kept separate because many students and mages weren't qualified to get their hands on them for their own safety. The book I had needed fell into the former category. Rudra Muralin's diary. Otherwise known as the book that helped save the Seven Kingdoms from enslavement by Sarad Nukpana and the Saghred.

Lucan Kalta and I had ended up toe-to-toe at the checkout desk. Lucan didn't want the book leaving the library. Mychael needed to see that book, and I was determined to take it to him.

Mychael's timely arrival had separated us before it progressed to a magic-slinging showdown. Though I wouldn't have used magic; I would have gone with fists. Always lead with the unexpected.

Oh yes, this place was just packed with fun memories.

"Do not concern yourself about my brother's lack of regard for you, Miss Benares," Vidor said. "He doesn't like me, either."

Justinius's letter and his seal gained us an immediate audience with Lucan Kalta.

His office was through the opening in the center of the monolithic checkout counter, then down a long, black marble–

lined corridor to a predictably imposing pair of dark wooden doors.

Vidor gave a sigh of contentment. "I've always felt so at home in my brother's office."

I blinked. "You have?"

"I'm a nachtmagus, dear. It reminds me of a particularly well-appointed crypt."

I snorted.

A robed librarian sat at a small desk to the side of the office doors. The gatekeeper, no doubt. He looked as though he didn't want to be here, either. I had to wonder if anyone did.

"I'm Raine Benares. I'm here on behalf of the archmagus to see Chief Librarian Kalta." I handed him the sealed letter.

He accepted the letter, saw the seal, and a single eyebrow arched above the rim of his round spectacles. Then the other eyebrow rose at the sight of Vidor and the Guardians aligned behind us, giving the librarian the appearance of a startled owl.

At least we'd made an impression.

"One moment, please."

The librarian knocked twice and opened one door just enough to squeeze through. Minutes went by.

"He's making us wait," I murmured without moving my lips. Kalta was probably watching us via spy crystal right now.

"Yes, he's being childish," Vidor agreed. "That bodes well."

"It does?"

"It means he knows he has no choice but to cooperate. This is his only chance to flex his muscles. My brother is taking what he can get."

Five minutes later, the door opened.

Lucan Kalta stood in front of his imposing desk. The Scriptorium's chief librarian was tall, black-robed, and spectrally thin. His already thin lips stretched to virtual nonexistence when he saw me.

I gave him a smile without teeth or sincerity.

We both knew where we stood, nothing was going to

change that, so why bother with banalities neither one of us would believe or accept?

"Brother," Vidor said in greeting.

Lucan turned his attention to his brother without a change in expression.

"It's good to see you, too," Vidor continued. "No, no, don't bother to offer us a seat; we can't stay long."

"How unfortunate."

"Isn't it, though? Perhaps next time."

Now it was my turn. Oh goody. "Chief Librarian Kalta, the letter from Archmagus Valerian explains that we need—"

"But not why you need it."

"There has been an incident, and we have reason to believe it was perpetrated in your ink shop."

"My librarians are—"

"Not suspects at this time." One good interruption deserved another. "We merely need to interview them to clear them of any involvement."

"May I inquire as to the nature of this incident?"

"You may inquire, but I am not at liberty to tell. Archmagus Valerian does not want it known at this time."

"Yet you know it."

"As the investigator and the seeker on this case, I would need to."

Silence.

I waited it out. Like Vidor had said, Lucan knew he had no choice but to cooperate.

"I will accompany you during your investigation," he informed me.

I inclined my head in acquiescence. It was Lucan Kalta's turf, and Justinius hadn't stipulated in the letter that he couldn't tag along. True to form, the chief librarian had located the loophole. The man had missed his calling as a lawyer. However, if he interfered with what I needed to do, I'd have his big brother escort him out. Lucan Kalta was a talented mage, but if it came down to a confrontation, I had no doubt as to Vidor's superior skill. And according to Vidor, Lucan was well aware of his shortcomings in that area. I was the last person he'd want to be watching while big brother handed him his posterior on a platter.

Lucan Kalta would be annoying, but he wouldn't get in my way.

But I was sure that he'd try.

More good times for me in the Scriptorium.

26

Ideally, I needed the ink shop to be empty before I set foot in it.

Having the chief librarian sweep in would cause enough of a panic among the people working there. Add to that a man who looked suspiciously like their dreaded boss, along with six grim Guardians, the paladin's second in command, and the elf woman who had been bonded to a soul-eating stone, and the emotional imprint left in the room would be so thick it'd take me forever to work through the layers of panic to find what I needed.

A psychic needle in a chaotic emotional haystack was a good analogy.

The Scriptorium's ink shop and bindery was located on the building's first floor. There was a small office outside the closed shop door. The office door was open and there was a robed man inside. Things were looking up.

"Is that the shop manager?" I asked Lucan Kalta.

"Yes, Patric Notte."

"Good. I need to speak with him."

Lucan Kalta stood in the open doorway and cleared his throat. The manager looked up, saw him, and his face completely drained of color. I could hardly blame him.

I stepped up next to the chief librarian and introduced myself.

My instincts told me that Patric Notte was a good man who prided himself on doing a good job. I was honest with him as to why I was there, or at least as honest as I had been with Lucan Kalta. Though when I got to the word "incident," you'd have thought I'd said "bloody murder."

"Neither you nor your staff are being accused," I hurried to reassure him. "The archmagus and paladin are eliminating possibilities, and the ink shop is merely one of them. I'm a seeker."

Notte swallowed, quickly following it up with a nervous smile. "Yes, ma'am, I am aware of that."

That gulp told me he was aware of everything else that I was, too.

"I need some time alone in the shop to see if I sense anything out of the ordinary. Is there another way in or out other than that door?"

"No, ma'am. The windows can be opened from the inside, but only in case of an emergency, such as a fire. I lock and spellbind the door and windows personally at the end of each workday."

"Have there been any signs of forced entry—or attempted entry—in the past week?"

"None."

A single entrance and exit was good for another reason: no one could make a break for it out another door.

"Is there a room nearby where you and your staff could wait while I have a look around?" I asked him.

"Yes, ma'am."

"If you could round up your staff and take them there

now, I would appreciate it. Oh, and Librarian Notte, please don't let them take anything with them; I need access to *all* of the room's contents. I promise not to touch anything that I don't need to. It should take no longer than half an hour."

Patric Notte smiled, and it was genuine. "Thank you for your consideration, ma'am. When you're finished, if you have any questions, my staff and I will be at your disposal."

I returned his smile and nodded.

The manager opened the shop door and went to do as I'd asked while we remained in the hall. As the men and women filed past us, there was plenty of shock, but I didn't detect any guilty panic.

When they had gone, I stepped into the room. Lucan Kalta started to follow.

I stopped and turned around, blocking the doorway with my body.

"Chief Librarian Kalta, I need you to leave as well. Magic users are a distraction to me while working. As you no doubt understand, the archmagus needs me to get to the bottom of this now."

"Come on, Lucan," Vidor told his brother. "The lady needs privacy."

"Vegard, would you wait just outside the door?" I asked.

"Yes, ma'am. Do you need for me to close it?"

"Yes, please."

Within seconds, I was blissfully alone.

I could have done this with everyone still in the room, but I didn't want to risk missing anything. While I'd worked around nervous and guilty people before, I didn't want anyone with me now. I could talk to the staff afterward if necessary to probe for a sense of guilt—or merely understandable paranoia, considering they worked for Lucan Kalta.

But the main reason I wanted to be alone was that I hadn't attempted to use my seeking skills to this extent since the Saghred had taken my magic. Vegard knew this. Having him in the room, feeling anxious while I worked, wanting me to succeed…That would be even more of a distraction than a possible poisoner in the room.

I went to the exact center of the room, closed my eyes, and steadied my breathing.

I didn't know anything about ink-making, or how the ink could have been drugged, so I didn't know what I was looking for. I assumed that if this person was clever enough to have drugged the peace delegates' ink, they wouldn't leave a bottle marked "POISON" lying around. Imala had once said that she could track a Khrynsani by smell. I'd been in the Khrynsani temple, with all the associated incense. I wouldn't be so lucky here. There hadn't been a Khrynsani in full temple robes skulking around the Scriptorium's ink shop drugging the ink bottles meant for the peace talks. Someone hired by the Khrynsani, on the other hand, an expert at…

I gasped and opened my eyes.

The Saghred had been stolen for Sarad Nukpana by a master shapeshifter, thief, and assassin by the name of Nesral Hesai. The goblin had been codenamed Chameleon and rightfully so. Hesai could shift shapes *and* sexes. He'd shapeshifted into Mychael and even I had been fooled. I knew that what had been done here hadn't been Nesral Hesai's work. He was dead. I knew that because I'd killed him, indirectly. Hesai had been trying to push me through a Gate into Sarad Nukpana's waiting arms. I'd stabbed his foot through the top of his boot with a dagger he'd intended for me. The wound wasn't fatal, but the poison Hesai had put on the dagger had been.

But if the Khrynsani considered a shapeshifter to be such a valuable resource, they wouldn't have only one in their employ. That would explain how an outsider could have gained access to a building as secure as the Scriptorium. If that was what had happened, one of Patric Notte's workers was now dead. To assume another's identity, you needed to ensure they wouldn't appear at an inconvenient time and blow your cover. Working for the Khrynsani meant taking *no* chances. To the Khrynsani, murder wasn't a crime; it was a solution to an inconvenience.

The surveillance gem in the citadel's chamber had shown an older man refilling the ink wells and replacing the pens. Mychael had said his name was Niall Reeves. I remembered his face well enough to know that he hadn't been one of the people who had filed past me in the hall a few minutes ago.

I looked around the shop until I located the large bottles that looked like the one Niall had used to refill the ink wells. He wouldn't have wanted to risk drugging any ink other than that going to the peace talks. I hoped he hadn't had time to be tidy.

There were five empty bottles on a table next to an ink vat, and they hadn't been cleaned yet. Good.

I picked up the first one and gazed through the glass bottle, unfocusing my physical eyes and opening my seeker vision. I got an image of a hallway lined with offices, both unfamiliar. I let out a shaky breath of relief. My seeker abilities were working as per normal. At least something was going right.

I repeated that with the second and then the third bottle. One showed me more offices; the other a large room lined with long tables, illuminated with lamp-mounted lightglobes. There were a few students in the room. Most were studying; two had their heads down on their books, sleeping.

I picked up the fourth bottle and nearly dropped it.

The man accepting the small vial of liquid and pouring it into the ink bottle was Niall Reeves, or the Khrynsani-hired shapeshifter who had taken his place.

I knew the person who was giving him the vial.

Sarad Nukpana's mother.

Sandrina Ghalfari.

27

As much as I wanted to run back to the citadel and tell Mychael that Sandrina Ghalfari either had been on the island or still was, I needed to determine if we had a master shapeshifter on the loose.

I opened the door. Vegard was there, waiting. The others were further down the hall.

"Sandrina," I told Vegard out of the side of my mouth, and kept walking, moving quickly down the hall. I passed Lucan and Vidor and went directly to the room where Patric and his staff waited. I did a quick survey of the room. No, Niall Reeves definitely wasn't there. I gestured Patric aside.

"Was Niall Reeves supposed to be working today?" I asked quietly.

"Yes, but he hasn't been feeling well for the past few days. He was out three days ago, but returned yesterday saying that he was feeling better."

"When he came back to work, did you notice anything odd about him?"

"How so?"

"Not quite acting like himself."

"As a matter of fact, he asked which ink would be going to the citadel. We only make two colors here, due to the volume. The archmagus has always insisted on the midnight blue."

I nodded. "And Niall would know that."

"Absolutely, ma'am. He's always done the deliveries to the citadel."

I gestured Vidor over. Lucan came with him, and I didn't try to stop him. The damage had been done.

"Vidor, I need for you to contact Sedge Rinker and have him check…" I turned back to Patric Notte. "Would you tell Nachtmagus Kalta where Niall Reeves lived?"

The ink shop manager blanched. *"Lived?"*

I winced. Good old past tense. Way to be subtle, Raine. "I believe he may no longer be alive. In all likelihood, the person who returned to work was a shapeshifter. Vidor, would you go with Sedge and investigate what you find?" He knew what I meant. A dead body. A body that might be able to tell a master nachtmagus like Vidor Kalta who had killed him, when, and how.

I already knew why.

The murderer could have been the shapeshifter, or Sandrina Ghalfari might have paid Niall Reeves a personal visit.

"Of course," Vidor said.

Lucan Kalta snorted and started to say something. I cut him off. I did not have time for this. None of us did.

"Vegard, we need to get back to the citadel. Now."

Just a month ago in the Khrynsani temple, Sandrina Ghalfari had been moments away from achieving her lifelong dream— seeing her son destroy all of his enemies and ascend to the goblin throne, with her as the power behind it.

I'd shattered that dream the instant I'd shattered the Saghred. Her son, Sarad Nukpana, had conjured a monster to kill Tam. When I'd destroyed the Saghred, Sarad's concentration had faltered for an instant and he had lost control of his creation. The demon that Tam had summoned had seen its chance, and taken Sarad Nukpana back to the Lower Hells with it.

Within seconds, Sandrina had lost both her twisted dream of ultimate power and the tool she had used to achieve that power—her son Sarad.

Now she was putting her revenge into motion.

I didn't know how. I didn't know the full extent of the plan.

But I knew why—she blamed us all for Sarad's death and her downfall.

And I knew where she would be.

There was only one place on the Isle of Mid where she could be, where as a mother she would have to go.

The highest tower in the citadel, where her son's body was entombed.

Three days after the Saghred had bonded itself to me, to save Piaras, myself, and everyone I loved from death or worse at Sarad Nukpana's hands, I'd tricked him into touching the Saghred with his bloody hand. The stone had taken him as a sacrifice and absorbed him, body and soul. Weeks later, when Nukpana's soul had escaped from the Saghred, he'd regenerated his body using the blackest of black magic. Then, in an act of unspeakable cruelty, Sarad Nukpana had abandoned his own regenerated body to possess Tam's, to ensure that Tam would take the blame for the acts Nukpana would commit once the Saghred was his. The only way to force Nukpana's soul out of Tam's body had been to kill Tam. Tam had begged me to do it. I'd killed him with a crossbow bolt through the heart. At the instant of Tam's death, Sarad Nukpana had abandoned Tam's body for the newly dead body of his uncle Janos Ghalfari.

Sarad Nukpana's regenerated body was entombed in the

citadel's highest tower in a crystal coffin woven with spells to keep it from being opened from the outside—or the inside.

Justinius and Mychael hadn't wanted to take any chances.

One of the spells inside the coffin had been to preserve his corpse. The mortician who had prepared the body and worked the spell had called it "perpetual repose."

I called it creepy as hell.

When it had been done, I had gone to see him. Sarad Nukpana was still perfect, still darkly beautiful. He had a shadow of a smile on his face, as if he knew something we didn't, something that was about to bite us all in our collective ass.

I had no doubt that he did.

And now I knew what that was, or at least some of it. Regardless of what happened, his Khrynsani had a backup plan, a plan that would ensure they survived—and their enemies did not.

The stairs to the tower crypt could be revealed by a spell that only Mychael and Justinius knew. The circular room had one door, no windows, and had been lit bright as day.

That had been my request.

Goblins didn't like bright light. I did. And for some irrational reason, I had also liked knowing that Sarad Nukpana wasn't lying in the dark. Bad things happened in dark places. Sarad Nukpana had most definitely been a bad thing.

I'd wanted the body destroyed and the ashes scattered to the winds in the far reaches of all Seven Kingdoms. But we'd kept it. King Chigaru's late brother, Sathrik, had sent Justinius a letter stating that unless Sarad Nukpana's body was returned undamaged to Regor within the month, he would declare war against the Guardians, the Conclave, and the Isle of Mid, and come and get the body himself. Mychael and Justinius had no intention of returning Nukpana's body, but it never hurt to have an ace in the hole just in case. Hence the mortician's creepy reposing spell.

Sathrik was dead, Chigaru was king, and the Khrynsani had been overthrown.

Now Sandrina Ghalfari had come to claim her son.

Mychael was waiting for us at the gates of the citadel.

With our bond, he'd sensed something had happened and that I was coming back to the citadel as fast as our horses could get through Mid's streets.

I quickly dismounted and tossed my reins to a waiting groom. "It's Sandrina."

"I know," Mychael said. "Tarsilia and Imala determined the drug was—"

"No, I mean she's here. In the citadel. The tower."

"It's sealed."

"If she hasn't gotten in, she's tried. She's got a shapeshifter working with her."

Mychael spat a curse and started shouting orders. Within minutes the two of us, Vegard, and at least a dozen armed Guardians were running through the citadel to the north tower. When we got to what looked like a solid wall, Mychael murmured a brief incantation, exposing a door.

"The seal spell was still in place," he told me.

"That's good, but I still want to check."

He incanted a few more words and the door opened. "I wasn't suggesting otherwise."

I'd insisted checking the tower; Mychael insisted on going up the stairs first. Vegard and I were relegated to the middle of the pack.

I had no problem with that. I didn't need to get there first; I just needed to see that Sarad Nukpana's body was still there. I had no idea how Sandrina would have gained access to the tower or, if she had gotten in, how she could have gotten her son's body out. I only knew what my gut was telling me, insistently—that we were going to find something in the room at the top of the tower that we did not want to see.

Mychael and the Guardians in front of us reached the top, checked the door for any signs of entry or trap, and with Mychael on one side of the door and a Guardian on the other, Mychael reached out, opened the tower door, and cautiously leaned around to look inside.

He stood there for a moment, not moving. After what seemed an eternity to me, he went inside. More Guardians followed, and I ran the rest of the way up, Vegard at my heels.

Sarad Nukpana was still in his coffin.

I slowly walked to where Mychael stood next to it, looking down.

I stepped up next to him and sharply inhaled.

A thin layer of dust coated the crystal coffin. The only disturbance in the dust was where two thin trails of water had fallen on the coffin's lid and had run down the side.

Tears.

Next to the tears was a note. It was unsigned. It didn't need a signature. We knew who it was from. There were two short sentences.

You destroyed my world. I will destroy yours.

"We need to get a look through that Timurus rift," Mychael said. "Now."

It looked like my bachelorette party would have to wait.

28

Cuinn Aviniel and his colleagues had been working feverishly since we'd left his lab, determining the best and safest way to briefly open a rift to Timurus. Eamaliel was working with them. During his centuries on the run, he had apparently become quite adept with rifts. When you had a father who was close to a thousand years old, you didn't find out something new about him every day—it was more like every minute. He'd opened a rift before in exactly the place we needed to see—the Table of Iron overlooking the city of Astava. He hadn't lived as long as he had without being cautious. He told me that when he'd needed to travel, he'd always opened a small rift—much like a window—and looked before he leapt.

That was what we'd be doing—the looking part, not the leaping.

As to my plans for this evening, as much as I wanted a night out with my friends, Sandrina's threat of an impending invasion knocked my plans right off the table. While going out and drinking too much was exactly what I wanted to do, staying stone cold sober was what was needed. Not to mention, there was no way Mychael was letting me out of his sight with Sandrina Ghalfari and her master shapeshifter possibly still on the island. Under normal circumstances, I would have argued with him about being overprotective. Right now, I completely agreed with him.

Mychael stayed awake and alert all night, or at least he was that way every time I woke up from my fitful dozing on the couch in his office. Since speed was now of the essence, we'd dispensed with Guardian messengers and were using telepaths. A Guardian telepath was in Cuinn's lab, relaying regular updates to Ben, who'd taken up residence with his scrying bowl in Mychael's outer office.

Knowledge of what was happening on Timurus was only half of what we needed. If there was an army poised to invade, what could we do to stop them?

Tam, Imala, Justinius, Garadin, and Tarsilia were among those working on that.

It had been seven hundred years since the unknown invader had wiped out the population of Timurus. That didn't mean that the Khrynsani's new allies were the same invader. That army had invaded Timurus, killed the population, then taken what they wanted and left. Why would they come back to an uninhabited world?

However, when it came to a possible off-world invasion with our worst enemies acting as tour guides, chances weren't something we were willing to take.

Justinius had made a recommendation concerning who should be in Cuinn's lab when the rift was opened. While none of us really liked what he wanted to do, we had agreed that it was necessary.

The ambassador from each kingdom needed to be there.

If there was an invading army massing on the other side,

a representative from each kingdom needed to see the proof with their own eyes.

Proof we were really hoping wouldn't be there.

Just before dawn, Cuinn sent word via Ben that they were ready to open a window onto Timurus.

Justinius had personally made the rounds of the embassies last night to inform them of the possible situation. Some had taken it better than others. He'd told them a Guardian messenger would be sent when the rift was ready to be opened. Even with their usual Guardian escorts, the old man wasn't holding his breath that most of the ambassadors would get here on time.

We were in Cuinn's lab. Considering that I was about to look through a rift to another world and possibly see an invading army, I was appallingly groggy even though I had eaten and consumed enough coffee to float one of Uncle Ryn's ships. Maybe after the events of the past few months, it simply took more for my survival instinct to kick in, like a threat of immediate death. Either that or I was getting too old for this crap. Then I glanced over at my nearly-a-millennium-old father who, after being awake and working all night, was plenty perky.

Tarsilia and Garadin were there as the two newest members of the Seat of Twelve.

Isibel arrived next, followed by the Myloran, Caesolian, Majafan, and Brenirian ambassadors. Tam was standing in for Dakarai Enric. As Chigaru's chancellor and temporary heir, Tam needed to be here.

I knew Mychael didn't want Isibel anywhere near here.

Eamaliel was talking to the ambassadors. All of them had arrived except for Aeron Corantine of Nebia. No surprise. He was on his way, so we were waiting for him. In the meantime, the group was close enough for me to listen in.

"Our rift won't be stable enough for travel," my father said, trying to reassure the nervous Caesolian ambassador. "From either direction."

"But could someone try to come through?" the Caesolian asked.

"That would be ill-advised."

"But they could still try."

My father put a comforting hand on the ambassador's shoulder. "Professor Aviniel and I would slam the door in their faces."

"Where would that put them?"

Eamaliel chortled. "Somewhere that's not here."

"If anyone is close to our rift when it opens," Mychael quietly asked Cuinn, "will they be able to see through it?"

"Possibly. It largely depends on the angle at which they're standing. If they're directly in front of the rift, then yes, they will be able to see through to this room."

"It's an unavoidable risk, son," Justinius told Mychael. "And one we have to take."

"I wasn't suggesting otherwise, sir. Merely determining what defenses we need to have in place should it happen."

Justinius glanced back at his four regular Guardian bodyguards, then around at me, Mychael, Vegard, Tam, and my father. He grinned. "I think we have adequate firepower. No need to make the place any more crowded than it needs to be."

I turned away from the door. "Speaking of unneeded," I muttered.

Aeron Corantine had arrived, looking distinctly unhappy. Another dozen Guardians were stationed outside of Cuinn's lab, ensuring that only the ambassador of each kingdom was allowed inside. I glanced beyond the door. Yep, the Nebian ambassador had brought an entourage. I'd already pegged the Nebian as the type that couldn't feel important unless he was surrounded by people who were paid to treat him that way.

Tarsilia had said the drug used to taint the delegates' ink

was the kind that needed to be in near continuous contact with the victim's skin to remain effective. It'd been over twelve hours since we'd discovered the drugged ink and Justinius had dismissed the delegates for the day. Fortunately, no one had discovered that they had been drugged, and according to Tarsilia, twelve hours was enough time for the ink's effects to fade enough that the delegate would be back to normal, which in Aeron Corantine's case wasn't a noticeable improvement.

The Nebian ambassador apparently had a problem with something this morning and was making a beeline for Justinius. Two of the old man's bodyguards put their large selves in the ambassador's path, effectively stopping his beeline.

"I demand to see the archmagus," he said from behind the armored wall of Guardians.

One of the men turned to Justinius with a raised eyebrow. With a resigned sigh, the old man waved his hand, telling his guard to let the obnoxious twit through.

Justinius intercepted him before he reached us. I was grateful. I'd barely slept and was in no mood for Aeron Corantine. One side of Tam's upper lip twitched in a snarl, exposing a fang. I already knew Tam was not a morning person.

"Disappointed Justinius got to him first?" I asked.

"Some people are not worth the effort. Ambassador Corantine is one such individual. I was merely expressing my distaste at his presence."

"You really don't like him."

"And you do?"

An answer using words wouldn't suffice. I went with a snort.

"Precisely," Tam said. "The Nebian king would be better served by appointing another representative. A good ambassador shouldn't tempt other kingdoms to cut diplomatic ties."

Justinius raised his voice to address everyone in the room, but his eyes were on the ambassadors. "Once the rift is open, whoever is on the other side may be able to see and hear us, so no movement or talking."

The Caesolian ambassador blanched.

The old man might want to include no screaming.

"Or noise of any kind," Justinius added. "It's imperative that we remain quiet and still. Do you understand?"

The ambassadors nodded or verbally affirmed that they got the message, including Aeron Corantine.

The old man didn't bother with the Guardians or the rest of us. We'd had ample experience seeing, hearing, and experiencing things that'd turn your hair white.

My father moved into position on one side of where the rift would open. Cuinn stood ready on the other. Earlier, Mychael and Cuinn had positioned a spy gem to record everything for later analysis.

There were no words, no incantations, only the perfectly controlled manifestation of magic between the two powerful elf mages.

The rift opened, and I gazed in wonder on another world. I wanted a better vantage point, but I didn't dare move.

It appeared to be just before sundown on Timurus. Eamaliel and Cuinn had perfectly positioned the rift, giving us a clear view from the Table of Iron down to the snow-covered valley and the ruins of Astava.

A view filled with things we did not want to see.

Campfires dotted the valley floor, surrounding what was supposed to be an empty city. A city that wasn't empty any longer.

The glow of the setting sun striking the snow illuminated the valley, putting into sharp relief the tents, horses, and men that extended as far as our eyes could see and the rift's borders would allow. I blinked and focused intently on one of the "horses." The distance was too great for detail, but not for what froze the breath in my throat. The creature was taller than the men; that was expected. What wasn't expected or wanted was that the thing was taller than the tent closest to it. It wasn't a distortion due to distance; it was sheer size. The creature had four legs, but there was no way it was a horse. And there were so many of them, even in my limited viewpoint, that I couldn't count them.

I wasn't a general, and I'd never seen an army massing for an attack, but I knew that was what I was seeing.

Mychael's hand found mine and gripped it, confirming my fears.

Justinius didn't need to worry about any of the ambassadors talking. No one in the room was making a sound. No one needed to tell them what they were seeing. I'd known, and so did they.

A pair of flags flew from the top of what remained of the city's walls. I didn't recognize one, but I knew the other. The flags were large, and the distance great, but I'd seen the insignia on one of the flags often enough that I didn't need a close-up. The wind must have been blowing hard in the valley because both flags were standing out, making the insignia on each all too clear.

Two red serpents twining around each other on a field of black, battling for dominance.

The insignia of the Khrynsani.

Sound definitely carried through the rift. We all heard the wind roaring across the Table of Iron.

Smell carried, too. Or more accurately, stench.

I'd smelled it before, in the caves beneath the Khrynsani temple that had been the home of a family of sea dragons.

This was no sea dragon.

The rift window was three feet tall and five feet wide. The side of the massive head that now filled it was covered in armored scales, its red eye was as big as my head, and the interior of its nostril glowed deep orange with banked fire. The nostril flared as it took our scent, the slit pupil narrowed, and a growl shook the stone floor beneath our feet.

Oh unholy hell.

The rift vanished—or more to the point, Eamaliel and Cuinn slammed it shut.

29

It was a good thing that silence was no longer needed.

The room erupted.

"Battle dragon," I heard Eamaliel tell Cuinn through the chaos. "Just as big and ugly as I remembered."

That battle dragon was on the Table of Iron for the same reason the launch pad for the Guardians' sky dragons was on a cliff overlooking Mid's harbor. Dragon eyes were sharp. They were more than fighters, they were lookouts. And that one had seen us. Fortunately for us, dragons couldn't talk.

At least dragons on our world couldn't.

The battle dragon was gone, but its stench remained.

Justinius Valerian stood motionless directly in front of the closed rift, where less than a minute before, the massive head of a battle dragon would have been close enough to touch. He had to have heard the noise around him, but gave no sign, continuing to stare fixedly at the now empty air. The archmagus closed his eyes for a moment, and his shoulders sagged.

I knew Justinius was exhausted—in body, mind, and spirit. He had been battling to clean the Conclave of corruption since he'd first taken office. The Saghred had brought that corruption—and the traitors who fed it—out into the open. The stone itself was gone, but the corruption remained, and Justinius's efforts to clean the organization he so believed in had severely weakened it.

And now, an invasion.

To look at him, no one would have realized the toll it had taken, not unless they knew Justinius.

Tarsilia Rivalin knew him.

She went to stand beside him, and silently reached down and took his hand in hers, fiercely entwining her fingers with his. Justinius opened his eyes, his gaze searching her face as he solemnly raised her hand to his lips.

Mychael's command cut through the panicked voices. "I need your attention."

He didn't shout; he didn't need to. He let his spellsinger voice do the work, and it did it well. The room went silent; all eyes were on him.

"What we just saw confirms Sandrina Ghalfari's threat," Mychael said. "We have *not* seen our defeat. Fear and panic serve no purpose, and it only helps our enemy." He paused, his blue eyes coolly meeting the gaze of each ambassador. "And there is no doubt now that we have an enemy. Sandrina left that message to be found. She wants us to know that they're coming. She wants us to be afraid." He smiled the slow confident smile of a man who has seen his opponent—and sees them as a challenge to be met and overcome. "She forfeited their element of surprise to sow fear on top of the distrust the Khrynsani already planted. In the past months, your kingdoms had begun preparing for war against Sarad Nukpana, who had planned to use the Saghred's power to open a Gate large enough to drive the army under his command into any part of any kingdom at any time. Sarad Nukpana is gone. The goblin army he would have forced to do his bidding is now under the control of a king who will be eager to extinguish this last threat to what he wants for his people—peace." There was a calm, absolute certainty to his words. "Your kingdoms were preparing for a war against Sarad Nukpana. Now we will be protecting and defending our people against Sandrina Ghalfari and a largely unknown ally. We will continue to prepare; but I strongly suggest that instead of arguing with and fighting each other, that we come together to defeat a foe who wants nothing less than our complete destruction."

Aeron Corantine stepped forward. "Under your leadership, Tamnais Nathrach summoned the demon that carried her son to Hell, and Raine Benares destroyed the Saghred. So now all of us will be made to pay for your ill-advised actions?"

Silence.

I knew what Mychael wanted to do to Aeron Corantine. Tam wanted pretty much the same thing except with more violence, and his chilling smile said he was entertaining himself at this very moment imagining it in all its gory detail. I knew Tam well enough to know precisely what he was thinking and I approved wholeheartedly.

"Sarad Nukpana wanted the goblin throne and the Seven Kingdoms under his complete control." Mychael's voice was ice cold, but perfectly composed. "His mother would have been a power behind the throne, but make no mistake, she would have been a force to contend with. If Tamnais Nathrach had not summoned that demon, and Raine Benares not destroyed the Saghred, none of us would be alive right now having this discussion. All highly placed government officials would have been killed outright; or if they had magical talent, they would have been imprisoned to await their turn on the Khrynsani temple altar as Saghred sacrifices. Tam and Raine risked their lives and their very souls to prevent Sarad Nukpana from taking control of the Saghred and, in the reign of terror that would have followed, having every man, woman, and child in the Seven Kingdoms at his mercy. Gratitude is called for, Ambassador Corantine, not self-preserving, misdirected blame."

"The ambassador is from the Nebian coast where there is much sand," the Myloran ambassador rumbled into the tense silence that followed. "Perhaps for the past few months, he has had his head buried in it." Herryk Geirleif addressed his next words directly to Aeron Corantine. "This 'ill-advised action,' as you called it, would not have kept Nukpana from killing you first, since you don't have any magic to have made yourself even remotely useful to him. With your head in the sand, you simply wouldn't have known about your death until it happened."

Diplomats may have some redeeming qualities after all—at least this one did.

"I've heard enough," Aeron Corantine said. "You will lead these sheep to their slaughter, but Nebia will have no part of it."

"And this gathering has heard enough of your cowardly ranting," said a familiar voice from the now open doorway. "In a time of war, an ambassador puts the safety of their people first, not themselves."

Markus Sevelien was out of bed.

The director of elven intelligence was dressed from head to toe in his customary black. His dark hair was swept back from a high and pale forehead that was even paler than usual from being out of bed entirely too soon. I didn't blame him for wanting to be here, though; I would have done the same. I'd seen Markus look better, I'd also seen him look worse, but rarely had I seen him this angry. Dalis was standing just behind Markus at his right shoulder, and Brina was at his left side. Both women looked even angrier than Markus, if that was possible, and all of it was directed at Aeron Corantine. They knew who was to blame for Markus's insistence on coming here.

The Caesolian ambassador was closest to the door, and

quickly found a chair for Markus. The man may have had a questionable backbone, but he did have a heart.

"Thank you, Bastien," Markus said quietly, "but I have spent enough time in bed. And from what I have just overheard—I stayed there too long." He walked forward, his steps unsteady, Dalis and Brina by his side. "I was one of Sandrina Ghalfari's first targets," he told the ambassadors. "I was attacked by a Rak'kari while traveling here by mirror from Silvanlar. I died in the Void. Had it not been for the bravery of Paladin Eiliesor and Raine Benares risking their lives to free me, I would not be here. Then the paladin's astounding healing skills brought me back to life. And I would not have survived the first few hours without the paladin and the gifted healer and dear lady next to me."

"Why weren't we told of this?" the Caesolian ambassador asked.

"To avoid precisely what is happening now," Markus replied. "Blaming the present goblin government for the actions of Sandrina Ghalfari, the Khrynsani, and their allies that remain hidden among us, which is exactly what they wanted you to do. I refused to play into their hands, so I asked Paladin Eiliesor not to reveal the true cause of my absence." The elf turned to Mychael. "I take it the rift revealed the worst?"

"It did. There's an army massing on the plains of Astava. Their banner flies over the city as does that of the Khrynsani." Mychael turned to Eamaliel. "Was the banner the same?"

"Unfortunately, yes. So was the battle dragon."

I tensed. How my father knew what he knew wasn't something we had planned to explain. The ambassadors needed to know what we were up against, but at the same time, we didn't want to shout my father's identity from the rooftops. Not to mention, who would believe that he was over nine hundred years old?

"What do you mean by 'was the banner the same'?" the Majafan ambassador asked.

I gave an inward cringe. Here we go.

"In addition to being an expert on rifts," Mychael said, "Professor Anguis is a military historian. Professor, would you briefly explain what you told me and the archmagus?"

Smooth. Not a lie, but not the whole truth.

"The world of Timurus was invaded approximately seven hundred years ago," Eamaliel said. "Few records exist detailing the war, but the invaders were not from Timurus. For one, the invaders had battle dragons, and Timurus had no dragons of any size. As you just saw, this army also has battle dragons and they match the historical description. The insignia on the flag we just saw was the same as the invaders from seven hundred years ago. It was unknown why they originally came to Timurus and what it was that they wanted, so it is also unknown as to why they have returned. The people of Timurus had mages and magic, and while they were not to our level of ability, they were by no means helpless. The invaders, on the other hand, were said to have magic different from anything that has ever been recorded." My father paused. "When scholars revisited Timurus years later, no human life remained."

Even Aeron Corantine had nothing to say to that.

"Bastien, I will now accept your offer of a chair," Markus said. The chair was brought and Markus eased himself into it with Dalis's assistance. "Mychael, do you believe any of our kingdoms separately stand a chance to defeat or turn back this invader?"

"Based on what I saw and what I know of Timurus's fate the last time this army was there...No single kingdom could hope to defeat them."

"And if we fought together?"

"The invaders' exact numbers, armaments, and magical powers are unknown, as is how they will get such a large army onto our world."

Markus smiled slightly. "It seems they have overcome that difficulty by getting to Timurus not once, but twice."

"Unfortunately, true."

"In your military opinion, Paladin Eiliesor, the only way we would stand a chance of avoiding Timurus's fate of total annihilation would be to form an alliance and combine our armies, yes?"

"That is my opinion and belief."

Markus sat back. "Then you will have Pengor's army at your command. I will have to obtain my queen's approval, but considering the circumstances, I am certain I will encounter no difficulty getting it. The elves will stand with you and your Guardians."

"You didn't even see through that rift," Aeron Corantine objected, "yet you would—"

"And I do not need to," Markus replied, each word sharp and distinct. "If Paladin Mychael Eiliesor tells me that we have an invader on our world's doorstep, I believe him without question. There is no one—elf, goblin, or human—whose word I trust or whose expertise I respect more than his. If you wish to believe otherwise, Ambassador Corantine, I do not have the strength or patience to expend attempting to convince you otherwise. None of us has the time. You and your people will help defend this world, or you are a liability. At this critical point, your opinion and willful divisiveness matters very little to me, and is a waste of all of our valuable time." Markus paused and took a shaky breath. "My fellow ambassadors, we can draw up the documents later, but for the sake of expediency, I would like to request a show of hands…"

Tam stepped forward. "No hands necessary, Markus. I too must confer with my king, but I am certain that the goblin army will gladly and eagerly meet the Khrynsani and their new allies on the field of battle."

"The warriors of Mylora's clans will be honored to fight beside you," Herryk Geirleif said.

One by one, the ambassadors pledged their kingdoms and armies to meet the invaders and defend our world.

Except Nebia.

Aeron Corantine turned on his heel and, without a word, left the room.

"In the vernacular of my people," Herryk Geirleif said after the Nebian ambassador, "fu'qut yiu."

I turned to Vegard. "What does that mean?" I whispered.

"Exactly what you think it does." He grinned. "I told you my people get to the point."

30

Mychael and I were to be married tomorrow morning.

For the past few weeks, I had been thinking of tonight as the make-or-break event between myself and my future in-laws.

However, nothing puts things in perspective like an impending invasion.

Impending, not immediate.

Magic makes noise. It doesn't matter what kind. The sound of a spell being woven is less noisy than an incantation to create a magical construct. However, tearing a rift big enough for one of those battle dragons to fit through would deafen every magic sensitive within a hundred miles.

Tam and the Caesolian ambassador had proposed a theory that sounded more plausible with every passing hour. There was an uninhabited continent to the west of Rheskilia and Caesolia across the Sea of Kenyon. Explorers from both kingdoms had visited it over the centuries and found it to be dry, barren, and inhospitable—which was why no one had ever bothered to claim it. No one wanted to live there, but for an off-world invader looking for a base of operations from which to launch attacks on the Seven Kingdoms, it would be perfect. The Khrynsani would know about it, and a rift opened there would be far enough away that it wouldn't be heard.

Perfect for an invader; better for us because it would give us time. Not much, but it was something.

Mychael and I had decided that unless the invaders were pounding on the citadel's gates tomorrow morning, we weren't putting off our wedding again. We'd get married and then prepare for war. All of us were overdue for a night off. Brant and Edythe Eiliesor had met me—now it was time for them to meet my family.

I had been dreading this moment since Mychael had asked me to marry him. Now, I was kind of looking forward to it in a finally-getting-it-over-with kind of way. I wanted everyone to like each other, or at least pretend they could get along, but there were more important things in my life right now, and at the tip-top of that list was Mychael Eiliesor—the man I loved, the man who loved me, and the man who was going to become my husband tomorrow morning. That made me unspeakably happy, and how my family and in-laws did or did not like each other no longer mattered. I couldn't control it, I couldn't change it, so I wasn't going to concern myself with it any longer.

We'd be having a reception after the ceremony tomorrow for those attending the wedding, which meant our families and closest friends. Tonight's party was to have been more of a political necessity. Mychael was paladin of the Conclave Guardians, sacred protector of the archmagus, the Seat of Twelve, and the Conclave of Sorcerers. I loved the archmagus, I adored half of the new Seat of Twelve, but the senior members of the Conclave who I'd met so far weren't what anyone would call sociable. I told Mychael that if he could tolerate them for a few hours, so could I.

We had also extended invitations to the peace talks delegates. This morning, the Seven Kingdoms' ambassadors had gotten a good look through that rift at what was coming for us. Between that and the peace talks, they deserved some fun. The delegations had accepted our invitation with the exception of the Nebians. No surprise there. The rest of the delegates actually seemed to be becoming friends. The threat of annihilation had turned antagonists into allies. The drugged ink had helped the Caesolian ambassador find his courage. The later realization that he'd gotten into a heated debate with Tamnais Nathrach and survived had helped him keep it. Though the first thing he'd done on arrival this evening was to apologize to Tam for his uncalled-for behavior. Tam had apologized in turn for any of his words that might have caused offense. Each graciously accepted the other's apology— mostly because, thanks to the drug, neither remembered anything they'd said.

One thing we hadn't bothered with tonight was a "no weapons" declaration. Asking any of my family to go anywhere without weapons would be like asking them to show up naked. Phaelan wouldn't have minded—the naked part, not being weaponless—but the rest of my relatives wouldn't have been amused.

Tonight was about celebrating a marriage, not laying down a bunch of hopefully unnecessary rules. Considering that these were mostly our family and friends, no one should be drawing steel on anyone else.

There were at least a hundred people gathered in the closest thing the citadel had to a ballroom. We'd told our families and friends what we had seen this morning through that rift and what it meant. We also warned them that Sandrina Ghalfari and her shapeshifter could still be on the island. Of the guests, fourteen belonged to the Benares family, all of whom could and would kill with steel. Then there was my adoptive family, all of whom could and would kill with spells—and of course, Tam who would gladly drop a hopeful assassin with one word. Rounding out our party guests were some of the most powerful mages in the Seven Kingdoms, and enough Guardians to make me feel warm and fuzzy. Vegard was close by and keeping watch, but not so close as to impose on any conversation.

Tonight I was wearing one of several gowns Alix had made for me. I was about to become the paladin's wife, and there would be occasions that required—or at least strongly suggested—formal attire. I'd wear gowns for those events, and Alix had made them to my specifications. I'd had the Guardians' armorer make an armored bodice for me that would fit under any of Alix's creations. Sometimes a girl felt safer wearing a little steel between herself and a potentially hostile outside world. Considering that we were on the verge of an invasion, tonight was one of those times. In addition, the present fashion of long, voluminous skirts left all kinds of options open. For the foreseeable future, my idea of formalwear would involve form-fitting trousers under detachable skirts. Yes, you heard me. Detachable. My life was worth more to me than any snooty mage or professor's idea of propriety. Not to mention, as far as I was concerned, my body was absolutely nothing to be ashamed of. For confirmation on that opinion, I'd gone straight to the top. I'd asked the paladin himself. He'd wholeheartedly agreed that I could shuck my skirts anytime I wanted to, and would look good before, during, and after I'd done it.

The particular gown I was wearing this evening didn't have the detachable skirt option, but it did have room for my armored bodice, and pockets in the side of the skirt that would let me access the daggers strapped to my thighs. The gown itself was a stunning shade of peacock blue, my hair was up in an intricate twist, and for the first time in a long time, I felt gorgeous. Mychael came up behind me and nuzzled my neck. Again, the paladin wholeheartedly agreed.

"So far, so good," he murmured against my neck.

"At least there hasn't been any bloodshed."

"And there won't be any. I think it's going exceptionally well."

I had to agree.

We'd started Mychael's parents out light by introducing them to Garadin and Tarsilia. That had gone well, so we moved on to Eamaliel. He'd utterly charmed both of them, so we'd thrown caution to the wind and introduced them to my Uncle Ryn and Aunt Deira, and then to Phaelan and his brothers and sisters. However, as long as the peace talks were underway, we couldn't introduce Mago as a Benares. Isibel introduced him to her parents as elven diplomatic attaché, Mago Nuallan, and the last I'd had seen, he was working his magic on them both.

Mychael stole another kiss, then sighed. "We don't want any of our guests to feel neglected, so we need to try to speak to as many as we can. I'll go to the right, you go to the left, and we'll meet at the bar. How does that sound?"

"It sounds like a plan. I have to do some small talk, but there's a reward at the end."

"Me?"

"And a stiff drink."

I started on my rounds. Markus was here and feeling much better than this morning. The director of elven intelligence had two dates this evening—Brina and Dalis—and neither was about to let him out of their sight.

Thanks to the Rak'kari infesting the Void, Brina Daesage had only had the clothes on her back, so I'd given her access to my wardrobe, and she'd chosen an outfit of head-to-toe black. Leather. We were about the same size, but let's just say that Markus's bodyguard was more abundant in certain areas than I was. So while my leathers fit, we'd had to adjust the lacings. The results had not gone unnoticed—especially by Phaelan, who'd just come up beside me.

"Who is *that*?"

"Brina Daesage, Markus's chief of security, and the woman who will run you through if you so much as look at him wrong."

Phaelan flashed a quick, wicked grin. "What if I look at her right?"

"She'll probably run you through twice."

Phaelan's eyes glittered in unspoken challenge.

"Uh, what about Isibel?" I asked.

My cousin's eyes stayed on Brina as his brain tried to process what I was asking—and who I was talking about. His brow creased with the effort. Phaelan was a brilliant tactician, a cunning strategist, and you did *not* want to play cards with him, but when he saw a woman he was interested in…Well, his mind didn't cease to function; but all his cunning and brilliance was rerouted to below his sword belt.

Phaelan looked at me, his dark eyes surprisingly lucid. "I'm a pirate. It's all I know how to do, and I'm good at it."

"Very good," I agreed, a little confused as to where this was going.

"Isibel Eiliesor is an ambassador. It's what she's always wanted to do." Phaelan glanced over to where Isibel and Mago were laughing at something the Caesolian ambassador had just said. "And she's good at it," he added quietly. My cousin's smile was wistful. "Could you in all honesty see the two of us together?"

I smiled fondly and tucked my arm through his. "Don't take this the wrong way, but no."

Phaelan nodded toward his older brother. "I could see Isibel and Mago together."

I considered the possibility for a moment. "Me, too."

My cousin lowered his voice. "He told me that if Markus's offer is still good, he'll turn in his resignation at the bank."

"Really? I knew he was thinking about it. He's 'thought' about changing careers before, but it's never gone any further."

Mago and Isibel were making their way through the crowd, and my cousin's hand was on the small of Isibel's back.

My smile broadened.

It appeared my cousin the banker wouldn't be a banker for much longer. The threat of war made you realize what was important, and sitting in a corner office playing with other people's money wasn't it. Mago could do a lot of good working for Markus. I stifled a chuckle. I could only imagine what the possibility of another Benares with another Eiliesor would do to Edythe.

Phaelan straightened his doublet. "I should pay my respects to Markus."

I glanced over to Markus—and Brina—and raised an eyebrow. "To Markus?"

"Yes."

"I'm sure he will appreciate your consideration."

My cousin picked an imaginary bit of lint from his velvet sleeve. "I thought he would."

Phaelan cautiously made his way to where Markus was seated. Brina's eyes locked on his approach. Her hand didn't need to go to her sword's hilt; it was already there. Phaelan judiciously kept his hands palms forward and away from any of his weapons. It wasn't how most men would begin a courtship, but Phaelan wasn't most men—and Brina Daesage wasn't most women.

I stood on tiptoe to see Mychael. He was already halfway to the bar. As paladin, he'd gotten to be an expert at small talk and efficiently working a room.

This isn't a competition, I told myself.

I spotted Edythe through the crowd—and she spotted me.

Oh crap. So much for getting to the bar first.

I'd already spoken to her and Brant twice. Brant was fun and friendly. Edythe was not. I still had no idea how she felt about me, but I thought I was about to find out. I wondered if I could get Vegard to go to the bar and bring me that drink. I took a deep breath and moved aside to one of the few clear spots on the floor that was also near an open door leading out onto a terrace, or whatever it was called in a fortress. There was cool air flowing in. My gown wasn't hot, but all these people in one room were, and if Edythe was finally ready to speak her mind, at least I'd be comfortable while she did it.

I glanced over to where Vegard stood. He'd seen Edythe approaching. He gave me a questioning look; I replied with a nod. He backed off a little farther to give us privacy to talk, but not before giving me a thumbs-up and an encouraging smile.

Edythe walked toward me, smiling brilliantly, and holding out her arms. "My dear, I've been meaning to tell you how lovely you look this evening."

Brilliant smile? My dear? Incoming hug?

Her lips were smiling; her eyes were the flat black of a shark. My right hand went into my skirt's pocket and came out with a dagger.

This was not Edythe Eiliesor.

It was Sandrina's shapeshifter.

31

"Clever girl," the fake Edythe murmured. *"Let's take a nice* walk outside."

I slowly circled off to the left. "I don't think so."

The woman stepped off to the right. "I am but one of many here."

More shapeshifters.

The blade of her small stiletto was concealed in the palm of her hand. The blade was wet, whether with drug or poison didn't matter. Either way I didn't dare take my eyes off of her. While both of us were wearing gowns, the shapeshifter had the misfortune of having had to copy Edythe's dress, down to the heavy brocade skirts.

She angled the stiletto's tip toward me. "I'm merely here to deliver a gift to the bride."

"Another of Sandrina's specialty poisons?"

"My you are a clever little thing. Come with me and your paladin lives. Raise an alarm and he dies."

I stopped circling her. "Threatening Mychael was the wrong thing to do."

We were attracting attention, meaning she was running out of time and she knew it.

She attacked.

I let her.

I quickly pivoted to the side, letting the weight of her skirts carry her past me. She stumbled, but didn't fall—at least not until I kicked her.

I knew from past experience that it took a lot of pain for a master shapeshifter to lose their assumed form.

Pain. Or unconsciousness.

I went for whichever one I could get.

Though until I had landed a good punch to the side of her head, I didn't realize how this looked to everyone else.

The bride and her mother-in-law were having a catfight.

"She's a shapesh—" I managed, before taking an elbow to the jaw.

And the gloves were off.

The fake Edythe and I turned into a snarling, cussing, punching, and kicking mass of silk and brocade rolling around on the citadel's ballroom floor.

I'd lost my dagger at some point, and I sank my teeth into her wrist, making her drop the stiletto, as a strong arm locked around my waist and lifted me off of her.

With the help of a guest, the woman stood and made the mistake of smirking—until I kicked out and the heel of my fancy silk shoe took her right under the chin.

She lost consciousness—and her glamour.

An elven mother-in-law turned into a Khrynsani temple guard, complete with the serpent tattoo on the left side of his face.

So there.

The arm that held me belonged to Vegard. I had to get enough air in my lungs before I could speak. Stupid tight bodice.

"Sandrina's shapeshifter." Gasp. "Poison dagger." I panted, and tried to look everywhere at once. "Mychael's next."

I didn't have enough air to speak, let alone shout a warning that could be heard more than two feet away. Vegard didn't have that problem. He also wasn't going to let propriety get in the way of saving his paladin. Vegard sucked in what had to have been half the air in the room and bellowed as if he were on a battlefield.

"Shapeshifter! Assassin!"

Those two words cut through and went over every voice in the room, and alerted not only Mychael and every Guardian in the room, but also all of our family and friends with steel or spells and a desire to use them. They knew exactly what those two words meant. Sandrina's other shapeshifters had just become mice in a room full of hungry cats—and I was the hungriest one of all.

For the second time today, a room erupted into chaos, except this was chaos with the intent of violence. I quickly scanned every face I could see. I knew that Vegard had my back, so I concentrated on locating Sandrina's other shapeshifters.

I didn't expect to see Sandrina herself.

In a crowd of angry or fearful people, Sandrina Ghalfari stood out because her expression was utterly blank. No emotion whatsoever. Her complexion was glamoured to pass for human, and the tips of her ears rounded, but I knew it was her. She was headed away from me and toward where I'd last seen Mychael.

She wanted revenge, and she wanted to do it herself.

She wasn't giving up.

Neither was I.

"Sandrina's going for Mychael," I told Vegard. I drew my second dagger and held it to the side of my skirt so I wouldn't stab anyone who didn't need stabbing as I quickly wove my way through the crowd. Vegard was right behind me.

"Take them alive!" I heard Mychael shout.

I moved faster.

The crowd thinned and I supplemented my personal armory by snatching the carving knife out of the roasted boar as I sprinted past a buffet table.

I couldn't get any closer to Mychael, but Sandrina had—and somehow she'd gotten a rapier, the last few inches of the blade dripping with what could only be poison.

"Mychael!" I screamed.

Another rapier's blade neatly parried Sandrina's, and I nearly dropped my carving knife when I saw who was wielding it.

Edythe Eiliesor. The real one.

My mother-in-law had Mago's rapier in one hand, the train of her gown in the other, and was forcing Sandrina Ghalfari back with a furious series of moves, her blade a silver blur.

"Damn," Vegard blurted.

Sandrina grabbed a small bowl from the buffet table and flung the contents at Edythe's eyes. Not all of it hit, but enough of it did. Sandrina darted around a column and out the door that went down to the kitchens—and led to countless ways out of the citadel.

Oh. Hell. No.

I caught sight of Mychael surrounded by his father, Justinius, his four bodyguards, Tarsilia, and Piaras.

Mychael was safe.

Sandrina was not.

And from what I could see, neither were any of her shapeshifters.

There was more than enough steel to go around. I'd asked my family to go out of their way to be polite, so they were sharing their blades with lesser-armed guests. A Benares wouldn't set foot out their door or off their ship with only one weapon.

If there was an incident, I'd asked them not to kill anyone unless absolutely necessary. A couple of chairs had been broken in the melee, and Phaelan's younger sister had a chair leg in each hand. Phoebe always did have a thing for clubs. Her twin brother had a shapeshifter in a headlock, a shapeshifter who'd lost his shape due to Phoebus clamping his forearm around the Khrynsani's windpipe. And panicked flailing from overhead drew my attention to a temple guard stuck to the ballroom ceiling. That would be Lucan Kalta's work. As chief librarian and a senior Conclave member, we'd had to invite him. Now it looked like I might actually have to thank him for something.

The situation wasn't under control yet, but it would be. As much as I would have loved to have stayed and enjoyed the show, I had a score to settle.

Cuinn was helping Edythe clear her eyes of dipping sauce. She saw me and pushed his hands away. "Where did she—?" she began.

"Through the kitchens," I told her. "Cuinn, she'll be using a rift to escape. I need your help."

The three of us took off after her together.

Vegard had gone to check on Mychael, and I heard his shouts for me to stop. If I did, Sandrina Ghalfari would escape, close that rift after her, and we wouldn't know where it had been until she decided to use it again to pay us another visit. That was not going to happen. We needed to know where that rift was and close it permanently.

Sandrina had a good head start, the kitchen was crowded, and she'd left chaos in her wake. I couldn't tell if any of those who had been knocked to the floor were wounded or not. I wasn't a healer, so what help I could have offered wouldn't have done anyone any good. I was a seeker and a pissed off bride-to-be, and the woman I was chasing had just tried to murder my soon-to-be husband, and wouldn't stop until she and her army had killed us all. Those things qualified me and gave me the right to hunt her down and make her sorry she hadn't kept running since that night in the Khrynsani temple.

Sandrina Ghalfari had passed two exits from the kitchens

that would have taken her out of the citadel. That meant she was going down into the citadel's sub-basements, which confirmed she'd used a rift. There were no tunnels down there that led to the outside. I'd made it my business to know the citadel's layout like the back of my hand—especially during the time when Carnades Silvanus had been trying to have me imprisoned in the sub-basements' containment rooms, until he could have me executed. Once down there, the only way out was up to the main level.

And once down there, it was like a maze. A maze that was kept lighted, but still a maze.

I held up my hand to signal Edythe and Cuinn to stop at an intersection of five narrow hallways. They were marked with numbers indicating what section of the citadel they went under, but that didn't tell me which one Sandrina Ghalfari had taken.

Then I smiled in realization. Oh yes, it did.

Section three contained the highest tower in the citadel—where Sarad Nukpana's body was entombed. Mychael and Justinius had magically disguised the door on the outside of the tower, but its footings were down in the sub-basements. There must have been a door down there that had let Sandrina gain access to the tower without tripping any of the alarm spells on the tower's exterior.

If Sandrina's escape rift was under that tower, I couldn't continue chasing her with only a dagger, a carving knife, my armed and apparently dangerous mother-in-law, and a mirror mage professor. The assassination attempts had failed, and neither Mychael nor I were dead. Sandrina was a smart woman. She wasn't going to risk capture now and ruin everything she'd arranged on Timurus. I couldn't risk that there wouldn't be a nasty surprise waiting for us, but if the Khrynsani had a rift in the citadel, that was the worst security breach imaginable. We needed to know where it was to ensure this was their last visit.

There was nothing wrong with my shields. I could protect

myself as well as Edythe and Cuinn, if necessary. When the Saghred and I had been psychic roommates, I could sling spells and fling fireballs with the best of them. If the Saghred's essence had been desperate enough to flee from the rock and into me, it was in its best interests to keep me alive. If I died, we'd both cease to exist. I needed a weapon and I needed it now.

I slid my dagger back into its sheath and turned my hand palm up in front of me.

Come on, fireball. Come on, come on.

A trio of sparks popped to life above my palm and began quickly circling each other, faster and faster, leaving thin strands of gold and orange light in their wake, until a ball of pulsing flame hovered just above my open hand. Light, but no heat. I wrapped my fingers around it, the surface buzzing against my skin like thousands of fireflies. I'd never made anything like this before, so I had no idea what it'd do if I threw it, but it looked fierce enough. If Sandrina had any ideas about attacking us, maybe it'd at least act as a deterrent. It was all I had, so it'd have to do.

I led the way down to the base of Sarad's tower.

There were several branches off of the hallway we were in, and my study of the citadel's layout told me that to reach the tower from where we'd started, we'd take a series of left turns. I also knew I was going in the right direction because I could now sense Sandrina. I could sense her like I'd been able to sense her son. In the past, the Saghred had helped me track Sarad Nukpana. But it was different now. I sensed...no, I *felt* Sandrina's emotions: rage, frustration, impatience—and now, eager anticipation. The sensation raised the tiny hairs on the back of my neck.

I knew she was at the rift.

I quickly handed the carving knife to Cuinn, and with that hand freed up, I fanned the fingers of my empty hand in front of us from wall to wall, summoned the strongest shield I had, and ran toward that rift.

After the next left turn, an ornate door stood open at the end of the hallway. A door that was far too fancy for a containment room.

Cuinn quickly stepped up beside me. He nodded toward the door and mouthed one word: "Rift." His head cocked toward the door as if he were listening. "It's about to close," he whispered.

We moved as quickly as caution would allow to the open door, and with my shield solidly in front of us, I peered inside.

There was row upon row of wine racks. The room was dimly lit with lightglobes set in sconces along the walls, and while I couldn't see the rift, I could sense Sandrina. We went in, shields and fireball ready. The far corner of the room was illuminated by a glowing seam that ran from floor to ceiling. Unlike the rift in Cuinn's lab, we couldn't see through to the other side of this one. I didn't want to. The scene on this side was nightmarish enough.

Four seemingly disembodied arms reached through the rift, lifting Sarad Nukpana's corpse to take it through to the other side. The goblin's dead eyes were open and staring. Sandrina's arms were around her son's knees, pushing his body the rest of the way through.

A scream rose in my throat, and I pushed it right back down.

I wasn't the only one with a shield. Sandrina had put one between us and her escape, so using my fireball to incinerate that waking nightmare wasn't an option.

Sandrina looked back at us, her mad eyes glittering in the rift's glow. "We didn't get all that we wanted, but my son is enough. For now. I will return, and when I do, I will bring many who are eager to enjoy all this world has to offer. Enjoy your life, my dear. You won't have it—or anyone you love—for much longer." The goblin's smile was pure evil. "And since you didn't get my first wedding gift, we'll leave you with another."

As Sandrina and the legs of her son's corpse passed through the rift, the seam closed and folded in on itself, and the glow winked out.

I started breathing again. "What did she mean by—"

A tremor started in the corner of the room where the rift had been and worked its way up the walls to the ceiling.

Cuinn went white as a sheet. "They used the wall and ceiling to bear the rift's weight. Collapse the rift—"

My stomach dropped to my feet. "Collapse the ceiling."

A spiderweb of cracks appeared in the ceiling, cracks that fanned out, coming toward us and through the wall out into the hallway. The door slammed shut seemingly on its own, and chunks of ceiling fell just outside to block it.

I'd been in a similar situation before, under the elven embassy. It had taken me and Tam and the Saghred running at full power to keep the ceiling—and the embassy above it—from collapsing on top of us and a group of imprisoned teenage spellsingers. I didn't have Tam and I didn't have the Saghred, at least not in the way I'd had the Saghred before. All I had now was an anemic-looking fireball and no clue what it could do. But if I didn't do something and do it now, the three of us would be squashed like bugs, I would never get married, and Mychael would be a widower before he was a husband.

I swore.

Dust began to fall along with chunks of stone, and the fireball I clutched in my hand suddenly grew heavy, the flickering lights solidifying into what looked like molten lava.

Lava. Liquid rock.

And I couldn't use it unless I dropped the shields protecting us. Shields were good against spells, not tons of falling rock. I dropped the shields and screamed in terror and rage as I thrust my hand and the fireball it held toward the fractured ceiling, pushing with everything I had, willing the liquid fire I'd created into the cracks as I created more and still more lava, filling every fissure in the room and the hall beyond, visualizing the lava cooling, solidifying, becoming part of the ceiling and walls, stopping the collapse.

I was gasping, panting, and tasting blood. It was either a result of taking an elbow to the jaw, or I'd just ruptured something. My vision grew dark, and I felt myself falling. Slender arms went around me, supporting me and holding me up.

Edythe.

I must have passed out for a moment. When I came to my senses, I was utterly spent, my head lying back against Cuinn's shoulder; his arms were around both me and Edythe. We all looked at the ceiling, at the lava that filled the cracks, cooling, fading from orange to black, and solidifying, becoming part of the rock itself. The fracturing stopped, the rock ceased to fall, and the dust settled.

32

I leaned against a cask while Cuinn checked the door. The stone archway the door was set into had been cracked and my lava had mended it off-kilter. That door wasn't opening anytime soon, and even if it did, there was a pile of rock outside. I'd seen it in my mind's eye while I'd worked. Actually, while the Saghred and I had worked.

It hadn't been ready to die yet. That was good, because neither had I.

"Things are probably under control upstairs by now," I said between breaths. "They're looking for us. It shouldn't take them long. Mychael knows that wherever the explosion is, chances are that's where I am."

I looked around, seeing for the first time where we'd ended up. It wasn't just a room with some wine; it was a wine cellar. A very nice wine cellar. I carefully removed the closest bottle from a shelf and brushed back a thin layer of dust. I read the label, and even more carefully, put the bottle back.

"I'd say we're in the middle of Justinius Valerian's private stock."

Cuinn glanced around. "Unbelievable. Nothing's broken."

I would have happily sacrificed even the two-hundred-year-old bottle of Mhetil Caesolian red that I'd just carefully replaced in its wooden nest.

"Mychael will be down to unblock the door as soon as he can." I told them.

"How will he find us?" Edythe asked.

"Did Mychael tell you I'm a seeker?"

"Yes."

"When it comes to me, your son has a similar talent. He's in the citadel. We're in the citadel. It'll be easy for him." I tossed a meaningful glance at the rapier Edythe held with a light, professional grip. She'd had to put it down to keep me off the floor, but she'd picked it back up again. "Probably a much easier time than you had keeping that skill of yours a secret from everyone. By the way, that rapier looks familiar."

"Mago Nuallan tossed it to me. A very nice young man."

"That he is. Does Brant know he's married to a swash-buckler?"

Edythe was standing utterly straight and perfectly still, the stance of a practiced and skilled swordswoman. She was half in the shadow of one of the racks of wine, but I saw it.

A very slow smile crept over her lips.

I reached behind me and pulled a bottle out of an open case at my feet.

Rum.

Oh yes.

I didn't recognize the name or where it'd come from. It was also a fancier bottle than rum usually came in.

The three of us both deserved and needed this. I was sure Justinius would approve of Mychael's bride, mother, and the elf who would be sealing the Khrynsani rift in his wine cellar partaking in a little refreshment while we waited to be rescued.

I looked around. There was a corkscrew, but no glasses that I could see.

"Do you want a drink?" I asked both of them.

"Want and need," Edythe actually said.

I looked around some more. "No glasses."

"No problem," Cuinn said.

"And no seats." I shrugged and slid down the delightfully solid wall to the floor, bottle in one hand, corkscrew in the other. When I landed, my skirts poofed around me, skirts that had stayed out of my way and not gotten me killed. Thank you, Alix. Yes, the floor was hard, but I was sitting down and no one would be trying to kill me—at least not for the next hour or two. Hopefully.

I smiled up at them both. "While we wait, why don't we talk?"

Edythe slid down the wall to sit next to me, the rapier diagonally across her lap within easy reach, if needed. I admired her caution. The rift was closed, but it wasn't sealed yet.

I waved Cuinn over. "Now's not the time to be shy. Have a drink with the bride and mother of the groom. You've earned the rest of the night off."

Without glasses, we drank the way friends did—take a sip, pass it down.

"The archmagus keeps a fine cellar," Edythe said after she'd sipped.

Cuinn took more than a sip and his face contorted.

"Yeah, it's really strong for rum," I agreed. "If you're not used to it, it can be a little much."

He nodded, then shuddered, but when it was his turn again, he took another, even bigger swig. "That's all I'm going to have until I get this rift sealed." He went to the corner and got to work.

Edythe settled herself against the wall and began to talk. Hers was a story that'd been repeated all too often in the aristocracy, minor nobility, merchant class, basically wherever there was money and a family member careless or stupid enough to lose it.

The "careless and stupid" in Edythe's case had been her younger brother. Her father had been a very successful merchant. Her brother had inherited the money and business. Her brother was a very bad and extremely unlucky gambler.

"Eadweard gambled the house and what was left of the money right out from underneath us. He said he couldn't lose." Edythe took another drink. "Well, he did. We all did."

"I am so sorry." And I was. It was also a sorry situation that'd caused it. Edythe was the oldest, but just because she was female, the property passed to her younger (and foolish) brother. It wasn't elven law, but it was elven tradition. In my opinion, it was a tradition that needed to be kicked into the nearest cesspit. Sex or age should have nothing to do with inheritance; it should be concerned with who is the most qualified to manage it.

"Judging from the way you handled that blade," I ventured, "you did something about it. What was it?"

Edythe's lips twitched at the corners. "My father thought he was paying for dancing lessons for me. The dancing master he hired *did* teach dancing—but he also taught fencing."

If we'd had glasses, I'd have clinked mine with hers. Since I only had a bottle, I raised it in salute. "A woman after my own heart."

"I learned enough dancing to pass inspection, but most of my time was spent with blades."

"A much more useful skill."

"My brother had lost the family estate and most of the money. My two younger sisters and I were left with a small town house next to what used to be our family business."

"The idiot lost that, too?" I winced and backtracked. "Sorry, I didn't mean to call your brother an idiot."

Edythe waved a hand dismissively. "I called him worse; and believe me, he was worse."

"Was?"

"He couldn't stop gambling, but he did try to start cheating to win back some of what he'd lost." She took another drink and passed the rum back to me. "Unfortunately, he was an even worse cheat than a gambler—and even worse than that with a sword."

"Let me guess, he was one of those who thought a true gentleman didn't need to fight."

"Essentially. I, on the other hand, could fight *and* ride. Our town house was next to a stable. The owner had been a dear friend of my father. He loaned me the fastest and most fearless horse he had." Her eyes held an equal measure of pride and sadness. "I wore a mask and took to the highway. I did what I had to do to survive and provide for my sisters. When I'd taken enough money, I bought back our family business and ran it until my sisters were old enough to run it themselves. Unfortunately, the taxes that year were much more than we'd expected. So I took to the highway again, hopefully for the last time."

"You met Brant."

Edythe nodded. "And robbed him. He later told me it was rather thrilling." She smiled, wistful and warm. "I may have stolen his money, but he stole my heart. He was minor nobility who did courier work for elven intelligence. Apparently I attacked him when he was carrying an especially important packet." She let out a little laugh. "He said he'd stand, but he wasn't about to deliver, at least not without a fight."

"You won?"

"I think he let me. He gave me the money. Then he offered me the ring off his finger, and told me that if I wanted to see him again, to be at the Spring Ball that next month and wear the ring."

I was grinning like an idiot. "That is *so* romantic. You went to the ball?"

She nodded. "And wore the ring."

"Why didn't Mychael tell me this story? I love it!"

"Because he doesn't know."

"What?"

"My family background, my circumstances. Neither he nor Isibel know."

"Why not?"

"Many of the people I robbed have estates around ours."

"Oooh, that's awkward."

"Yes, it is."

"Okay, I can see why you wouldn't want Mychael and Isibel playing with the neighbors' children and telling them about how Mommy and Daddy met—and then having *their* mommies or daddies overhear." I paused, baffled. "But they're grown now, why keep it a secret? By the way, only my opinion, but your family is way too fond of keeping secrets from each other."

"Raine, how do you tell your children that their mother turned to highway robbery to buy back the family business their uncle lost gambling?"

"In my family, that's called a bedtime story. A good one. It would've been our favorite."

Edythe gave me a little smile. "I do like your family—and you."

"Really?" I suddenly felt warm all over. Then again, it was probably the rum. This stuff was seriously strong. "I'm so glad."

"You are not a suitable wife for a noble landowner, and I thank God that you are not. My son is not suited to be a landowner, and with what is coming, I again thank God that he is not."

"He may not be a landowner, but he is noble." I didn't mean aristocratic, and Edythe knew it. Mychael was noble in that he put the needs of others above his own and he fought for the greater good.

"Yes, he is," she said quietly. "And you are the perfect wife for such a man."

I couldn't help it, and didn't even try. I didn't just smile, I beamed. "Thank you, Lady Eilie—"

Edythe held up an imperious finger. "Edythe. I insist."

I nodded. "Edythe. Mychael said that when you insist, there's no fighting it."

"My son has grown to be a very wise man."

"He would say that he's merely a strategist who knows how to pick his battles against a superior opponent." The bottle felt suspiciously light in my hand. I took a look. Empty. "That bottle went way too fast."

I heard what sounded like a snore from Cuinn's end of the wall. Edythe and I leaned forward and looked over. The elf mirror mage was curled happily against a cask, either sound asleep or marginally unconscious. The rift wasn't glowing and the wall looked solid, the way a wall should look. Asleep or unconscious, whatever it was, Cuinn Aviniel deserved the rest.

When someone started pounding on the door, I thought I was going to die. But when they started shouting, I knew they were going to die, because I was going to kill whoever it was if they didn't stop.

Though first I had to remember how to stand up.

It took entirely too long to get the door open, with entirely too much noise.

Cuinn slept through all of it.

"We only drank a little." I was barely whispering. Heck, even moving my lips hurt. If I'd spoken any louder, I was fairly sure my head would explode.

Mychael was there, along with Brant, Justinius, Vegard, and Phaelan.

My eyes were squinting against the glow of a single lightglobe, but I couldn't miss Justinius Valerian's eyes going wide at the sight of the empty bottle I held in my hand. Edythe held the other empty. It was the first time I'd seen that particular expression on his face.

Awestruck.

"The rum in the case next to the cask?" he managed.

"Yes, and it was delicious."

"*Two* bottles?"

I blearily glanced down. "It appears that way." I tried to look at Edythe. "Is yours empty?"

Michael's mother held up the bottle in front of her face. "To the last drop." She sounded proud of herself and slightly pained.

Justinius was aghast. "And you're still standing?"

"This shelf I'm leaning against is helping *a lot,*" I admitted.

Phaelan shouldered his way to the front. "What was it?"

"The label said rum," Edythe told him.

"It was a really pretty bottle," I added, handing him the empty.

Phaelan saw the label and gasped. Another first.

"This is legendary," he managed. "It's not supposed to actually exist."

"It exists, all right," Justinius told him. "And I have two cases."

Edythe grinned. "Minus two bottles." She draped an arm across my shoulders and I gratefully leaned away from the shelf, which seemed to be moving, and into her. Fortunately a large cask was holding her up, otherwise we'd have both been on the floor. I giggled at the thought.

"You're only supposed to drink one sip at a time," Justinius told us.

"That's what we did," I said. "Then we had another sip at another time. Unfortunately, those times were only a couple seconds apart."

"It's a wonder you're still alive."

Edythe gave my shoulders a proud squeeze. "Benares and Eiliesor women are built of tough stuff. We can take it."

"Obviously."

I vaguely saw someone who looked like Vegard—actually he looked like two Vegards. Both of them took one look at us and burst out laughing.

I winced and held the side of my head with the hand not attached to the arm that was holding on to Edythe.

My bodyguard, bless him, immediately recognized our

sorry state and clapped his hand over his mouth. It didn't stop him from laughing, but I was grateful for the muffling.

Note to self: Kick Vegard later when you can feel your legs.

Mychael appeared behind him.

There was only one of him. Things were looking up.

"Mother?"

"Darling!"

It was all Mychael could do not to laugh. "I was going to ask if you're all right, but it's apparent that you are."

"I feel splendid," she pronounced with a grand sweep of her arm that nearly sent us both to the floor. "Though I suspect in the morning I will pray most fervently for death."

"Yes ma'am, you certainly will," Vegard heartily agreed.

Edythe turned on her son. "How could you allow this lovely girl to think I wouldn't adore her and her absolutely charming family?"

One of Phaelan's eyebrows nearly arched up into his hairline. "Charming?"

Mychael gaped at her. "I never said—"

"You didn't have to say; you assumed. And you assumed incorrectly."

"He may have assumed incorrectly," I said, "but it was because he didn't have all the facts."

"I've kept things from my children." Edythe heaved a despondent sigh that only the truly drunk could carry off. "What kind of mother keeps secrets from her children?"

I thought for a foggy moment. "All of them?"

She put her hand to her forehead, suddenly unsteady on our feet. "Oh dear. If you gentlemen will excuse me, I need to take a nap."

Like the true lady she was, Edythe Eiliesor gracefully sank to the floor.

Being unified in drunken sisterhood, I followed.

33

The morning of my wedding dawned unnecessarily bright.
And the bride had a hangover.

I didn't say it out loud for fear of excruciating pain and possible death. I didn't think anyone had ever died of a hangover, but I wasn't going to risk it because there was a first time for everything. If Edythe felt anywhere near as bad as I did, we were going to be quite a pair. That thought made me smile. It hurt, so I stopped.

Mychael and I had slept separately last night, and wouldn't see each other until the ceremony later this morning. We'd had enough bad luck lately, so I didn't want to tempt Lady Luck further by letting the groom see the bride before the wedding. I'd always thought that was a stupid custom. Though bad luck for a normal bride would be rain on her wedding day, or tripping on her dress and tearing it. We had an invasion by an off-world army and our on-world archenemies hanging over our heads. Bad luck for me could be the worst possible luck for everyone.

The ceremony would be in the citadel's chapel. I'd chosen it because of its relatively small size and beauty. The beauty was provided by its stained-glass windows. Windows that later this morning would be sparkling with head-splitting color as the sunlight streamed through.

Imala and Tam were probably still at the goblin embassy. I wondered if it was too late to send a messenger over to ask if she had an extra pair of what no nocturnal goblin would face a bright day without.

Sun spectacles. I needed a pair desperately. It could be my something borrowed. For a wedding present, Imala had already given me my something blue—five blued-steel goblin daggers that I'd had incorporated into my bouquet, the beautifully ornamented grips adding a special touch to the floral arrangement. I didn't understand the point of carrying only a bunch of flowers.

There was a knock at the door, and it was all I could do not to drop to my knees in agony. I opened the door as soundlessly as possible. It was Phaelan. He was smiling.

The bastard.

"Cousin, you're even worse off than I thought you'd be."

"Shhh."

He was still smiling. Even his teeth were too bright.

"Loud talking hurts, huh?"

"Shut up."

He looked more closely, though he didn't need to. I knew what I had; he didn't need to remind me.

"That's a beauty of a black eye."

I smiled. At least I tried to. It probably looked more like a lip spasm. "You should see the other guy."

"I have. By the way, they're not talking—at least not the two who are still alive."

None of the Khrynsani shapeshifters had been killed by

any of our guests—including my family, which was a major accomplishment. As soon as they knew there was no escape, eight of the shapeshifters had swallowed poison. Two had been knocked unconscious before they had the chance. The fake Edythe had been one of those taken alive.

Phaelan came in and closed the door. Quietly. "By the way, congratulations on bonding with your new mother-in-law last night."

To hell with the pain. I smiled. We had bonded, and those memories made me unspeakably happy.

He held up a bottle.

I held up my hands. "No, no, no."

"It's not hair of the dog. You drank from Justinius's cellar. I couldn't steal anything that good. It was good, wasn't it?"

"Very."

"Damn. I hate that I missed it."

"What's in there?"

"For me? A noxious and vile brew. For you, the thing that's gonna get you down the aisle."

"Do I want to know what's in it?"

"Absolutely not."

"You sure that won't poison me? I've had it with poisons. Besides, Mychael would kill you."

"Mychael would be at the front of a long line. And most of the people in that line could turn me into something with eight legs. If it makes you feel any better, it's Tarsilia's recipe."

I took the bottle. "It does."

"I thought it would. I'm here to be the man who keeps the bride from throwing up on her silk shoes. As to being here early, I knew you'll soon be overrun with women intent on getting you fed, bathed, dressed, and ready. You like these ladies and wouldn't want to bite their heads off, so I got here early with what you need to keep your friends."

I took the bottle. "How much of this swill do I need to drink?"

"A couple of shot glasses' worth. And definitely do them like shots." He flashed an entirely too bright smile. "Toss 'em back so you don't throw 'em up."

"Lovely." I uncorked the bottle, took a sniff, and willed my stomach not to flip. "You were with Markus and Brina when all hell broke loose last night. What happened?"

Phaelan's smile broadened into a grin. "I helped."

"I'm almost afraid to ask. What did you help do?"

"Protect and defend the director of elven intelligence."

"A shapeshifter went after him?"

"Oh, hell, no. One thought about it, but changed their mind."

"I take it the ring of rapiers surrounding Markus changed it for them?"

Phaelan nodded proudly. "Brina and I make a good team."

I shuffled over to my bedside table in search of a glass. "So it's 'Brina' now, is it?"

"I think she likes me."

"How do you know that?"

"She hasn't tried to kill me yet."

"For you, that's a promising start."

Phaelan shrugged. "I'll take it."

I tossed back the first dose of Phaelan's—excuse me, Tarsilia's—hangover cure and my entire body promptly spasmed to get rid of that nasty concoction.

"Yeah, the first dose is always the worst," my cousin said. "Go ahead and toss the next two back and I promise you'll start feeling better."

"Tarsilia made this."

"Yes, Tarsilia made this. Trust me, it works."

The only alternative to trusting Phaelan was killing him for making me feel even worse, which until now I hadn't thought was possible. I wasn't up to killing, so that left trust. I didn't think my taste buds survived the next two doses, but the rest of me did. And true to Phaelan's word, I started feeling better. Immediately.

"Wow."

My cousin was nodding and smiling. "Wow is right. Today of all days, I would not steer you wrong."

I stood up straight and actually felt like it. Within another minute, the pounding in my head stopped, and I didn't have to squint against the little bit of light that I'd been barely able to stand. I might never taste again, but considering that less than five minutes ago, I'd felt like I was weakly scratching on Death's door, it was a small price to pay.

There was a knock at the door and I didn't clutch my head and drop to my knees. It was a definite improvement.

"I may live," I said. "Thank you."

Phaelan came over and actually gave me a peck on the cheek on his way out. "Just remember to do the same for me on my wedding day." He didn't give me a chance to ask what he meant by that before he opened the door. "She's all yours," he told Tarsilia and Alix as he left.

My friends took one look at me with identical expressions of horror and disbelief. They looked amazing. I did not.

Alix was wearing a stunning gown of pale blue that set off her blond hair and blue eyes to perfection. Tarsilia was wearing robes that befitted her new station.

"We've got our work cut out for us," Alix noted.

Tarsilia stuck her head back out in the hall and told one of the Guardians on duty outside my room to get Dalis down here now. I heard boots running down the hall. Even if Justinius hadn't already announced the new members of the Seat of Twelve, I think that Guardian would have run just as fast to carry out Tarsilia's order. I didn't even try to stop her. While I knew Mychael loved me unconditionally, I didn't want to put it to the test in front of all our friends, family, and guests. I didn't want to see anything except love in his eyes when he lifted my veil.

Dalis came, did her usual exceptional work, and left. The area around my right eye was still tender and slightly blue with bruising—which would turn lovely shades of green and yellow over the coming days—but at least it was no longer black.

Between Tarsilia's hangover cure, Dalis's healing work on my eye, and a hot bath—I emerged looking and feeling almost lifelike. The silk confection of a gown that Alix had made for me completed the illusion.

I may not have felt my best, but I certainly looked it. Cuinn Aviniel's gift was a completely deactivated, detached, full-length mirror allowing the bride to admire herself to her heart's content. And admire I did.

Vegard was waiting outside my room to escort me to the chapel. He was attired in his formal Guardian uniform. My eyes went a little wide at the dozen identically uniformed— and armed—Guardians with him.

"An honor guard, ma'am," Vegard assured me.

I scooped up my bouquet of blades and blooms. Tarsilia and Alix were right behind me. "To make sure the three of us don't get into any trouble on the way to the chapel?"

He took one look at the bouquet and snorted. "We can try, but some things simply aren't possible."

The trip from my room to the citadel's chapel was thankfully uneventful.

My father and godfather were waiting for me outside the chapel's doors.

I simply stopped and stared at the two of them. They were the newest members of the Seat of Twelve, and they looked it.

Garadin glanced down at his fancy, new robes in resignation. "I know. Alix said if I made you look bad, she'd kill me. And as a newly minted member of the Seat of Twelve, I had a standard to live up to."

"You look amazing."

Garadin grinned and shrugged. "I clean up well."

Eamaliel looked perfectly at ease and perfectly elegant in his formal robes.

"Mom would have approved," I said softly. I looked to Garadin and then back at Eamaliel. "And I think seeing the two of you here together would have made her so happy."

Eamaliel's gray eyes glistened with unshed tears. "I wish she could have been here. She would have been so very proud of you."

I smiled. "Who's to say she's not?" I passed my bouquet to Alix and linked my arms through theirs. As she handed it back to me, Garadin saw my customized floral arrangement and rolled his eyes. I grinned at them both. "Shall we?"

The citadel's chapel was glowing with the late morning sunlight. Thanks to Tarsilia's magical elixir and Dalis's healing, no squinting or sun spectacles were needed.

Then I saw Mychael waiting at the end of the aisle; it was a sight I wouldn't have missed seeing crystal clear for the world.

As I made my way down the aisle, my father and godfather on either side, I couldn't help but think how perfect my life was, how right. Yes, there would probably be an invasion; and yes, if there was, war would come as a result. But we had something we'd never had before in the entire history of the Seven Kingdoms—a peace treaty signed by six out of the seven, and the promise of an alliance in which we would fight together against any and all invaders.

Tam and Imala would be returning to Regor to organize a joint Caesolian and goblin expedition to the continent that lay to the west of Rheskilia. If the Khrynsani and their allies were staging there, Tam had vowed to find them. Uncle Ryn had ships in the Sea of Kenyon, and had pledged them as escort for the goblin and Caesolian vessels.

What would happen tomorrow, next week, or next month was unknown. How my new magical power would help me face it was also largely unknown. It didn't matter. I had family and friends both old and new who I knew would stand with me and fight beside me. Whatever came, we would face it together.

It was all I could have asked for and then some.

It was the same with my life. I now had all I had ever hoped for and more.

And as I reached the end of the aisle, I was met by a man who adored me and who was nothing short of my dreams come true.

When Justinius asked us to repeat the vows we had written to each other, Mychael and I spoke the words in unison, our joined voices giving them strength, power, and permanence.

"I promise to be your lover, your companion in life, your ally in conflict, and your partner in adventure. I will strive every day to be worthy of your love. I will be honest with you, kind, patient, and forgiving. I will love you, hold you, honor and respect you, in sickness and in health, through loss and victory, for all the days of my life. I promise to help shoulder our challenges, for there is nothing we cannot face—and nothing we cannot do—if we stand together. These are my sacred vows to you as I join my life to yours."

Justinius declared us husband and wife.

As we kissed, our magic flared, met, and melded with a power I knew would see us through whatever tomorrow brought—and would last for a lifetime.

ABOUT THE AUTHOR

Lisa Shearin is the *New York Times* bestselling author of the Raine Benares novels, a comedic fantasy adventure series, as well as the SPI Files novels, an urban fantasy series best described as *Men in Black* with supernaturals instead of aliens. Lisa is a voracious collector of fountain pens, teapots, and teacups, both vintage and modern. She lives on a small farm in North Carolina with her husband, three spoiled-rotten retired racing greyhounds, and enough deer and woodland creatures to fill a Disney movie.

Visit her online at lisashearin.com, facebook.com/LisaShearinAuthor, and twitter.com/LisaShearin.

CPSIA information can be obtained
at www.ICGtesting.com
Printed in the USA
FSOW02n0131220216
17209FS